Just
One Day

AUTUMN

Also by Susan Buchanan
Sign of the Times
The Dating Game
The Christmas Spirit
Return of the Christmas Spirit
Just One Day – Winter
Just One Day – Spring
Just One Day – Summer

Just One Day

AUTUMN

SUSAN BUCHANAN

Copyright

Dedication

For Antonia and Luke, without whom life would be considerably less interesting
Love, Mummy xxx

About the Author

Susan Buchanan lives in Scotland with her husband, their two young children and a crazy Labrador called Benji. She has been reading since the age of four and had to get an adult library card early as she had read the entire children's section by the age of ten. As a freelance book editor, she has books for breakfast, lunch and dinner and in her personal reading always has several books on the go at any one time.

If she's not reading, editing or writing, she's thinking about it. She loves romantic fiction, psychological thrillers, crime fiction and legal thrillers, but her favourite books feature books themselves.

In her past life, she worked in International Sales as she speaks five languages. She has travelled to 51 countries and her travel knowledge tends to pop up in her writing. Collecting books on her travels, even in languages she doesn't speak, became a bit of a hobby.

Susan writes contemporary fiction, often partly set in Scotland, usually featuring travel, food or Christmas. When not working, writing, or caring for her two delightful cherubs, Susan loves reading (obviously), the theatre, quiz shows and eating out – not necessarily in that order!

You can connect with Susan via her website www.susanbuchananauthor.com or on Facebook facebook.com/susan.buchanan.author Twitter @susan_buchanan and on Instagram @AuthorSusanBuchanan.

Acknowledgements

Thanks go to

Wendy Janes, my amazing friend and editor –
www.wendyproof.co.uk

Claire at Jaboof Design Studio for the final cover in this series
and for all of my advertising graphics, and for keeping me topped
up with coffee – claire@jaboofdesignstudio.com

Trish Long for proofreading – trishlong3ok@gmail.com

Paul Salvette and his team at BBeBooks Thailand for
formatting – www.bbebooksthailand.com

Catherine Ferguson, Katy Ferguson and Barbara Wilkie for
agreeing to be beta readers

My ever-expanding Advance Review team

Clare Swatman for providing Autumn's cover quote

Leah Tonna for providing me with the name Elijah for a
character in Autumn, and Lesley Garety for choosing Elodie

Rachel's Random Resources for my fabulous cover reveals and
blog tours for this series, and for engaging all the wonderful
bloggers – thanks to them too

Thanks to the following Facebook groups:

Lizzie's Book Group, run by the amazing Lizzie Chantree, for
constant support

The Word Wranglers

The Friendly Book Community

Chick Lit and Prosecco, run by Anita Faulkner

Fiona Jenkins and Sue Baker for organising my launch day party

And thanks to all my readers for their wonderful comments
about the series, and for investing in it. I hope you love Autumn.

Chapter One

Monday 4 October

To-do list
Buy books on twins
Start looking at twin clothes – to cheer myself up. They'll be cute at least.
Check out blogs about mums having twins
Check out blogs about mums who're 40+ having twins
Ask the Book Nook to recommend any books on twins

'Oh my God, how am I going to cope?' I put my head in my hands, fighting back tears.

Wendy puts her hand on my shoulder. 'Lou, you'll be fine. Women have taken this kind of thing in their stride for centuries. In fact, in the past, families were far larger.'

I glare at her. 'Not helping. How can I go from three kids to five? I hadn't even planned on having any more, never mind two more.'

Wendy sighs. 'Breathe, sis. I know it's a shock, it was to me too, but you'll manage. Heck, you'll only have one more than me.' She smiles, but I don't reciprocate. I'm feeling sick again and it's nothing to do with being pregnant. Well, unless you consider the end result of two new babies being in my household by early next year.

I hold onto Wendy's granite worktop as if for support, my untouched cup of decaff before me. 'Wen, I keep telling myself it'll be fine, but deep down, I know it won't. I can barely cope with three kids–' I hold up my hand to stop her interrupting when she goes to speak '–I know you have four, but I have no idea how to go from three to five, particularly as I near forty. Maybe that nurse was onto something after all, when she called me a geriatric mother.'

'Midwife.'

'Huh?' I say.

'It was the midwife who said it when you went for your first scan.' Wendy gives me a long, thoughtful look.

'Don't split hairs. Perhaps if I was younger with fewer commitments, it would work, although five children in one family these days is unusual. Four is acceptable, but five?'

Wendy remains silent. She knows I'm right.

'But how am I, honestly, going to juggle this, or do any of it well? I've just signed a contract with Cerulean to work with Fabien, plus I have Wedded Bliss to manage.'

Wendy moves to interrupt, but I hold up my hand again to silence her. 'I know Mum's working with me now, but although she's been quick to learn, it's not the same as having two of me.'

Wendy nods then takes a sip of her drink. 'I know you're full of hormones–'

'It's not the hormones making me say this.' I'm trying hard not to let my composure slip.

Wendy stares at me until I look away in discomfort. 'Let me finish,' she says. 'You have to start looking at the positives.'

'Yes, yes, I know.' I glare at my coffee cup. 'Come

February, I'll have two bouncing bundles of joy, and I'll have swelled the family ranks. They'll smell of talcum powder, they'll gurgle, coo and generally be fabulous.'

'You're taking this so well,' Wendy says dryly.

I sigh. 'I'm just trying to be honest here.' I look directly at my sister's kind face. 'I'm freaking out!'

Wendy holds my gaze and then grabs her bottom lip between her thumb and forefinger, pulling on it lightly, a sign I recognise means she's deep in thought, pondering a dilemma with no quick answer to it.

Then it's her turn to sigh. 'Lou, it is what it is. And you will manage. We'll all rally round. We're a family. That's what families do. That's what this family does.'

I feel ready to burst into tears. Usually, Wendy gets me, but today she's throwing platitudes at me. Since she's on annual leave this week, I thought it would be a good idea to come here and talk things through with her, confess my misgivings, my fears. Is it the hormones, after all? Am I being unreasonable? Should I be, given the shock of discovering I'm having not one surprise baby but two?

I was in so much shock when Ronnie and I left the midwife, and then we had the housewarming party to prepare for and hold, that I barely had time to reflect even for a second. Now all I'm doing is reflecting. Well, that and panicking.

But honestly, how will I fit everything in? Even with Ronnie home, he's away some of the week in Aberdeen, and he has to be in his 'office' by nine, so can't do the school run. How will I handle two newborns and the school run? Thank goodness Gen at least is at high school and can do her own thing.

Plus, Mum has pretty much been firefighting at

Wedded Bliss whilst I learn the ropes with Fabien for the Cerulean side of my job. Typical. I land a partnership with a huge firm, which in itself is a crazy amount of work on top of my own business, and then I discover I'm pregnant – with twins. You couldn't script this.

Fabien had talked of further opportunities to go abroad or travel and give training courses, meet clients. How will that work now? It would have been very difficult with one new baby, even for a couple of days, but nigh on impossible for more than that. Mum may have managed to look after one baby once I was no longer breastfeeding, but two? Not likely. And even if I am able to plan ahead, and when Ronnie's been in his new job long enough to take holidays, he wouldn't be able to look after two new babies. Heck, it's hard enough for me to trust him with two dogs.

I've seen mums trying to handle twins. It's rugby-hold breastfeeding, one on each side. How can I do that whilst running, in effect, two businesses and managing three other kids?

It's simple. I can't. A wave of sadness washes over me. I won't be able to breastfeed. I could just about have managed one baby, maybe. But two? I'd never be able to do anything else. And I'd be leaking all over the place. That would be attractive at meetings. Professional. No matter how progressive the workplace is meant to be these days, no one, including women, want to see you with a wet blouse from where your breast pads have slipped and you're lactating. OK, I know I'm obsessing.

'Lou.'

I glance up to find Wendy staring at me.

'You went into a wee world of your own there. Look, it won't be easy, no one's saying it will be, but it will be fine.

And so will you, and the kids, and Ronnie. I promise.' She pulls me into a hug and I try not to bawl my eyes out there and then.

Once I'm back in the house, I revel for a moment in the silence. It won't be like this for much longer. The kids are at school, Aria thankfully settling in better than before, so I only have the two dogs to contend with. I bend down and scratch Patch's ears as Bear lopes up to me and rubs himself against my leg. Somehow that familiar action undoes me and I burst into tears. Damn these hormones.

I sit at the window and look out over the garden, trying but failing to come to terms with my new future. Rain batters the window and the wind picks up, howling as if sensing my mood. Thunder and lightning should follow if it's to truly mirror it, or perhaps a monsoon. The latter would represent the number of tears I've shed since I came out of shock mode.

Ronnie has been busy with his new job, and I know he doesn't get it. Doesn't get the issue, the problem. It should affect him more, particularly now he's back on the mainland working, and thus home at night. I can't decide whether to be narked at him or admire him for taking all of this in his stride. Why isn't he horrified? I'd go as far as to say he was overjoyed. Probably thought it meant he had supersperm or something. No doubt the boys will make some joke about that. Ha bloody ha. Let's see them laugh if they had to bring up five kids. Nope, no matter how many times I think of us having five kids, I can't make it seem any easier or reconcile it with my life. I sigh and start to draw stick men on the condensation on the bay window.

Two big ones and three medium ones and then two tiny ones. For good measure, I add two more, with tails. Can't leave Bear and Patch out.

I haven't slept well since the night after the party, and even then I only slept because I was exhausted by the news I was having twins, the party itself, the late hour we went to bed, not to mention the fact I'm pregnant.

Maybe if I made a list, a plan of action, I'd feel more able to cope, more organised, but the truth is, I'm terrified. Terrified it will show how insurmountable a task it is. And this is my life, will be my life. There's no getting away from that fact.

It worries me that confiding in Wendy didn't bring me the solace I'd usually feel at having offloaded. That's bad. We always have each other's backs. Me, Wendy and our other sister, Jo. But this is so much bigger than anything I've ever had to deal with, and I don't know where to start with it.

I rub my stomach and talk to my babies for the first time. Again that plural strikes me in the heart. 'Mummy's sorry. It's not that she doesn't want you, she does. She just doesn't know how to cope or how to give you both the life you deserve.'

I think of how they'll always have each other to confide in, look out for, share a secret language with and other twin stuff. How will that affect our other kids? How will that impact their bond with us, me especially? After giving birth to three kids, I'm used to, and like, having a special relationship with my children. They may love their dad, but they're closer to me. Always have been, always will be. I guess it's a symptom of him working away for so long.

The letter box rattles and I head over to pick up my

mail. That reminds me, I need to send a card to my nephew Jackson, as I may not see him on his birthday.

I leaf through the post: gas bill, Next bill, various pieces of junk mail, a letter from SAGA offering insurance for the over fifties – they're a tad early – and a brown envelope. I have an aversion to brown envelopes. I open it. Another medical appointment. Oh well, I suppose I had best get used to those. There will be plenty of them to come.

I decide not to resume my staring out the window and instead choose to do some work. Mum wasn't able to come into work today, she had arranged to take a friend to a hospital appointment. I settle down to make the most of the 'free time' I have, even though it's work, and crack on.

By the time the school run comes round, I'm feeling more positive. I've sped through my emails, done the banking, arranged some things for Cerulean, delegated some tasks to Mum for tomorrow and the rest of the week for Wedded Bliss and even managed to run the hoover round. Dear God, I hope being pregnant, especially with twins, doesn't make me become some house-proud nut. I mean, I like having a few dust mites around. I don't need to be able to eat my dinner off the floor. A home should look lived in, right?

OK, gotta go. Keys, purse, bag, dogs into kitchen and go.

'Mummy!' Aria lunges for me the moment she sees me in the playground. A few other mothers, some of whom I know, others I don't, smile at her enthusiasm.

I swoop down to give her a kiss. I can't pick her up and swing her around as I'd like to, and that both saddens and irks me. The pitfalls of being pregnant. I hate having to be so careful. 'What did you do today?'

She tilts her head to one side as if considering my question carefully. 'Well, first we did some Halloween sums, then I drew a picture of a witch on a broomstick – she had two black cats on it with her. Then it was playtime…'

I listen to her prattle on, enjoying hearing about her activities and antics. Kids are so literal. I should have realised she would give me a blow-by-blow account. She wraps up by coming back to the sums.

'And I got all my sums right.'

'That's excellent. How were they Halloween sums?'

Aria rolls her eyes at me as if this is obvious. 'I had to add three pumpkins and eight pumpkins, ten witches' hats and four witches' hats, and five broomsticks and six broomsticks.'

Ah, I see. 'Sounds fun.'

'Yes, it was. We're getting more tomorrow.'

Distractedly, I think how the beginning of October seems a tad early to be wheeling out the Halloween activities, but what do I know? I do know Aria will be fed up doing them by the time the thirty-first comes round. How will the teacher keep the topic fresh for four weeks? Aria has a low attention span. She craves new activities all the time, not more of the same.

'Oh, and I have a letter for you.'

I scrunch my eyebrows. 'A letter?' I'm already praying she isn't in any trouble. She's been at school six weeks and has already caused a stir by falling and breaking her wrist. She got a little too used to the fame that came with that too, if I'm honest. I'm hoping she hasn't done anything to add to her notoriety. Unless it's something positive, like she's been awarded the Children's Nobel Prize, or she's discovered a new planet. I'm joking, but you get the idea. Aria's unpredictable.

She hands me the letter and I glance at it. Phew! It's just a Halloween disco, but again I wonder why they're sending us the info so early. I shouldn't complain. It's better they're organised, and at least they're getting a Halloween disco. Last year it was cancelled because of budget cuts, and the PTA didn't have the funds to cover it.

'So, Mummy, I was thinking. I'd like to go as a zombie princess.'

I screw up my face. 'A zombie princess? You're five, Aria. Can't you go as a witch, or a witch's cat, or a girl wizard or something?'

She crosses her arms across her chest. 'No.' I half expect her to stamp her foot. 'I'm going as a zombie princess and that's that.'

Oh, is it? 'We'll see. I'm not sure they make zombie princess outfits for your age group.' Over my dead body, no pun intended, will my daughter attend her first Halloween disco as a zombie princess.

Aria smiles sweetly. 'That's OK, Mummy. You can make me one then.'

I have no comeback to that. Sometimes it really sucks to have clever children.

'Hey, Mum.' Hugo saunters over to Aria and me, no jacket on, despite the fine drizzle. What is it with kids that they can't wear the clothes we pay lots of money for? I know he won't catch cold – a myth – but he will get wet through, and for what? So he can carry the jacket I bought him around rather than wear it?

'Hi, darling.' I lean in to kiss his cheek, but he glances around and I see him look nervously at two boys standing near the school gate, smirking at him. Their parents aren't with them. I don't know them. They must be new to Hugo's class. I hate how at each year end, the school mixes the classes, so the children who were in your child's class the year before aren't necessarily in it the following year. And it screws with the friendships. Not ideal, and sometimes catastrophic.

'Good day?' I ask instead, as I pretend I wasn't leaning in to kiss him. I have feelings too.

'Not bad,' he mumbles.

Dear Lord, no. I can't have a monosyllabic nine-year-old. I'd expected to wait until he was at least twelve or thirteen. This is my lovely sweet boy. He can't disappear overnight, surely.

It has been a decent day from a homework perspective. Hugo applied himself the minute we arrived home, and Aria only moaned four or five times, before the promise of marshmallows and me enduring two episodes of *Shimmer and Shine* with her was enough of a lure for her to do as asked. I think the homework's too easy for her, and she's bored.

Patch and Bear set up a chorus of barking, announcing Gen's arrival. I glance at my watch. Yeah, she's right on time. Once again I'm thankful Gen's responsible enough to take the bus home on her own, as the frenzied journey from Ferniehall to Hamwell to pick her up any time after school closed for the day doesn't bear thinking about.

'Hi, Mum.' Gen beams at me as she skips into the

kitchen, drops her bag on the floor and opens the fridge door before extracting a carton of apple juice.

'How was your day, hon?' I ask as she passes me to grab a glass from the cupboard.

'Good, really good.'

'I don't imagine you were doing Halloween activities like Aria, so what made it so good?'

She blushes. Ah. Not schoolwork-related then. Silly me.

'It was just good,' she says, flipping her long honey-coloured hair out of her eyes. I know when she has no intention of being forthcoming, so I give this particular reconnaissance mission up for lost. I will win the battle though.

'Oh, I forgot.' She pulls a letter out from her jacket pocket. 'This was behind the door when I came in. Patch was jumping up at it so I thought I'd better bring it in.'

I frown. The post has already been today. Maybe the postman put the letter through someone else's door by mistake.

As Gen hops up on a stool beside me, I study the envelope. I frown again. It's from the insurance company. My heart drops. Please don't let them be taking away the extra money they finally stumped up for this place. I can't face having to move yet again.

With some trepidation, I slice open the envelope and read.

Dear Mrs Halliday

Following further investigations, the surveyor and building control have definitively found that your property is viable for reconstruction, and have advised us that this should be possible by the end of the year. The construction firm, Beeson, will be in touch with you in due course.

Please do not hesitate to contact us with any questions you may have.

Edith Holmes
Claims Handler
Prendergast Insurance Services

Oh my God, I can't believe it. Our house isn't going to be demolished. I grab Gen and hug her to me, tears in my eyes. Wait till I tell Ronnie!

Chapter Two

Wednesday 6 October

To-do list

Call insurance company for further details

Read Ace your To-do List – a guide to streamlining your life – God knows I need it, especially now

Order bus passes for the kids – gives them free travel

Send out Arlington and Veitch pocketfold wedding invitations by courier

Talk to printer about blurred menu cards for Graham wedding – the rustic woodland birds theme looks like a blob now

Two days later, I'm still flying high with elation. I can't help it. Even though it will involve packing up this place at some point and transferring our belongings back to our house, the smile hasn't left my face since I received the letter. Ronnie occasionally smiles at me, indulges me, but more often than not I catch the fleeting look of exasperation at me still going on about it. But I'm so happy I can't contain myself, borne out by the fact I've called all my family, my friends, and pretty much anyone else who'll listen. In fact, the only person of note I haven't told is

Martha. I can't wait to see her face. She'll be overjoyed, and it'll be lovely to see her too. I'm heading into the heart of the village on Friday as I have a few errands to run, so since I'll be halfway there I've decided to pop in for a surprise visit. It hits me suddenly how much I've missed her. She's like a second mum.

But first I must get a handle on this lot. I have a whole heap of work to get through, both for Wedded Bliss and for Cerulean. Fabien has a show next month in Hertfordshire and he wants me to both be involved in the rest of the arrangements and also attend it and man the stand, along with a couple of other colleagues. I've been too blown away with the revelation about having twins to really work out how I'm going to manage the logistics of it all: Ronnie's usually out of the house long before school drop-off, then there are pick-ups and after-school clubs, not to mention the simple day-to-day running of our life, and the dogs. Mum and Dad will take the dogs surely. Is it bad I'm just as concerned over who's caring for the dogs as the kids?

I'm looking forward to it apart from that. Fabien is putting us up in some swish hotel called Melbourne Lodge, in the countryside, and it's all expenses paid. I can't help wishing this had happened to me before I became a mum, or at least pregnant – again – with twins, but better late than never. I'd really like to have more time to look forward to it, enjoy the show and then luxuriate in a claw-foot bath after several glasses of champagne, whilst reflecting on a productive day's work. Instead, I'll probably be trying to head off an argument at the pass with Gen and Hugo, negotiating with Aria over doing her homework, fielding calls from Ronnie over where Gen's leotards and Hugo's tae kwon do belt are hiding, and what Aria is going to wear to school. I'll leave him written instructions, but it won't be enough. Although I've rarely been in this position, my business trip to Madrid in the summer gave me a taster of what to expect from my beloved husband.

The only upside is that Ronnie has been much more switched-on and attentive lately, and I don't just mean he's taken the bins out without being asked, or coughed up the remote control, instead of hiding it. He's genuinely been a help. Sounds ridiculous, doesn't it, that that's a breakthrough instead of a given, but it is, and I appreciate it.

Patch barks and jumps up on the dining chair next to me. 'OK, I get it, you need taken out.' I slide my feet into my trainers and grab his lead. This one still isn't to be trusted not to shoot off, unlike Bear, who can't be bothered with all that malarkey any more.

As Patch does his needs, I reflect on how it will be nice once the babies come to be able to do 'baby stuff' with Sam. With her baby – note baby, not babies – due in January, and mine in February, it will be lovely to have them so close in age. They'll hit their milestones at the same age, and hopefully end up as good friends as me and Sam.

The babies will bring to-do lists all of their own. My to-do lists don't seem to be working. I've started reading books on to-do lists. Who knew there were so many different systems? There's the 3 + 2 (3 big tasks, 2 little ones); the 1 + 3 + 5 (1 big task, 3 middle-sized tasks and 5 little ones); the project-based lists (kind of what I do at the minute, as I have lists for home, work and other), the 3 MIT (most important tasks); and my latest one – the kanban list – reminds me of production in a large factory, but basically where you have a wall full of Post-its (I like Post-its, a lot!) and they move from 'to-do', to 'doing', to 'done'.

Surely in the next four months, I can trial some of these and find something that works for me, as something has to give. I've barely survived on the system I set myself with three children, but the balls I'm juggling won't stay in the air with the current system when I have five.

Anyway, I'm always open to learning new things, proven by the fact I've taken on a partnership with Cerulean, although the timing couldn't have been worse.

I've only just returned with Patch when the front door goes. Ooh, a delivery. I'm waiting on some scalloped card. It's been delayed and has set me back with a couple of jobs, so as soon as I can, I need to get stuck in.

Ronnie's working a half day at the office today, so he's picking up the kids, which is great as Sam asked me if I could meet for a coffee at the Café on the Cobblestones, although this time I'm hoping there's no momentous news. I'm beginning to think the place is a jinx. Last time I was there with Sam I realised I was pregnant. Unless I'm going to discover I've won the lottery when I'm there, I'd rather have no more revelations, thank you very much.

I'm so looking forward to discussing baby things properly with Sam. Even though we've gone to aquanatal a few times together, more often than not I've missed it, plus, it's not exactly as if you have a great deal of time to talk to each other when you're jumping about like a loon amidst a gaggle of pregnant women in a swimming pool.

I want to be talking buggies, bootees and baby carriers.

I feel lucky that she's going through the same, or similar, experience to me at the same time.

Nicky said if Valentin could watch Xander for an hour, she'd try to join us, but she also had a conference call planned with Fabien, who has been helping her business stay afloat, as a favour to me, by ensuring her clients whose weddings were booked before her accident have a photographer for their big day. He has been an absolute godsend and I don't know what either of us would do without him. I actually miss seeing him as regularly, now we're no longer living in the hotel. If you'd told me a year ago I'd rather be living in a house doing my own cleaning and laundry, cooking my own meals, instead of having a three-course meal put down to me and my family each night, a maid who came in to clean daily and laundry service on tap, I'd have thought you were two sandwiches short of a picnic, but I'm definitely much happier in the new house, temporary though it may be. And so are the kids, and Ronnie, I think.

The kids can now nip out to the park, which is one sweep of a road and they're at the gates; Hugo is out on his bike a lot more, and even Gen goes for walks with the dogs more, or with her friends. Being cooped up in the hotel, living on top of each other, high-class hotel though it was, really affected us, and made us appreciate much more the space and freedom we have in our home. And Benedict's house, although not as homely to us as our own was, is working well for us.

I tear open the package the postman has delivered. Yes, it's the card materials I was waiting on. Thank goodness. I can probably make some of the vintage flower invitations before I meet Sam. Time to get cracking.

'No, Patch, that does not mean it's time for you to play up, or play, or get fed. It's time for me to do some work.' He makes puppy eyes at me. Easy, when you're an actual puppy. 'Oh for goodness' sake, Patch, I will never get this done. Fine, five minutes. C'mon.' I collect his tennis ball and his grabber and head out into the garden where I stand under the oak tree and toss his ball to the other side of the garden. Patch tears off down the garden at speed, his tail wagging happily as he searches for the ball amongst the many leaves that have fallen from our tree. I love the crunch of autumn leaves underfoot, and we're lucky to have loads in the garden. We've been drawing round them for Aria to learn about trees and their growth cycle, and they've come in very handy when we've been painting.

Patch bounces back over the leaves, crunch, crunch, crunch, and I can't help but smile at his enthusiasm. As I launch the ball for him once more, I realise that although I'm looking forward to returning to my house at some point, I'll miss this garden. It has to be said, it's a little better than ours. Wilder, larger and with more character. The kids love playing hide and seek in it, and I loved being able to find a shady spot under this very tree when it was too hot in summer to sit out on the chairs.

It's peaceful too. As we're one street back from the rest of the village here, the only sounds I can hear are birds and the occasional trundle of a lawnmower. The traffic, when I do hear it, is either a neighbour, or the very muted tones of cars and lorries heading towards the village's main street. But it's more of a gentle burr than anything else. Somnolent. Crikey, thinking about this and the repeated action of throwing the ball for Patch is making me sleepy. I'll be needing that coffee when I meet Sam. I might even have a real one, just the one. I'm not a saint. I can do without caffeine most of the time, but sometimes needs must. And today is a needs must kind of moment.

I finally settle down to work on the new invitation suites I've been designing for Cerulean, completely separate to my own range, and before I know it, three and a half hours have gone. However, I'm pleased with the results, and I know Fabien will be too. I've also checked and parcelled up again, ready to send out, the marble blush samples that came in. Charles, Fabien's biggest client, can't fail to be delighted by them. They're gorgeous. I'll courier them over today. We're meeting when I get back from Arran with Wendy, Jo and the kids, our belated sisters' getaway for Jo's birthday last month. With everything that happened: the lorry crash, moving into a hotel, all the upheaval and emotional trauma too, Jo felt it made sense to wait. I have to say, I'm glad now she suggested that, as I couldn't have appreciated it then, and I'm really looking forward to it now. I also thank the Lord that Mum and Dad decided to buy a property in Arran. It's such a gorgeous island, and the house is fabulous. I can't believe we haven't been there since the spring.

Gracious, is that the time? I'm going to be late.

Luckily, as it's less than five minutes away, I reach the café bang on time, and only slightly out of breath. This rushing when you're five months pregnant isn't ideal.

'Sam!' I call as she rounds the opposite corner, heading towards the café at the same time.

'Lou!' She comes forward and hugs me, which is a little harder than usual as both of us have bumps now.

'Ha, ha, that's hysterical,' she says. 'I feel like one sumo wrestler trying to hug another.'

'Don't you go grabbing me by the belt. No one needs to see my pants. The image would never leave them.' I shudder. Pregnancy's beautiful, they say, whoever they are, and some women do have the glowing skin, dewy complexion and look radiant. Me, I'm more of the sweaty harassed mess kind of pregnant. Or maybe I'm like that most of the time, and I simply happen to be pregnant at the moment.

The café's busy, and at first, I think we won't find a table, but then I spot two elderly ladies standing up and gathering their bags. We loiter, in as polite a way as possible, until one says, 'Oh, are you girls looking for a table?'

We nod and the one with pink hair says, 'We're just leaving. Enjoy. June, bring those cups so those girls have a clean table.' Her friend obliges, in her ancillary role as waitress, and I watch as she deposits them on the bar.

We shrug off our coats and I relax into the warmth of the café. I hadn't realised it was cold outside, not really, until I came in here. It's positively tropical.

When the waitress comes over, we order then settle down for a good old natter. Soon the conversation, inevitably, turns to all things baby-related.

'That was good you were able to get the afternoon off since you were at the midwife.'

'I know. I feel quite jammy, actually, but then I do put in quite a few extra hours,' Sam replies as she adjusts her coat on the back of her chair. 'So, Erik's asked if he can have first dibs on a boy's name. He's hoping to be able to name it Henrik, after his father, who passed away last year.'

'That would be a nice tribute.'

'Yeah, that's what he thought, and it would carry on his name.'

I gulp the water the waitress brought over before taking our order, whilst I wait for my coffee. Being pregnant is certainly making me thirsty. I've been drinking gallons since I found out, possibly more since I discovered it was twins.

'And are you happy to leave the boy's name to him then?'

'Well, I do still get first crack at naming the baby if it's a girl. And I don't want to be too selfish. I chose Ava and Emily's names if you recall, although Erik liked them too.'

I nod. 'Is it terrible that I can't exactly remember how much input Ronnie had?'

Sam laughs. 'No, I'm putting memory loss down to baby brain. I can remember my first day at school at the moment, but not what knickers I put on this morning.'

'Oh, I can. Big Mummy ones. Bridget Jones has got nothing on me.'

Our drinks come and I take a sip from my latte and pronounce a satisfied 'Aah.'

'I'm jealous. I've sworn off caffeine completely, and the decaff simply isn't cutting it for me.' Sam's mouth downturns at the corners.

'I know what you mean. Some brands aren't so bad, but some are little better-tasting than chicory.'

Sam grimaces. 'Oh my goodness, I remember that stuff. The granules were like sand. My gran used to buy it out the pound shop. They should have paid us a pound to drink it.'

'It is pretty gross. That's why I'm allowing myself one or two proper coffees a week. It didn't do me any harm with the other three. And I didn't touch it for the first trimester.'

'I'll stick to my camomile tea. Anyway, I meant to ask, have you had any more thoughts on names?'

'Well–' I lean forward, my excitement spilling over '–since I found out it was twins, my ideas have gone in a totally different direction.'

'Oh?' Sam tilts her head in interest.

'Yep, I was thinking, Elijah if it's a boy, and if it's a boy and a girl, I'd like both of them to have the same–'

Pharrell Williams' 'Happy' blasts out of Sam's bag. She flushes red. 'I'm so sorry, let me get this. I'll kill Ava. She keeps playing around with my ringtone and turning it up top volume too. That's it, I really need to change my password. Kids are too good with technology.'

'That they are,' I say, thinking of my three.

She wrestles with her bag and finally turns it off and adjusts the ring tone and volume. 'Oh, do you know, talking about names, I've narrowed my choices down to two. Amelia and, wait for it, Elodie. Actually, Elodie's my favourite, and Erik prefers that too. I have a new pupil in my class and that's her mum's name and I just love it. What do you think?'

My smile dies on my lips. How do I tell her? I can't. 'Lovely.'

'Anyway, sorry, what were you saying?' She frowns as she tries to recall. Please let her have forgotten. She did say she had baby brain. 'Oh yes, Elijah and you'd like them both to…what?'

I take a deep breath. 'Have names starting with different letters. I know some people like to do it with the same one for twins, but I'd like them to be more distinct.'

'I get that.' Her head's almost bobbing in her attempt to agree with me.

It's a pity it isn't true then. And right at that moment, much as I hate myself, I curse the fact one of my best friends will give birth before me, because the name she's chosen for her baby girl, out of all the names in the world, is the same as the one I've chosen: Elodie. I started reading a novel the other day by one of my favourite authors and her protagonist was called Elodie, and I fell in love with it immediately. And now it's been snatched away from me. What do I do? Am I being silly? Do I tell her? But what if that causes a rift between us? I sigh. Why is nothing ever simple?

Chapter Three

Friday 8 October

To-do list – the 3 +2 method. I almost did it, but I had to add an extra about packing for Arran. Oh well, it's 3+3
Buy flowers for Martha
Steak for dinner from butcher
New gymnastic shoes for Gen
Set up direct debit for Behind the Mask – Aria's drama club – find form
Buy new water bottle for Aria – hers is cracked
Start packing for Arran trip

I can't believe the kids finish up today for ten days. It feels as if they only started back at school a few weeks ago. Where has the time gone?

Ronnie's heading into the office later today, so I'm taking advantage of that to take both Bear and Patch for a walk, at the same time, whilst the kids are still asleep. A fine early morning drizzle coats my face as I head down past the park and along towards the central part of the village. I love being out at this time of day. No one around except the van that drops off the newspapers to the two shops that stock them. I'm a little too late to catch the milkman. He tends to do his round at four thirty, for some unfathomable reason. I used to keep the window open in the summer until the predawn tinkle of milk bottles and the slow trundle of the milk van woke me daily. After that, when it became exceptionally warm, I wore ear plugs, and when it was cool enough, I'd close the window.

It's still dark as I wander through the village. Dawn won't make itself felt for another hour or so yet. It's the one thing I hate about autumn, and winter, it being dark for so long. I don't actually mind the rain, except when it's a torrential downpour. And I love the smell that lingers in the air after it has rained. One of my favourite smells of all.

I chuckle as I consider I'll be coming along this way later. I have some tasks to do and, of course, I'm looking forward to seeing Martha and giving her the good news. I walk along Main Street, past the church, the bookshop – oh, they've redone their window display. I must pop in later. Dad would like the new Michael Connelly. I glance in the window of A Cut Above and tug my hood over my head self-consciously. I am long overdue a haircut. I've been snipping it a little here and there when it becomes a bit too unwieldy and wild, but I need to make an appointment. Funny how I rarely forget to ensure the kids have hair appointments.

I think back to the last time I was here, with Gen, for her makeover. Such a great day. I could have had it cut then, but I wanted the day to be all about her and her transformation. I pull my hood down slightly and study myself in the shop window. A slightly older than I'd like version of me returns my gaze. Hmm. I might have to actually make more of an effort. I do for meetings with clients, but otherwise I'm very much a dress-down person.

It comes from living in a village, and I'm lucky we don't seem to have that rivalry between the school-gate mums, to be dressed to kill. Not that that would influence me to follow suit, but I'd rather not look like a total scarecrow.

Just before I reach our house, I glance at Martha's. Her curtains are already open. Early start this morning, Martha. Too early still for me to visit, and I have the kids to see to anyway, but early start all the same.

I walk the extra few metres to our house and stand in front of it, drinking in every detail. There does seem to have been some progress. Different pieces of machinery stand like sentinels waiting for their operators to return. Pallets of bricks and sandstone, if I've made that out right, peek out from under the flapping tarpaulin. Plus a few minor things do seem to be underway already. My heart lifts both at this development and at the fact we should be home by the end of the year. Home. I smile. I can't help it. So many memories here. I stand, one lead in each hand, the dogs obediently sitting at my feet as I stare up at the house and try to think of only happy moments we had there, and not the awful evening when a lorry crashed through our living room. It occurs to me suddenly that my friend Nicky must have flashbacks to this all the time. It may have been my home that was lost that night, but Nicky lost so much more: her mobility, her confidence, her livelihood, almost her life. I shudder and turn away, but not before I determine that only good memories will come from the house from now on.

I stroke my stomach, conscious of keeping a tight hold on Patch's lead, and tell my babies, 'This is your home. This is where you're going to live and grow up, just like your brother and sisters.' Then with a small smile, and chiding myself for being so maudlin a moment earlier, I turn for home – my temporary home – back beyond the park. As I pass Icing on the Cake, the church bell strikes the half hour, and I glance up at the tower in all its Gothic glory.

Is that the time? I'd better get a move on.

'Morning!' Ronnie says when I shake the rain off my coat and hang it up to dry. 'Want a coffee?'

'Yes, please, decaff.'

The edges of Ronnie's mouth turn down. 'Oh, I'd forgotten. Of course.'

I hide a smile. That's my husband's way of saying he wished he hadn't asked. Now he has to make two different types, although he *will* only be spooning a teaspoonful of instant from a jar for me.

'What's the weather like out there?' Ronnie asks as he passes me the cup.

'Drizzly, but not bad. Nice for walking in.'

'You are weird, you know.' He smiles. 'I hate drizzle. It gets in your face, and even though it's not that much water, it makes you feel cold and soaked through.'

'Each to their own.' I stick my tongue out at him. 'I walked up as far as the house.'

'Oh really? How's it looking?'

I hesitate for a second. 'It's definitely coming on. I love it here–' I throw my hands out to encompass the house we're currently in '–but I can't wait to go home.'

Ronnie says nothing, but comes forward and envelops me in a hug. The solidity of his chest against my face still makes my heart leap, even after all these years. And he smells divine. It's only a fruity body wash but I don't care. It's heavenly.

'I'm going to see Martha today,' I tell him as we move apart. 'Give her the good news.'

Ronnie frowns. 'Don't you think it would be better to wait until we know for sure?'

Now it's my turn to frown. 'Well, we have it in writing, and we've told everyone else.'

Ronnie gives a faint smile. 'You mean you've told everyone else.'

'Details, husband, details.' I dismiss his statement with a wave.

'Aria, you need to eat your breakfast. We'll be late for school otherwise.'

No answer.

'Aria. Breakfast.' I'm resorting to one-word sentences like they did in caveman days. Maybe I'll get a better response rate. Nope. Seriously? Have my children gone on strike or something today, or are they just being pig-ignorant where I'm concerned?

My patience is beginning to wear thin. I pause Aria's episode of *Shimmer and Shine*. I knew getting a TV for the kitchen was a bad idea.

'Aria.'

She turns to look at me, her big blue eyes full of innocence. Perhaps she didn't hear me before. Perhaps monkeys can fly. 'Yes, Mum?'

Hmm. When did I go from being Mummy to Mum in her eyes? And how come I've only just noticed this? Or is this the first time?

I realise she's waiting for me to speak again. 'Breakfast. You need to get dressed in five minutes.'

'OK, Mummy.' She picks up her spoon.

And relax. I'm still Mummy. It's not the end of an era yet. Far from it. I have two more children arriving in February.

Five minutes later, I'm dressing Aria. She turns her back to me so I can put on her tie. I've always found it easier that way. 'Mummy.'

Oh no. I recognise that tone.

'Yes, Aria?' I finish her tie and turn her to face me so we can put on her pinafore.

'You know how you said you'd still have time for me and love me when the baby came?'

OK. Not what I thought she was going to say. I assumed she wanted an extra Freddo for her lunch box or something.

I stroke her hair. 'Yes. I remember.'

'Well, now there are going to be two more babies, will you still have time for me?'

Be still my beating heart. How can a child as gregarious and uber confident as Aria be so insecure? It really goes to show, we never really know what's happening inside their little heads.

'Aria–' I rest my hands on her shoulders '–I will always have time for you, always, no matter if I have ten babies.'

'Ten! I thought you were having twins. What even are ten babies called?'

'Aria.' I pause because I realise I can't explain what I meant to a five-year-old. Although clever, I don't think 'figurative' or 'metaphorical' have reached her vocabulary yet, and right now is not the time to rectify that. 'I'm only having two babies.'

She rolls her eyes as if to convey two babies is more than she'd like.

'And two babies is quite enough,' I continue.

She nods. 'Yes, no more babies, Mummy, after this one, I mean, the two babies. That's quite enough now. You're just being greedy.'

I can't help it, I burst out laughing.

Aria puts her hands on her hips. 'Mummy, I'm not kidding. No more babies. Some people have no babies, so if you have any more, they can have them.'

I have no comeback to that at present and decide to wrap things up with a little reassurance. 'Aria, I will love you, and the two new babies, and your brother, and Gen, just the same. The same amount. So will Dad.'

She eyes me suspiciously. I'm not off the hook yet. 'How do you know? Did you ask him?'

Her tone suggests she might ask him if I don't say yes. 'Dad told me,' I fib.

Fortunately, she seems mollified by that, so I jump at the opportunity and say, 'Right, shoes. We need to go. Hugo!'

'Coming!' comes the response from upstairs. Gen left earlier to catch her bus, or she could have helped me fend off Aria's barrage. Either that or she would have sat and sniggered into her phone, eyes down to avoid being drawn into things.

I will have to be mindful, not only of Aria's needs and emotional state around the topic of the twins, but her siblings' too. Hugo, in particular, isn't the best, especially now, at conveying his feelings; instead he covers it up with humour, and Gen, well, Gen's at that difficult age, and I don't want to leave her to get on with it simply because she's more mature than her brother and sister. She needs me in different ways now.

With these thoughts flying around my head, I shepherd my youngest two out of the house, into the car and off to school.

When I return from the school run twenty minutes later, I slump into my chair for a second. Mum's due any minute. We have a morning briefing scheduled regarding what's what with Wedded Bliss, before I head out to do some shopping in the village and visit Martha. We're still finding our feet with regards to who does what and how much of Wedded Bliss Mum will handle whilst I get to grips with working for Fabien and Cerulean. I hadn't expected to throw having twins into the mix too. I sigh. I'm sure it will all work out, or am I just telling myself that to make myself feel better? Hard to tell.

I fill my water bottle from the fridge dispenser and settle down to attack my to-do list before Mum arrives. I have two more designs to finalise for Fabien, and I'd also like Mum's opinion on them before I show them to him. Mum's always been my biggest supporter and if not my harshest critic, she'll at least steer me in the right direction when I'm about to screw things up. So I trust her judgement.

'Hi, darling!' Mum envelops me in a bear hug then follows me into the house. Her hair's slightly damp, she clearly hasn't dried her hair after showering, and it tickles the side of my face.

'Morning, Mum. Tea?' I start the familiar ritual of heading for the kitchen and switching the kettle on. Soon, we're ensconced in the living room, each with our notepads and pens, as we transfer some of my to-do list to Mum's and she updates me all things Wedded Bliss she's been working on that I need to know about. Mum's been handling more of my company business than I have the past few months, since the crash and since I signed on to partner with Cerulean. It's difficult for me to let go of the reins of my baby, but at least I know the company's in good hands. The best. But I can't help the occasional twinge of guilt or thinking she'd be enjoying her retirement more if it wasn't for having to step in to help me so often.

Once Mum and I have sorted the tasks for the day, I prepare to head into the village for a few things.

'Right, Mum, I'll see you later. Would you like me to pick anything up for you when I'm in the village?'

She shakes her head. 'No, but please do send Martha my love.'

I smile. 'I will.'

This time I go on my own, no dogs – Mum's there to fuss over them anyway – and I stride purposefully towards Main Street.

What a difference a few hours can make. The drizzle has cleared, the sun is out and the village looks totally different.

I pass the man who helped me with Patch on the night of the crash. Oh my goodness, I've forgotten his name. How embarrassing. 'Lovely day now, isn't it?' I say.

He dips his head, then stops for a moment. 'How's that young pup of yours doing? I haven't seen him around much.'

'He's getting into scrapes as usual. We have to enrol him in puppy training classes. We just haven't had much time, what with everything else.'

What the 'everything else' is remains unspoken between us. No need to dredge up the details of that terrible evening.

As we part ways, I notice a scarecrow sitting on the wall off to the left. I didn't notice him this morning. Well, Amy's certainly quick off the mark this year. She's usually one of the first to put her scarecrow out, but the festival doesn't start for another week. I suppose, Amy is on the festival committee, so that's probably why her multicoloured patchwork-dungareed creation is already sitting out front. I smile. Good on her. Everyone needs a boost. And although I was already in good spirits today, the scarecrow's presence and reminder of the festival to come has boosted them further.

The kids love the festival and have been to it every year since its inception. Now there's a whole programme of events, including a scarecrow parade. Many of the houses and local businesses put miniature scarecrows in their shop windows in the run-up to the festival to show support for it.

Oh, before I forget, I want to buy that book for Dad. He's such an unassuming sort is my dad, eclipsed in the shadow of my wonderfully effusive mum. So I like to make a fuss of him when I can. And whilst Mum has found her métier with Wedded Bliss, and now they've decided to go cruising far less so they can spend more time with all of us children and grandchildren, Dad is a little lost sometimes. But one thing he does enjoy is a good action novel.

The bell tings as I enter the Book Nook.

'I'm in the back. Just be a sec,' calls a voice.

A minute later, the owner, Geraldine, comes out. 'Sorry about that, Louisa. Delivery.'

'No problem. I'd like a copy of the book in the window, *For Forever and a Day*. It's for my dad,' I add unnecessarily. 'I didn't see it on the displays.'

'No, it's just in. I'm still unpacking them. Ooh, he'll love it. My dad finished it the other day. Said it was brilliant. Really fast-paced. He's given it to me to read next. I did try pointing out I work in a bookshop and can have my pick of books, but there was no telling him.' She wraps up the book in brown paper for me, which makes it look as if I've bought something off the top shelf in a dodgy newsagent's.

I grin. 'Parents, eh?' I think of Mum. I'll pop across to Blooming Marvellous and get some flowers for both her and Martha. 'See you later, Geraldine.'

'You too, Louisa.'

I navigate the little traffic there is to cross to Blooming Marvellous. Susan, the florist, is already out arranging bouquets in colourful buckets.

'Hi, Louisa, haven't seen you for a while. All good?'

'Morning, Susan. Yep.' I lean forward slightly as if whispering a secret. 'Our house is being rebuilt and should be ready for the end of the year.'

'Oh, that's marvellous news.' Then she seems to realise what adjective she's used, looks above her head, points to her sign and says, 'Blooming Marvellous.'

I smile. 'It is indeed. Can't wait to move back. In fact, I'm just on my way to tell Martha. I'm looking for a bouquet for her and one for Mum. What do you recommend?'

'Well, we have these, of course.' She points to the slim bouquets she's putting in the coloured buckets, or, if you want something truly autumnal, I can make you up one of dahlias, chrysanthemums, I even have Chinese lanterns, some protea and kniphofia.'

That's easy for her to say. She lost me at Chinese lanterns. I thought they were those things we used to send up into the sky at New Year, to be trendy, then realised it was terrible for the environment. I love flowers, love looking at them, that is. I don't grow them, am not in the slightest green-fingered, nor have plans to be, and I honestly have no idea what she's talking about. I can just about remember what dahlias look like.

'Whatever you think, Susan. You're the specialist. Can you make me two slightly different ones?'

'Of course.' She bustles around, talking to me, although she'd be as well talking to herself, as she tells me what pairs best with what. I think I'd be as lost if she was discussing calculus. I really hated calculus.

'Oh, and do you mind keeping Mum's until I'm on my way back from Martha's? I don't want to pitch up with two lots of flowers, plus I need to nip in to Icing on the Cake and the butcher's too.'

'Absolutely.' She waves a hand to show it's no problem at all and I'm not to give it another thought.

We chat as she works, and soon I head off along Main Street towards Martha's, eager to see her and also to check if work is going on in our house today.

I spot another couple of scarecrows along the way. Initially, I wonder how I didn't see them earlier, but it was still dark, and it's not as if they're sitting front and centre. One is sitting on a bench underneath someone's windowsill – dressed in military garb – another is against a white wall, which doesn't help as it's a snowman scarecrow. We may have to up our game with our costumes this year for the parade, but how? We're going to Arran in three days' time for a week.

When I reach Martha's, I'm dismayed to see no one is currently working on our house. No diggers. No drills. No bricklayers. Nothing. I'm not sure what I expected, but I expected something, especially since the insurance company has advised we should be able to move back by New Year.

Oh well, I'm not going to dwell on it. It probably takes a few days for the info to filter through from one company to another. As long as it's not because there aren't enough tradespeople to go around.

I ring Martha's bell. I wait. No answer. I ring again, expecting to hear the smack of her slippers as she plods along the runner to the front door. Still no answer. Surely she isn't out? It's a bit early to go for lunch, and if she'd been in the village, I'd have passed her. Maybe a friend has come to pick her up. Drat, I've missed her, haven't I? I take a pen and some paper out of my bag and scribble her a note, which I pop through the door. Then I prop the flowers up against the front door, and head back the way I've come. I knew I should have called ahead. Oh well, I'll catch up with her over the weekend, hopefully.

In the butcher's, I'm waiting whilst George prepares my steaks and cuts me two pounds of sausages. Something's niggling me about Martha's. Nope, I can't remember. I guess it will come back to me at the most unhelpful time, like three in the morning.

'Has Martha been in today, George?' I ask. The words are no sooner out of my mouth than realisation slaps me on the back of the head. Isn't Martha in Australia at her son's? I don't even hear George's reply. I'll have to go rescue those flowers and give them to someone else who deserves them.

'Sorry, George. I didn't hear you there.'

'Not yet. She came in on Wednesday and asked me to order in some lamb's liver for her. She was meant to pick it up yesterday, but she must have forgotten.'

A shiver runs down my body, and I think I'm going to throw up. 'George, I need to go. Something's wrong with Martha.'

Chapter Four

I turn and flee the shop. I know what was niggling me, and it wasn't that she'd be at her son's in Australia, but that there were two full milk bottles outside her house. Martha would have taken her milk in if she'd gone out. Not only that, but Martha only orders a pint of milk each day, not two. And our usual milkman is on holiday, so his replacement wouldn't have necessarily noticed anything amiss. Dear God, no!

This time, I throw her gate open and rush round the back. The back door's locked. I look in the windows. Nothing. I go round the front and peer in there. I can't see anything. Am I overreacting? Is pregnancy making me overprotective? I don't think so. I have a moment of doubt, then I thrust open the letter box to shout through it and glance down – there are several letters there. The postman doesn't come until around half past one, so that's not today's mail.

I know she could simply be away staying at a friend's overnight, although this would be out of character, but I have this awful sense of foreboding. I shout through the letter box. Nothing. I try again. Nothing. By now, Martha's neighbour on the other side, Malcolm, has come out. He mainly keeps himself to himself, but I have seen him talk to Martha now and again.

'Malcolm, Malcolm!' I call.

He looks rattled at me shouting at him, but I don't have time for niceties. Something's wrong. I know it. I can feel it in my waters.

'Louisa?' He registers who I am.

'Malcolm, have you seen Martha the past few days?'

He thinks for a minute, although it seems an age before he replies. 'No, I haven't. The last day we spoke was Monday.'

Monday! Four days ago. Oh my God!

'Malcolm, I need to break the glass in Martha's door. Something's wrong. Do you have something I could use?'

He eyes me warily.

'Malcolm, I promise, I'll take full responsibility, but if I'm right, Martha's hurt and there's no time to lose.'

He nods and goes round the back of his house, presumably to his shed to fetch something suitable. Meanwhile, I continue to shout through Martha's letter box but with no response. Then I hear something. I'm sure of it. 'Martha!' I call. 'Are you there?'

Nothing. Then I hear it again. It's very faint, but someone's in there, and I know I'm right.

Fortunately, Malcolm returns then with a crowbar, which I almost snatch out of his hands in my hurry to check on Martha.

I've never done anything like this before. I may have sounded as if I was talking a good game when I asked Malcolm for something to break the glass with, but I honestly have no idea what to do. Do I jimmy the door? How do I jimmy the door? In the end, which is probably only after a few seconds, I hold the crowbar in one hand, the sleeve of my jumper around it to protect my hand and I smash the glass. I wait a split second. No alarm. Good. I don't want to have that to deal with too. I use the crowbar to bash in enough glass so I can get my hand to the lock of the door. Lucky I've been in Martha's so many times, I know exactly what type of lock she has and what she doesn't have. She doesn't use the safety chains, despite my pestering her to do so. She has a single lock which I easily unlock by means of reaching my hand in through the broken window.

Soon, I'm in. I kick aside the letters scattered behind the door. Please, God, let her be all right. 'Martha!' I call. 'Martha, it's Lou. Are you here?' I go into the living room. Empty. I check the kitchen and I'm about to rush up the stairs to check if she has tripped up there and been unable to get help, when I hear a sound again. I shove open the kitchen door and hear the noise again. It's coming from the pantry. Martha has one of those old-fashioned walk-in ones my granny used to have. It's more like a small room. My heart speeds up and I fling open the pantry door to find Martha lying prone on the floor. Her skin is grey.

'Martha, I'm here now.' No response. Heart in my mouth, wondering if I imagined the earlier noises, I put my fingers to her wrist. At first I can't feel anything, then finally and with a sigh of relief, I note a faint pulse. Oh, thank goodness. She's alive. I don't know what's happened here. 'Martha,' I say to her, stroking her cheek. 'Martha'. No response. If she did make a noise and I didn't imagine it, then it clearly took all of her reserves of energy, as she's unresponsive now.

I take out my mobile and dial 999. I give the call

handler my name, Martha's, her address, what's happened that I can see, and that I don't know how long she has been there. Yes, she has a pulse, but it's faint, and no, she doesn't appear to be conscious. Yes, I'll wait. The responses tumble out of me automatically as I continue to answer their questions. I'm told not to move her as we have no idea what's caused her to be unconscious. Given she's in the pantry, she could have fallen trying to reach something high up, or she could have had a heart attack, a stroke, or there could be any number of other reasons.

Until the paramedics arrive, I'm going to keep talking to her, hoping subliminally my words get through. 'I'm here, Martha. You're going to be all right. The ambulance is on its way.' God, I hope I'm right. Life without Martha in it doesn't bear thinking about. The world is a better place with Martha in it. She's kind, selfless, funny. I stop myself. I'm being maudlin. She's going to be fine. I've found her in time. Whatever's wrong, the doctors will be able to fix it. Fix her. She looks so pale. So old. I mean, I know she is old, but she's never seemed old before. I feel sick.

'Louisa.' Malcolm.

'Come in, Malcolm, but watch the broken glass,' I shout. 'I'm in the kitchen. She's here.'

I hear Malcolm pick his way over the glass and shuffle towards the kitchen.

'Oh my goodness,' he says as he takes in the sight of an unconscious Martha.

'The ambulance is on its way.' I try to reassure him. He and Martha have been neighbours for more than thirty years.

'Why didn't I check on her?' he mumbles. 'Poor Martha.'

'Malcolm–' I lay a hand on his arm '–you couldn't have known. She could have been visiting friends. For a moment, I thought she'd gone to her son's in Australia.'

'Not for another three weeks,' he mutters.

'Poor Martha.' I reiterate Malcolm's thoughts.

'Malcolm, can you do something for me?' I say, suddenly practical. 'I'm going in the ambulance with Martha. Can you call a glazier to come fix the door so the house is secure? I'll square it with the police and the insurance later. The glazier can call me for my credit card details, if necessary, but we'll need to secure the house.'

Malcolm waves his hand at me in dismissal. 'Don't you worry about that, lass. I'll take care of it.'

Martha's son. For a moment I'm torn. Do I tell him or do I wait to see what happens? His number is in my Filofax at my house. Yes, I still keep a Filofax, in case the internet melts. Brett? Is that his name? My brain feels more than a little fogged with everything that's happened.

With shaking hands, I call Mum. 'Mum. It's Martha. Something terrible's happened.'

Not long after I end my call with Mum, the paramedics arrive and they are marvellous. They manage to be both professional and chipper at the same time, although Martha doesn't regain consciousness whilst we're in her house. Soon we're whisked away in the ambulance to the hospital, me sitting beside Martha holding her hand. Sirens blaring, lights flashing, the ambulance races for the city as I gaze down at Martha and do the only thing I can. Pray.

Mum calls me back with Brett's number when I'm at the hospital. It's so frightening to see Martha attached to all these monitors and machines. I've never seen her so frail. I didn't even have the presence of mind to pack her a bag.

'She's in the best place, Lou. Thank God you found her.'

I nod even though I know she can't see me. I can't bear to think of what might have happened had I not decided today was the day to tell Martha we were moving back. Tears threaten to fall as I consider the possibility of returning to our home without Martha being next door.

I wish we knew more about what was wrong with her. She still hadn't regained consciousness by the time we reached A & E. Fortunately, the paramedics zipped her straight through to triage. They allowed me to go with her as I explained her only son was in Australia and I'm the nearest thing she has to family.

After debating it for a while, I decide to wait until I have a little more information before calling Brett. I don't know which part of Australia he's in. Is it Melbourne? How many hours ahead are they? Will I be ringing him in the middle of the night if I wait?

I pass on my misgivings to the nurse. She shakes her head and gives a sad smile. 'We'll know more once the doctor's been. We're just stabilising her for now.'

'How long will that be?' I ask.

'Hopefully, not too much longer,' she says.

I wonder how often she has to repeat that each day.

Whilst I wait, I glance up at Martha in the bed beside me. Her skin is paper-thin, the veins visibly criss-crossing her skin like a route map. I shake my head in disbelief and stifle a sob. Then I chastise myself. I'm not lying in the bed, Martha is. And she needs us. Her family needs us.

I make the call. 'Brett, it's Louisa, your mum's

neighbour.'

As soon as he hears my voice, he breaks down. It must be hard being so far away. Quickly, I hasten to reassure him, in case he fears the worst. The situation's already bad enough, but she's still with us. She's still with us. I keep that thought uppermost in my mind. I tell Brett what I know, and that I'll keep him updated.

'I'll book a flight. I have things to organise, but I can take care of that once the flight's booked.' He's babbling, and my heart goes out to him.

'Do you have someone there with you?'

'My girlfriend lives twenty minutes away. I'll call her. She can help me sort things.'

'Call me if you need me, Brett, and I'll let you know as soon as there's any news.'

I disconnect the call and realise I need to let Ronnie know. Mum will have probably texted him, but someone will have to pick up the kids. Maybe Dad could do that. I don't want them hearing it through the grapevine. They're all so close to Martha. She's known each of them since they were born: another reason our house is so important to me. My kids' childhoods are tied up with Martha and her house.

And I must let Nicky and Sam know, and Wendy and Jo. God, I'm supposed to be going to Arran with my sisters on Monday. I can barely think straight. What's taking so long? Don't they realise this is an emergency? She hasn't regained consciousness yet. How long has she been unconscious? How long was she there on her own? And as these questions flit through my mind, the tears finally come, and the sobs, and then I'm a sobbing, snotty mess, and I don't care.

'Mrs Halliday, is it?'

I glance up to see a man in a white shirt, no tie, I note. His name badge reads Dr Cross. My addled brain takes this in and tries not to smile as he's the least cross-looking man on the planet. Professional and perhaps sombre given the occasion, but he exudes positivity.

'Yes.' I fumble nervously with the hem of my jumper, terrified of what he might be about to tell me.

'Mrs Crawford is stable at the minute. We're not entirely sure what the full extent of her injuries are yet, but she has broken her hip. It could be that she's unconscious as she passed out from the pain.' He winces. 'Since we don't know how long she was lying there, it's hard to tell. But she may have fallen, rather than something more sinister having caused her to fall.' When I continue to stare at him, he clarifies, 'Like a heart attack or a stroke.'

I sigh with relief, although I'm not sure why. She's not out of the woods yet.

'There's no indication she's had a heart attack. The observations we did are clear from that perspective. And there's no obvious sign of a head injury: no bruising, no bleeding, no lumps or bumps. So now we just have to wait and see if she wakes up soon. It may be that her body shut down temporarily to deal with the pain. She's breathing more easily now, although we've given her a little help in that department.'

I try to process this, relief and anguish mixing in equal measure. 'And do you have any idea how long that will take?'

Compassion crosses the consultant's face. 'Sadly, no. These things take time, but I can assure you, as soon as we know anything, we'll let you know. I trust the family has been informed. They're in Australia, I believe.'

'Yes, her son's catching the first flight, but obviously it will take a day or so for him to get here.'

He nods. 'Right. Anyway, we'll keep you posted.' He gives a wry smile and turns to go, his thoughts no doubt already on his next patient.

'Thanks, Doctor.'

I slump down in the chair and exhale loudly, then when I'm sure the doctor has gone, I let it all out again. The tears, the frustration, the anger. Why didn't I check on her before? She's an old lady. I know I'd tell anyone else not to waste energy on recriminations, but following my own advice is *hard*. Martha is so dear to me, and I've been lax in keeping in touch since the crash. I've turned inwards, concentrating on me and my family. Not that that's wrong, but it shouldn't be to the exclusion of all else, and now I feel I'm paying for it. Poor Martha.

To take my mind off my self-reproachful thoughts, I bash out texts to Brett, Mum and Ronnie with updates.

I'm blowing my nose noisily when a nurse comes by. 'Would you like a cup of tea?'

I nod silently then smile. I don't trust myself to speak. My voice would croak more than Kermit's at the moment. I'm thankful I'm in this odd little triage waiting room, and not in the main waiting room in A & E which was chockful when we passed through it.

My phone buzzes. *Wendy.*
I just heard. Oh my God, is she OK?

I take a deep breath and type back. *Doctor's just been. He's ruled out a heart attack. Thinks it was a fall x*
Which hospital is she in? x
The Queen Elizabeth. The Royal was full, apparently x

Are you staying or coming home? x

No hesitation in my reply. *Staying x*

I'll be right there. I don't want you being on your own x

I stifle a sob again. Wendy. My sister is amazing. She's always there for me. Her kindness and humanity make me want to weep with gratitude. If ever there was a time I needed my sister's shoulder to cry on, it's now.

I type back one word. *Thanks x*

The nurse brings my tea and it's the best tea I've ever tasted. It must have about four sugars in it. Belatedly, I realise I was, I am, in shock. I just hadn't had time to realise it. Whether it actually works or is purely a placebo, the tea does wonders. After I finish it, I feel more rational. I try to recalibrate as I send texts, answer messages, field calls about how Martha is. Mum passes on the best wishes of what seems half the village. That's the thing about villages: news spreads like wildfire.

I'm burying myself in work emails when Wendy blows in, her coat flying behind her like a cape. My sister doesn't really do things at regular speed, particularly when someone she cares about needs her. Not that I'm the slowest person in the world. We're more alike than I'd realised.

As she comes towards me, I stand and walk into her open arms, which she enfolds around me. It's how I imagine being in the womb: cocooned, safe. I sob silently against Wendy's chest as she strokes my hair. When I finally draw back, she asks, 'Any more news?'

I shake my head. 'Just a waiting game now.'

'I've asked Brandon to collect the kids.'

I nod. She thinks of everything.

'Have you eaten?' she asks as we sit down next to each other.

'No, the nurse gave me some tea.'

She opens her bag. 'Here.' She passes me an energy bar. 'It'll keep your strength up.'

'Thanks.' I rip it open and take a bite.

'What a mess.' Wendy runs a hand through her hair. Although Martha's my neighbour, Wendy has become fond of her over the years too. 'She won't be allowed out until they have a care package in place, I imagine, since she doesn't have any family here.'

I hadn't thought that far ahead, but that would be the case. Poor Martha. 'I wonder how long Brett will be able to stay for.'

Wendy shrugs and shakes her head at the enormity of it all. 'Will we cancel the Arran trip?'

I stare at her long and hard, biting my lip. 'I don't know. I can't think past the next hour at the moment.'

'We're not going until Monday. Brett hopefully will arrive Sunday. If you wanted to stay here for Martha, I could take the kids and you could join us later.'

'I don't know. Sorry, Wen, I really can't compute all this right now.'

'No worries. I shouldn't have brought it up.'

'No, it's not that.' I want to reassure her. 'I just can't process information at the moment. Can't think ahead, not where my life is concerned, work, yeah, maybe, but me, the kids, not yet. Not until I know how Martha is.'

My phone beeps. Brett. *Flight will arrive in Glasgow at 12.45 tomorrow. I'll go straight to the hospital. Thanks for everything.*

I let out a breath. Brett is on his way. He'll be here in slightly less than a day. Hopefully, Martha's condition will have improved by then.

Wendy and I sit side by side, chatting, playing trivia games on my phone together, killing time until we have an update on Martha. A dinner lady passes by with a trolley and the smell from the roast beef wafts into the waiting area. Both Wendy and I almost physically rise to follow its smell like the Bisto Kid in the ad. My stomach rumbles then Wendy's does, and we share a laugh. A rare moment of levity.

Ten minutes later, the same dinner lady passes. 'You girls want some food? I have a few leftover portions. Couple of patients who were discharged before lunch.'

'That would be lovely, thanks,' Wendy says, and we gratefully accept the trays the woman passes us, then devour their contents as if we've never been fed. It must be the stress.

A few hours later, I'm on the verge of finally insisting Wendy goes home – I've been telling her to for ages, but to no avail – when the doctor from earlier comes into the waiting room, a smile on his lips.

'Good news. Mrs Crawford is conscious and asking for a cup of tea.'

A gurgle escapes my lips. It's somewhere between a laugh and a cry. Wendy thanks the doctor, since I seem unable to speak. I smile back at him and croak 'Thanks.'

He smiles. 'You can see her for five minutes if you like.'

If I like? If I like? Of course I want to see her. I can't get out of my seat fast enough.

Chapter Five

Friday 8 October

'Martha, how are you feeling?' I ask as I take her hands in mine.

'Like I've been hit by a lorry,' she rasps.

I wince, and her eyes flutter closed a second. 'Sorry, that was thoughtless of me. Not great. But I'm still here.' Her trademark twinkle along with some steely determination returns to her eyes for a second.

'You're still here.' I don't want to tire her out too much, so I get to the point almost immediately. 'Brett's on his way. He'll be here tomorrow.'

Martha sighs. 'Oh goodness, he didn't need to do that.' However, from the way her body slumps almost imperceptibly against her pillows, I can tell she's relieved.

'Yes, he did,' I say firmly.

A few minutes later, I tell her I'll be back tomorrow, but she has to rest. Better I go now before some nurse throws me out.

As Wendy drives me home, my thoughts return to the progress with the house. At least soon we'll be home again and able to keep an eye on Martha, as we've always done in the past. This whole crash, temporary rehoming in a hotel then a new house has taken our routine away from us all.

'Penny for them.' Wendy glances across at me in the passenger seat. When I raise my head, she adds, 'You've been very quiet, and you don't usually do quiet.'

I smile. 'True. Just thinking about when we move home. Can't wait.'

Wendy nods. 'Yeah, it'll be great to have you all back where you belong.' She fills me in with details of how her job's going, the works' night out she has coming up and how Brandon's on track for another promotion. For all I think my brother-in-law isn't good enough for my sister, most of the time, he is exceptional at his job.

'Wen,' I say, my thoughts meandering once again. 'What would you have done if one of your best friends had chosen the same baby name as you?'

We're stopped at lights. She turns to me. 'Sam?'

I nod. 'She wants to call the baby Elodie. She and Erik found out the sex at the scan, but didn't tell anyone at the time. It's a little girl. But I'd already decided that if the twins are a boy and a girl, I'd like to call them Elodie and Elijah. I just hadn't told anyone yet.'

'Ah.' Wendy's one-word reply says it all.

'I can't call the baby Elodie, can I?' I say sadly.

'Nope. How about something else beginning with E? Eloise? Elenor? Emmy?'

'No, although Eloise is OK. I just felt Elijah and Elodie went well together, and I kinda had my heart set on them. And now I feel…' How can I say this out loud? I've barely admitted it to myself. 'Now I feel…resentful of Sam.' I clap a hand over my mouth as if it will stop any more incriminating words tumbling out.

Wendy gives a wry smile, whilst keeping her eyes on

the road. My sister's not the safest person in our family for nothing.

'That's only natural. And remember, you have all these hormones raging through your body at the minute. Little things can seem enormous things when your hormones are off kilter.'

'Hmm, I guess. But what do I do? I haven't told Sam, obviously, but the thought of meeting up again and listening to her going on about baby Elodie makes my blood boil.'

Wendy laughs.

'I know. I'm a terrible person, and then we have all this with Martha, and reality kicks in with what's important, but I can't get it out of my head,' I confess.

'Lou, I wouldn't worry about it. You may change your mind nearer the time, and in any case you may have two boys.' She pauses. 'Are you going to find out if they give you another scan at any point?'

I shake my head. 'No. My mind's made up on that. Surprise is best.'

'I agree.'

Gen throws the door open and runs down the drive the minute the car starts to pull in. 'How's Martha?'

'She's conscious now.'

'Oh, Mum! Thank God.' She buries her face into my neck and within seconds my neck is soaked with her tears. 'I've been so worried. Thank goodness you went to visit her.'

I've been thinking about that a lot too. Someone up there must have been watching out for her, and us. Gen adores Martha. Since she's the eldest, Martha has spent the most time with her, so it's natural it has affected her more than her brother and sister.

Soon Aria and Hugo join their sister. Aria's arms wind themselves around my legs, whereas Hugo buries his face into my stomach, not wanting me to see his tears, but the jolts his sobbing cause reverberate through my body, so there's no doubt he's upset. My poor, sensitive little man.

I stroke his hair and say, 'She's going to be OK.' Whilst I'm not entirely sure of this, she's certainly better than she was this morning, and I think I'm exhibiting strength and positivity in the hope that by osmosis my hopes shall come to pass and Martha will be back home in jig time.

'Wendy, you coming in?' I ask, peeking my head through the open passenger door. Wendy shakes her head, and tells me she'll call. We all wave as she drives away, then taking Aria by the hand, I shepherd the three of them indoors where I can see Ronnie waiting at the window.

'Kids, go play whilst I talk to Daddy, then we'll have a movie night. I think we need it.' And then some.

'You OK?' Ronnie asks, coming up to me and wrapping his arms around me. I deflate against him, and it's good to let it all out for a second. Today has been a pressure cooker of a day. And strangely, though Martha is conscious, I don't feel elated. Maybe I'm just wrung out.

'Honestly? I'm shattered. Emotionally and physically,' I say as I step out of his arms after a moment of resting against his chest.

Ronnie's eyebrows raise. 'I'm not surprised. It's been quite a day. I dread to think what could have happened if you hadn't gone to visit her.' He blows out a breath.

'Don't. I've already been down that road, and I really

don't want to think about it.'

'No. Hey, why don't you put your feet up and I'll make you some tea. If you're lucky, there might be some of those cookies left your mum brought round earlier.'

'How's Mum? I haven't even had a chance to speak to her recently.'

'Worried about Martha. Worried about you.' He gives a wry smile.

'I'll give her a call later.'

'Fine. Oh, and George brought over the stuff you ordered and left in the shop. Plus, Susan gave him the flowers to bring over too. You and Martha have been quite the talk of the village today.'

I manage a faint smile. Only in a village would a butcher and a florist give you such personal service.

'Right, time to chill. You need it.'

'Aye, aye, Captain.' For once, it's Ronnie waiting on me hand and foot, and right now it's exactly what I need.

Saturday 9 October

To-do list
Drinks and snacks for Martha
Update everyone on Martha
Phone butcher to thank him
Nip in to see Malcolm and check on the replacement glass
Decide what's to happen about Arran trip – liaise with Wendy and Jo
Call garage about car's service

'Have you phoned the hospital yet to see how she's doing?'

Ronnie asks me as I walk out of the bathroom, fresh from the shower, towelling my hair.

'Not yet. I was on the phone to Jo earlier. She was asking for an update and also to see what's happening about Monday.'

Ronnie hesitates. 'Monday? The Arran trip?'

'Yeah. Obviously, I can't go now. I'm trying to work out whether it's fair to let Jo and Wendy take the kids, and if the three of them and all their stuff will fit in their cars, or if I bite the bullet and tell the kids we're not going.'

Ronnie's eyes widen. 'Lou, you can't not go.' He rests his hands on my upper arms. 'This trip has already been postponed once. Your sisters and the kids are looking forward to it, and I know you are too.'

I nod. 'I am, of course I am, but I can't leave now, not with Martha in hospital. I just…can't.' My voice cracks with emotion and I sniff.

'C'mere.' Ronnie pulls me towards him and I sob into his chest.

'I can't bear to see her like that. She looked about ten years older, and she was grey, Ronnie, grey.'

'I know. What's happened is terrible, but she's in the best place, and she's conscious. The only thing you'd be able to do is visit. And Brett's here now, isn't he?'

'He's arriving today. I said I'd pick him up from the airport, after I've checked in with Malcolm about the replacement glass, then I'll drop him off at the hospital and go back and see Martha later. Gives them a bit of family time together.'

'Louisa, you're an angel in a stressed-out mum's clothing.' Ronnie smiles at me. 'But there's only one of you, and you need a rest, especially–' he pats my stomach

'–since you're carrying not one but two babies.'

I sigh heavily. 'I don't want to let her down. She's been there for us so much, including after the crash.'

'And we will be here for her,' Ronnie tells me gently, cupping my face in his hands. He drops his hands back down and says, 'Lou, here's the deal. First of all, I'll go see Malcolm about the glass. You're already doing enough today. Secondly, you need a rest, you need this break. I'm at home. I can easily substitute you in the visiting schedule. Brett will be staying nearby anyway, so I can coordinate visits with him, pick stuff up, and I can also keep Brett company in the evening. Take him down the pub for a pint, or invite him over for a few beers and a curry.'

I debate this internally. Technically, that could work, but it wouldn't be me visiting Martha. The fear that ran through me when I found her is almost indescribable. Can I hand over responsibility for her care to Brett and Ronnie? I know Brett's her son, but I'm the one who, usually, is on hand when she needs anything, since he lives on a different continent. Part of me knows it's the control that I'm worried about giving up. It's like if I give up control, something bad might happen, kind of like when you were little and you really wanted something to happen, or not happen, and you told yourself if you reached the next lamppost before the bus passed, or whatever, then it would, or wouldn't happen. I know I'm rambling, but it makes perfect sense to me.

I blow out a breath as I struggle with myself over this. I know the kids need the break, and I definitely do, but I don't want to be ditching Martha to go and enjoy myself. And that's sort of how it feels. But Ronnie's stepping up and handling more, generally, and now he's made this offer, it seems foolish not to take it. OK, I've made my decision.

Twenty-five minutes. That's how long I've been waiting at International Arrivals at Glasgow Airport. Finally, the doors open again and a man pulling a maroon trolley case exits.

I wave to attract his attention. 'Brett, how are you doing?'

'I'm OK, thanks. You? Expecting another baby, I see. Mum didn't tell me that.'

'That's not like her. I'll have to pull her up about not keeping you in the loop.'

He smiles. He's a tall, rangy guy with naturally wavy light-brown hair, which has some parts more bleached by the Aussie sun than others. His tanned face, although smiling, shows signs of stress and strain in the wrinkles around his eyes and the dark circles ringing them. My heart goes out to him. As an only child, and with the vast distance separating him from his childhood home and mum these days, this must be taking its toll on him.

'Thanks, Louisa.' He squeezes my arm gently. 'I can't bear to think–'

'I know. Me too.'

We both exhale noisily then start to laugh at our being in synch.

'She's lucky to have you next door.'

'We're lucky to have her, more like, and we're not currently next door, but hopefully soon.'

Brett's eyes widen. 'I'm so sorry. I forgot all about the crash, what with all this.' He throws out a hand to encompass the many problems we're both dealing with right now.

'No worries. Isn't that what you say in Oz?' I chuckle.

He smiles again and I spot a tiny gap between his front teeth. I've never noticed that before. How bizarre. I've known him for years.

'It is. But that must have been hard on you, especially now.' He gestures to my stomach.

I sigh. 'It hasn't been an easy year, let's put it that way.'

We walk to my car, chatting away, catching up and all too soon we've arrived at the hospital.

'Just let me know when you want picked up, and I'll come get you,' I say. 'And tell your mum I'll be in to see her later.'

'I will. Thanks, Louisa.' He gives me a crooked smile before his face changes into a more serious expression as he walks away. I guess he's thinking about his mum's situation.

At four o'clock, I stride back into the ward. With half an hour left of afternoon visiting time, I'm going to take the opportunity to see Martha too.

Brett's standing in the doorway talking to a doctor when I arrive. She walks away, clearly finished, as I reach him. 'How's the patient?'

He pauses for a moment as if recapping what he's heard. 'The doctors seem happy with her progress. They can't find any indication of a medical reason for her being unconscious, other than being in a lot of pain from the fall. She has, however, broken her hip and fractured her right wrist, so it'll be a little while before she's properly mobile.'

I frown. That's not good, but it could have been much

worse news. 'So, what does that mean for her staying in hospital?'

'Don't know yet. They were talking about care plans and wanted to know if she had anyone here to take care of her long-term, like a live-in person, but I made it clear I've flown in from Australia, and although I can be on hand for a few weeks, short of moving back for several months, I can't be here in that way for her. And I didn't want to promise anything I couldn't follow through with.'

'Quite. And if they think they can discharge her, they will. It's all about freeing up beds these days, unfortunately.'

'Yeah. Things aren't what they used to be, that's for sure. Although, I have to say, the staff were lovely.'

'They always are, but underpaid and under-resourced. Same old story.'

He looks at me ruefully.

'Right, I'm going in to see her now. Is she awake?'

'She was last time I checked.'

'Great. Why don't you go find something to eat? You must be starving.'

'Good idea, Louisa.' He claps me on the shoulder and heads off down the corridor.

'Martha.' I lean forward to kiss her forehead and she tries to sit up.

'No, don't worry about that. Here, do you need me to help make you more comfortable?'

'Thanks, Louisa.'

'How you feeling now?'

She tries to shrug, but grimaces. 'I keep forgetting other

parts of me hurt, and when I move one part, it affects the other.'

I give a sad smile.

'Apart from that, I'm as fine as can be, given the circumstances. I was very lucky.'

Privately, I don't think her injuries constitute lucky, but she's braver than me.

'Lucky?'

'Yes, lucky. Lucky you found me when you did.'

'Oh, that. Yes, well, I'm glad I came along then too.' I clasp her hands in mine and we look at each other, so much being said without the need for words.

'So, do you know what happened?' I ask. 'I found you in the pantry.'

She sighs. 'Stupid old woman. I stood on that stool I have, you know, the one on wheels. I was sure it was close enough to the shelf that it wouldn't move, but then I realised the jar I was trying to get down was the wrong one. Then I spotted the right one, but it was a little bit further along, and I stretched, and…' She gestures down to herself and the hospital bed.

I roll my eyes at her to admonish her for being so foolish.

'I know, I know. It was a moment of madness. I should know better.'

'You should. You need to be more careful. OK, end of lecture.' I smile and she returns it.

My phone pings a few times whilst I'm in with Martha, but I ignore it, despite her protestations that I should answer it.

'It can wait. You're my priority right now, and if it was life-threatening they'd have called, wouldn't they?'

My use of life-threatening strikes me a moment later as perhaps inappropriate given the events of yesterday, but Martha doesn't seem to have noticed. Her head falls back on the pillow a little, and I can sense she's tiring.

'Right, I'm going to round Brett up. He must be exhausted after that flight. Hopefully, he'll have eaten by now, and he can go home, get a sleep and then if he wants, eat with us later. I'll be back in tomorrow afternoon or evening, once I've discussed it with Brett. OK?'

She nods and her eyes flutter closed. Poor thing. I press my lips to her forehead and her fingers come up and grasp mine, her grip surprisingly strong.

'You're a good girl, Louisa, you know that.'

I smile. 'Yeah, I'm awesome, Martha. You never let me forget. See you tomorrow.' I squeeze her fingers and catch a slight smile at her lips as I turn to leave.

I collect Brett from the cafeteria, and we head for Ferniehall, Radio Clyde on low as we chat.

Brett looks diminished somehow. Perhaps it's jet lag.

He huffs out a breath. 'That was a shock.'

I nod. 'Yeah, I was pretty taken aback yesterday, too.'

'No, not just seeing her with tubes and things in her. I hadn't realised how much she'd aged. I mean, I know she's eighty-eight, but she looks it now. She never did before.'

I know exactly what he means. Martha has always been good for her age, but now she looks more vulnerable than I've ever seen her and her voice is barely more than a whisper.

As I go to change gear, he places his hand over mine. 'Thanks so much, Louisa. I don't know what I'd have done if anything had happened to her.'

'Me neither, but she's going to be fine.' I hope.

'I don't know how to repay you,' he says as he produces a tissue from his pocket and wipes his eyes.

'You don't need to repay me. Knowing your mum is OK is all I need.'

He gives a sad smile. 'Me too.'

With the afternoon spent in a flurry of phone calls to my sisters – first to get their opinion on whether I should go, then to organise the Arran trip, and packing for it, as well as fielding the kids' many demands, as usual – it's late by the time I sit down with Ronnie. Hugo, for some reason, had difficulty getting off to sleep tonight, but finally he's down, as is Aria, with only Gen, ear buds in, listening to music as I retrieve her phone.

'Thanks, Ronnie.' I kiss him on the lips then nestle my head into his shoulder.

His head turns slightly. I sense the scrunch to his eyebrows. 'For what?'

'For making me see that I should go to Arran, and for offering to visit Martha in my absence.'

'Don't mention it. Besides, Martha's important to me, too. And you three are very important to me.' He places his hand on my stomach. This is becoming a habit. Thank goodness he's my husband as it freaks me out when total strangers do it to me: in the ladies' in a restaurant, my mum's friends that I barely know, or basically anyone who feels they have good enough reason – they don't – to get closer to my baby. Maybe I'm being touchy. OK, I am being touchy, but whatever happened to privacy? Right, I'm rambling again.

As I cuddle into Ronnie, I start to doze off, only to be awoken by the trill of my phone. What? Who's calling at this time of night? Martha! I hope it's not bad news. Oh God! Just when I thought she was all right.

I fumble around for my phone. Nicky? I glance at the clock as I answer. Ten thirty. She doesn't usually call so late. In fact, her MO is more text message, generally.

'Nicky? You OK?' Panic threads through my voice.

'Not really.' A string of expletives follow, and I only catch a few of the other words through Nicky's sobs.

'Nicky, what's wrong? You're worrying me. Calm down.' As if telling anyone that ever helped them do so.

She gulps a few times, composing herself. 'I've been out all day, and when I got back, I found today's post. There's a letter from my insurance company saying the lorry driver's insurers have cited extenuating circumstances, an act of God. They're trying to make out he had some cardiac issue, but that hasn't been proven.'

My mouth falls open. They're going to lie about this? After everything that happened? How dare they? A few expletives pass through my head too.

'But I don't understand, our insurance company has okayed the rebuild of the house. How can they be dragging their feet over your claim, when ours is being paid out?' I'm not trying to make her feel worse, but that simply doesn't make sense.

She bursts into tears again. 'I don't know. All I know is it's not going to be straightforward. I thought all I had to do was concentrate on my recovery and restart my business, but that might not be possible without the compensation.'

I don't say at this point that Valentin wouldn't see her short and would take care of her, as he's already doing. That's not what she wants, or needs, to hear right now.

Nicky's as independent as they come. She's had to be.

'And it's not just the money, Lou, although that would really help. It's the fact that if they don't make the driver and his company pay, in every sense of the word, what's to stop a tragedy like this happening again? I mean, I know I'm still here, but I could just as easily have died, as could you all have.'

I take a deep breath. That doesn't bear thinking about. She's right.

On impulse, I say, 'Do you want to meet me for a coffee in the morning? I'm going to the hospital to visit Martha, and the Arran trip's definitely going ahead, Ronnie's offered to visit Martha whilst we're away, but I could meet you early if you want.'

'Thanks, Lou, I'd really appreciate that. I know I can speak to Valentin, but I just want to rant at the injustice of it all. He just wants to fix it without actually listening to me.'

I sigh. Yep. I know the type, although I have to say, Valentin's more attuned to this than most.

'Try not to worry, Nic. Meet you in Jumping Beans at ten?'

'Sounds good. Thanks again. Goodnight.'

When I hang up, Ronnie says, 'It's OK, I heard. Yes, I'll watch the kids, and yes, that's crappy, and no, it doesn't make any sense.'

I smile. On the one hand, the fact he *gets* it is great, on the other, the fact he didn't let me tell him, in my own way, isn't.

I close my eyes, too tired to even trudge up to bed, and as I drift off, my mind swirls with thoughts of Nicky, lorries, Martha, Arran and that much-needed holiday.

Chapter Six

Sunday 10 October

To-do list – today I'm trialling the 1 + 3 + 5 method. The one big item is the packing, the three middle-sized are Halloween decs, midwife and power banks. Oh, damn it, I only have eight tasks not nine!

Make a note to call midwife tomorrow – I've lost the card with the next appointment on it

Get shoelaces for Hugo's trainers – have snapped again. What does that boy do to them?

Start buying Halloween decorations for the house, so don't get caught out with no availability of anything nearer the time

Pack – remember goggles and wetsuits for kids too

Sun cream – Arran's microclimate means we can have all four seasons in one day

Print off ferry tickets

Pack extra chargers and power banks – do not forget power banks. They will keep me sane.

'Nicky. Come here.' I hug her as she stands up to greet me. Her eyes are red and puffy, and I'm betting she didn't sleep much last night.

'Valentin dropped me off. Said to give him a ring when

we're done.'

'Right, let's get you something to boost your energy, however short-lived.' I glance towards the cake counter. 'I can highly recommend Jacinta's orange and coconut cake.'

'OK, sounds good. What you having?'

'Usual, for now, decaff latte and probably Jacinta's orange and coconut cake,' I say with a grin.

That coaxes a smile from her, although she's definitely not herself. Poor thing. As if she hasn't been through enough. We all have. Anger rises in me again at the thought of the insurance company shirking its responsibilities and trying to wriggle out of paying up.

Nicky, when prompted, shares everything she knows about her case. Apparently, it's not as straightforward as our case, as ours is property, whereas hers is personal injury. I'd have thought that would have made it a higher priority and the insurers would have even more reason to pay out without lengthy delays, but from what Nicky says, it's all sub-section 2b of article 1027 and other helpful jargon of that ilk.

'So, what are you going to do?' I ask as I wipe the froth from the latte off my top lip – I think Jacinta is trialling a part latte, part cappuccino combo.

She sighs. 'Well, Valentin is looking into things, of course. He has a great lawyer, naturally, with his business interests, but it's the sheer audacity of them that gets me. I wish I could get the driver and look him in the eye.'

I nod. She needs to vent. Despite the upheaval to our lives, it's been nothing compared to the agony Nicky has gone through. Sometimes I still cry with relief at night when I think how much worse the outcome of that crash could have been. I can honestly say I don't know anyone else who's had an articulated lorry crash through their house on a Saturday night and pin their friend against a wall.

I'm about to voice how the press would have a field day with a story like this, when I hit pause. Nope. Can't go there. Already did that, with disastrous results. Journalists aren't to be trusted. Hmm, how else to help? For once, I'm stumped, and I don't like not having a solution. Funnily enough, I'm often more able to help with other people's problems than my own.

'Anyway, enough about my woes, how's Martha? I can't believe how lucky she was, you finding her when you did,' Nicky says.

I fill her in, and once we've exhausted that topic, she says, 'Oh my goodness, I'm a selfish mare. How are you feeling? With the baby, babies, and everything?'

I smile. 'I've not had a great deal of time *to* think recently.'

'I can imagine. But have you and Ronnie discussed names?'

Ah. Do I tell her? Do I tell her Sam's chosen the same name as me? I can't quite decide if that would be disloyal. She would then know something that Sam didn't. Am I being unfair to Sam by not telling her? But surely that would open a can of worms.

Nicky picks up on my hesitation. 'What's wrong?'

Now it's my turn to sigh. 'I haven't really discussed names with Ronnie, but Ronnie tends not to get too involved. He's happy to go with whatever, unless I followed Bob Geldof's Fifi Trixibelle, or any of the other stars' more out-there names.'

'So, what's the problem then?' She frowns, causing a

tiny wrinkle in her otherwise unblemished and unlined forehead.

I bite my lip, as if doing so will help me decide whether to tell Nicky or not. Finally, it rushes out of me. 'Sam's chosen the same girl's name as me, and I don't know what to do.'

'What?' Nicky asks, her lips parted in dismay.

'She told me the other day.'

'But she might not have a girl,' Nicky says, trying to placate me. Uh-oh, I've put my foot in it. Sam hasn't told Nicky she knows the sex. How do I play this now? Do I tell her, or do I waffle about how the name will be an issue if it is a girl? Life, give me a break!

'True, but there's a fifty-fifty chance.' That much is true.

'What's the name anyway?' Nicky asks as she takes a sip of her latte.

'Elodie.'

'Aw, that's lovely,' she says before she's thought it through. Her face blanches when she realises what she's said. 'I-I-I didn't mean–'

I let her off the hook. 'Don't worry, it is a lovely name, and that's the problem. We can't both have it, and I love it.'

Nicky digests this for a moment. 'But either of you could change your mind before the babies arrive.'

I tilt my head to the side. 'Hmm, we could, but then again, we might not. And what do I do then?'

Nicky's emerald eyes bore into me, as if she can see right into my soul. It's rather unnerving. 'Lou, I think you know what you'll have to do if Sam names her baby Elodie.'

I blow out a breath. 'But I really want to call the baby Elodie.' I know I sound petulant, but I can't help it. Is this my hormones testing me?

'Lou,' Nicky says, her exasperation coming through. 'You need to stop torturing yourself with this. You might not be having a girl. Don't spend your pregnancy worrying about something that might never happen.'

'I can't help it!' I'm equally frustrated.

'I know,' Nicky says, her voice soft. 'But seriously, there are other great names out there. Have you thought of any others?'

I shake my head. I had a list earlier in my pregnancy, but now I'm having twins, I'd narrowed it down to Elodie and Elijah.

'Look, why don't we do a bit of brainstorming,' she suggests, pulling out her phone and tapping away on the keys. 'Here we go. Top baby names.' She glances at me hopefully, but I shake my head. 'OK then,' she says, tapping away again. 'Exotic baby names.'

'They're not alpacas, Nicky, they're my babies.'

I wince at the hurt that crosses her face. 'Sorry, I know you're only trying to help.'

She falls silent for a moment, then more tapping. 'Here, matching baby names for twins.'

I perk up a little. 'OK. What does it say?'

'Rihanna and Ronan.' She looks up. My silence says it all.

'Nuala and Norbert,' she says. I snort at this. So does Nicky.

I look over her shoulder. 'Patagonia and Peter? Who the heck is going to call their child Patagonia? I wonder why they chose that? Was that where they were conceived?

Were they copying the Beckhams with Brooklyn?'

Nicky's latte nearly comes through her nose. She splutters then recovers. 'Never mind that, the other child is to be called Peter. How much plainer can you get? Hard to know which child would suffer most in life, the one with the crazy name or the plain one. And how would the parents decide which one had the plain name?'

'God knows. What else is there? Leandra and Lionel. Yeah, that's not going to work.'

'Here, what about this? Oscar and Olivia.'

I blink. I've always quite liked the name Oscar, but I love Olivia and Oscar as a combo. Yes, I love it.

'Nicky, you're a genius. I love them. And I now have a backup plan.'

She grins. 'You know I've always got your back.'

When I return from the hospital later, the house is relatively tidy and Ronnie's running the hoover over the dining room carpet. Who is this man and what has he done with my husband? Hoovering? Next, he'll be donning an apron or brushing cobwebs out of the high ceiling corners with an extendable feather duster. I live in hope.

'Hey, how's it going?' I ask, tilting my head towards the hoover.

'Clean.' He smirks.

'So, what's brought this on?' I ask, pulling him by the lapels of his shirt towards me. 'I have to say I find all this domestic god thing a real turn-on.'

He laughs. 'Don't get too used to it. I just thought, since you've been running about going to the hospital and you're taking the kids away to Arran, I'd do a bit more around the house.'

Now I know my husband has been abducted by aliens.

I nod my head slightly. 'Well, keep up the good work. I'm impressed. Right, I'm going to finish the packing and check on the kids.'

'How's Martha? Brett called in earlier. Said he'd text you to see if she wanted anything brought in.'

'She's OK. I think she got a fright, but she's resilient. I wonder if we got more of a shock than she did. You know what she's like. She'll be charming all those young doctors and nurses, having them wait on her hand and foot, with her sweet little old lady act.'

'Except it's not an act, she is a sweet little old lady,' Ronnie says.

'I know, but she's a fighter too, and takes no nonsense. She told me she was reaching for a jar and fell. Hey, it's just occurred to me. She should have one of those personal alarms. You know, the ones you wear on your wrist or on a lanyard?'

'That's not a bad idea. You should mention it to her when you're in.' He slaps his forehead. 'You won't see her for a week. I'll tell Brett to bring it up when I see him.'

'Thanks. That way if anything happens again – and let's hope it doesn't – at least she can call for help.'

Aria wants me to colour in with her when I pop my head round the playroom door, and Hugo is determined to show me the new level he's reached on some Xbox game. However, I want to give Gen an update on Martha, and she's up in her room listening to music, so I promise to play later, once I've finished packing, and head up to Gen's room.

I've barely opened her door and indicated she should take her ear buds out so we can talk, when the doorbell goes. I'll let Ronnie get it whilst I fill Gen in. It's probably a courier delivery or something.

A few minutes later, having brought Gen up to speed on Martha, and having reassured her that she's doing well, I frown at the continued voices downstairs. That's not the kids. I listen on the landing for a second and my heart plummets. Annabelle. And Phillip. You have got to be kidding me? What are they doing here? Ronnie didn't say anything. The last thing I need today is my in-laws descending when I'm trying to prepare to leave for holiday tomorrow. What are they playing at? I plaster a smile on my face and trot down the stairs. Time to face the music.

'Annabelle, Phillip, what a surprise.' Note the omission of wonderful. I'd have loved to have a mother-in-law who I was besties with, but Annabelle doesn't exude warmth. She's fine with the kids, and naturally, my husband, who can do no wrong, but me, not so much. I don't think I've ever met her expectations, and I've often failed to live up to them. Surely even she must give me a brownie point or two though for being pregnant with two grandchildren for her.

'Louisa,' Annabelle says primly. 'We were passing and thought we'd pop in.'

They live in Edinburgh, well, as near as. We're hardly handy for them to pop in, and why couldn't they have phoned first? Has Ronnie not told them about Martha? I feel a stab of irritation at this possibility. And surely they must have known we're off on holiday tomorrow? Who drops in unannounced on someone the day before they go on holiday? Everyone knows it's a nightmare with last-minute packing, rushing out to buy items you'd forgotten earlier, or assumed you had but were proven wrong, or can't find. Plus, they've landed on us at the kids' dinnertime. Honestly. I have to concentrate not to roll my eyes.

'Oh, have you been somewhere nice?' I ask, not remotely interested, but doing my best to keep up the façade. I sense Ronnie's eyes on me. He knows I couldn't care less. But the sooner I can consider my daughter-in-law duty done and can escape, the better.

'We were at Pollok House with some friends, and since you're not so very far away…'

But not exactly next door either…

'Right,' I say over brightly. 'Well, I'll leave you and Ronnie to chat. I need to get the kids' dinner on and then finish packing.' I smile and leave the room. If they didn't take that mammoth hint, then nothing will make them leave this side of the kids' bedtime. Give me strength!

Chapter Seven

Thursday 14 October

To-do list
Actually, nothing. I'm on holiday.

The rain batters the living room windows, but despite the inclement weather, I'm enjoying my morning. The solitude. The time to rest. Me and my book. Shock horror, I'm taking a few days off, only looking at my work emails once a day for fifteen minutes. The out-of-office message is on, diverting emails to Mum. I'm still receiving emails from Fabien, but I'm keeping those to my strict fifteen-minute window. After everything we've been through this year, we all need a break. Ronnie's getting a break by being at home alone, with only Patch and Bear, and now Brett for company. I have my downtime with my sisters, which is almost as good as being on my own, and in some ways better, but I do relish this half an hour in the morning. I check my messages. Ronnie has sent me the latest on Martha, including a photo of her sitting up in bed. She has more bruising now than when she fell, and she is a painful-looking rainbow of yellow, green and purple. But Ronnie says she's in good spirits and in less pain. I wonder how much morphine the doctors have her on.

I'm sleeping well here. This is our third day and Wendy and Jo have been very good at letting me have a cat nap mid-afternoon when I've started to fade. And whilst the weather's horrible today, it has been unseasonably warm the past two days here, not a cloud in the sky either. Almost freakish for October. But then Arran has its own little microclimate. It's one of the many things I love about it.

Much as I love my dogs, I'm also enjoying being able to have a cup of coffee and read a couple of chapters of my book before having to do anything else, including taking dogs to the loo.

The plan today is to have no plan. Looks like it's just as well, given the weather. We've had a day at the beach, and mini-golf, then a visit to the castle and a walk on the other side of the island, near Lagg. I haven't really spent much time round there. It's very remote, and there's not a great deal there, but it was a beautiful day for a walk and the view was stunning, and the kids loved having a new beach to play on.

My phone buzzes with a WhatsApp. Sam. *How's it going? Missed you at aquanatal last night.*

I'm still feeling a bit guilty about not telling Sam about the whole name debacle. I know it's a silly thing, but I don't want it to become an issue, or cause any awkwardness between us.

Good. Enjoying the peace and quiet.

How you feeling?

Not bad. Less stressed than I was at home last week. Looking forward to being able to eat a runny egg again though.

LOL. Me too. And smoked salmon. I don't like it hot.

Ha ha. We should probably make the most of being able to eat a meal without having to feed a baby or change a nappy or sterilise a bottle or rock a pram at the same time, I type.

God, I'd forgotten about that. Not sure I'm ready for this.
You're not ready. I'm having two!

She sends me an array of smiley faces and a care emoji. They make me smile, but soon my thoughts turn to the future, and I can't help longing for when things were simpler. Soon when I go anywhere, I'll have a whole entourage and a mountain of paraphernalia to take with me – again.

It also strikes me that I'll have to start looking into nursery places for the babies already. Most places have waiting lists. I thought I was done with all that, since Aria's now at school, but nope, got to go through it all again. Fabulous.

And although I'm making more money now with the Cerulean contract, won't any extra be eaten up by nursery fees? Why has this only occurred to me now? Why hasn't Ronnie mentioned this? Why would I think Ronnie would? No, these thought processes are down to me, always. I can't help feeling a twinge of resentment towards Ronnie for unwittingly, at least I hope it's unwittingly, leaving me to manage things again, to keep the cogs turning. But why would I expect anything else? And I'm not the only mum in this position. I think of Brandon, with Wendy; Nicky – her ex is worse than useless. Thankfully, she has Valentin now. That would be ironic, wouldn't it, if I've taken on this contract, am spreading myself thin to cover everything, and then I'm actually not any better off financially. Plus, I'll lose time with the kids.

'Morning!' Jo says, inching the living room door closed again.

I smile. 'Morning. Sleep well?'

'Like you wouldn't believe. Must be the sea air.'

I don't like to tell my sister that technically it's not the sea, it's the Firth of Clyde, so I rein myself in. She probably won't appreciate me telling her that the minute she's woken up.

'What you reading?'

I show her the cover of the romance novel I'm absorbed in.

She squints then says, 'Ooh, I fancied that. Can I borrow it when you're done?'

'Sure. Do you want a coffee? I'm going to make a fresh one?' I pick up my half-empty cup, whose contents are now cold and uninviting.

'That'd be great. Can you grab me one of those pains au chocolat when you're coming too? I'm starving.'

'Back in a sec.'

I gaze out at the roiling 'sea' as I wait for the kettle to boil. The turmoil of the sea matches my mood and emotions at the moment. Of course I'm happy, although shocked, still, about being pregnant with twins, but I haven't fully reconciled myself to this being my life going forward. I think it's partly because the important people in my life are taking it too well, as if we'll all simply adapt. Easy-peasy. Well, I don't think it is, nor will it be. And that worries me. As I reach for the cups, I feel a flutter in my stomach. Maybe I'll have a croissant. I've been up for a while and I'm clearly hungry. I place the cups on the counter and then I feel it and it makes me gasp. A kick. That's the first time I've felt a kick this pregnancy. My eyes well up. Is this because the babies can sense my apprehension? I do want you, babies, I really do, I just know it's going to be hard.

The wind howls in time with the kettle boiling and I want to join in. I startle as Wendy puts a hand on my shoulder.

'Sorry, didn't mean to give you a fright. Is there enough water in the kettle for one more?'

I nod, not trusting myself to speak and will my tears back into my eyes before Wendy notices. Is there such a thing as antenatal depression?

She chatters away whilst we prepare a continental breakfast and coffee, then helps me carry everything through. I sigh with relief. She hasn't noticed anything. I wanted to have more time to reflect on the baby's or babies' first kick, but I guess I'll have to park that for now. I place my hand on my tummy and communicate telepathically with the babies. I'm here for you, even if I seem a little off and grumpy.

The rain is relentless. It's just as well we had a no-plan day as we would have been soaked through. Despite Lamlash being a relatively sheltered area of Arran, certainly more so than the busier Brodick, you'd never know it today. We're now on our third board game and Jo's been making everyone hot chocolate, and Wendy's been helping the kids make real popcorn, whilst I mediate over which board game's next. We've had Colour Brain – a game where you place colour cards down to indicate your answer – it's really good. Then a couple of games of Cluedo, and now they're debating over Harry Potter Cluedo or a Battleships tournament.

I'm reminded once again of why we each always bring

several board games with us on holiday. Something for everyone. Usually, I'd be miffed at the weather being as rotten, but sometimes it's nice, especially when you're pregnant with twins, to simply sit back, relax and have some family time indoors.

Some of the little ones are becoming a bit bored, though, so even though we're in teams, named after areas of Arran – Blackwaterfoot and Lochranza – they're toddling off and an adult meanders off every so often to retrieve them, coax them to sit down with a colouring book, or a toy that will keep them occupied for a bit, but which won't halt play of the board game.

Later, Jo and Wendy are making dinner whilst I bath Aria. My phone pings in my pocket. I wonder if it's Nicky with an update about her insurance claim. Nope, it's Fabien. Wonder what he wants. I'll call him back when I've dried Aria. True to my promise to myself, I've only been checking emails once a day.

After I've dried Aria's hair and she's looking all sweet and innocent, and sleepy, thankfully, I send her down to the kitchen to ask for her bedtime milk, and then I grab a moment to call Fabien back.

'Fabien, hi. Sorry I couldn't take your call. I was bathing Aria.'

'Louisa.' His voice sounds strained, so much so I could tell from a single word. 'Didn't you get my email this morning?'

'Not yet. I'm on holiday, remember? I'm only checking email once a day.'

I swear I hear him curse under his breath. 'Louisa, I need a favour. A huge one.'

Chapter Eight

Friday 15 October

To-do list

Remember to renew passport – now has only 10 months left on it

Call Fabien for more details on what's expected of me

Discuss meetings with Mum for next week – hope she can do them

Change meetings with the Millers and Flanagans for next week – advise them Mum will be there instead (seriously hate rescheduling and having to let people down)

Buy travel plugs – where the hell do they all go? Every time I go abroad, I can never find the ones I bought before

Get euros

'Flight FR 5834 is now ready for boarding.'

I drag my trolley case behind me, trying not to yawn. I still can't quite believe I'm off to Italy and at such short notice. I'd be looking forward to it, had I not been wrenched mid-vacation from my family, and if I weren't five months pregnant.

However, when Fabien called with an emergency, given everything he's done for us: having the faith to offer me the

Cerulean contract in the first place, and then housing us all in his luxury five-star hotel, at no cost, after the lorry crashed into our home, I couldn't say no. Even though I wanted to. Even though it's the last thing I wanted to do. Even though it meant leaving my kids with their aunts and cousins to see out the rest of the holiday, and even though it means my husband will have to take the train down or get a lift to Ardrossan on Sunday to then take the ferry to pick up the kids and my car from Lamlash. Even though my kids' expressions were like a stake driving through my heart. Gen scowled, Hugo did that thing where he swallows hard multiple times to prevent himself from crying, and Aria, well, Aria, let rip. She ranted and raved and threw an all-out tantrum at my imminent departure.

I'm not sure Jo got it, but Wendy did, which I was truly grateful for, not least because even on holiday, I felt a distance between us that I don't remember ever being there before. It started when I mentioned not knowing how I'd cope with the twins, straight after the housewarming party, but I've noticed something a bit off between us on occasion since.

Once again, I'm pulled in too many directions and I'm not really happy with any of the choices. Normally, I'd be delighted at going to Italy, to Bergamo. I've never been. I just know it's near Milan, and it's a walled city. Città Alta. Not that I'll see much of it at the trade show. These things are exhausting. I'll probably be happier to order room service from the hotel than go out for dinner after the show, which is the only time I'd have to see anything of the city. That reminds me, Fabien still hasn't sent me the hotel details. All I know is I'm meeting Charles' colleague, Lorenzo there. He's already at the show today setting up.

As long as I'm there from tomorrow for a few days to cover the wedding side of things, Charles, and Fabien by extension, are covered. The two women who were meant to be covering this section of the stand both had to drop out at the last minute; one has shingles and the other has an elderly mum in hospital who isn't expected to last the week. As it's Cerulean's first year at this event, neither Fabien nor Charles wanted to scrimp on the personnel. Cue me assuming the mantle.

Whilst it's encouraging that Charles and Fabien show such confidence in me by asking me to this show, after this, I'm seriously going to have to take Fabien aside and underline the terms of my contract. I can't be nipping off to Italy, leaving my three children, soon to be five, at a moment's notice, or indeed at all, until the twins are at least one. With that thought, I wave my boarding pass at the ground crew, take my seat on the plane and go to sleep until the pilot informs us we're landing.

The temperature on the clock outside the airport shows 21°C, and I tilt my face to the sun. I'm sure I could get a bus, but with luggage, being pregnant and having no idea where I'm going, and since Charles is footing the bill, I take a cab to the hotel. I pull up the name and address from the email Fabien has just sent me – nothing like cutting it fine. Relais San Vigilio. It's not one of Cerulean's. How remiss of them not to have a luxury hotel here. I must remember to pull Fabien up about that. Twenty minutes later, I arrive at the hotel in the Città Alta. It's nothing like I was expecting. I had assumed it'd be another smart yet essentially soulless five-star hotel. But this place is gorgeous, rustic, with high ceilings, wooden beams, topiary gardens, full of individual features. And it's actually touching the castle! I love it. I'm beginning to warm to the idea of this trip. I'm here now, so I may as well make the most of it.

No one's here to greet me. I ask at reception once I see the foyer is empty.

'Has anyone left a message for me?'

'*No, signora. Mi dispiace.* Would you like me to show you to your room?' the receptionist asks.

I'm slightly shaking my head at Lorenzo not being here to meet me when I realise what she's said. 'Yes, thank you.'

I follow her along a corridor to a sumptuous room. The hotel's really pretty deceptive from the outside. Inside, it's every bit as opulent as a high-end chain hotel. A lovely little boutique number. The fabulous cantilevered brick ceiling is the first thing I see when the receptionist gestures that I should enter the room ahead of her. The bed is enormous. It must be a super-king. I want to roll over and over on it until I reach the end. I think back to the bed in Madrid. They're probably about the same size. And whilst this room isn't as ostentatious as the one in Madrid, it oozes class. It's understated, whereas the décor in Madrid was very much over the top. I long to slide between the cool sheets and drift off. The receptionist clears her throat.

Poor woman. Hanging about whilst I'm daydreaming. '*Scusi, grazie,*' I say, dismissing her. Then I wonder if I should have tipped her. Aargh! Turning up and no one being here to meet me has thrown me off kilter. Wait until I get my hands on Lorenzo. He'd better have a good excuse. I haven't cut short my holiday and flown to Bergamo for him to mess me about. I stop and smile. Hey, I'm in ass-kicking mode. Must be the hormones. No one's taking advantage of me or my good nature.

After I've unpacked and checked my emails and messages – still nothing from Lorenzo or Fabien or Charles – I decide I'm not hanging about here. I send a quick message to Ronnie saying *The eagle has landed* then grab my bag and a cardigan and head downstairs.

At reception, I ask if I can leave a message for Lorenzo.

'Of course, Mrs Halliday.' The receptionist hands me pen and paper. I scribble 'Lorenzo, I was told you'd be here to meet me. I've settled into my room and am now going for a walk. You can reach me on this number when you get here.' I write my mobile number then fold the piece of paper and write Lorenzo on the front.

'Do you have a map of the city?' I ask the receptionist as I hand her the message.

'But of course.'

I ask her about the main places to visit and she indicates where we are on the map and then I venture out.

It's such a beautiful city. It did, however, take me fifteen minutes to leave the hotel as it has lovely gardens and viewpoints, but eventually, I figured I could see more of the hotel later, and I should really make the most of being here to see what sights I can.

I wander along the quaint cobbled streets of the Città Alta, literally the upper city, taking my time. Gorgeous independent shops nestle in amongst cute little cafés and I wish I could stop at each and every one of them. I promise myself I will visit a few on the way back, but as well as savouring the ambience of the small walled city, I'm keen to see the *duomo*. However, before I come across it, I reach an impressive church. The might of Santa Maria Maggiore towers over me, and the décor is so intricate it takes my breath away for a moment, although the most interesting thing is the pair of marble lions the columns of the basilica stand on. Unsure how much time I have, rather than go inside, I opt for continuing my walk to take in the awe-inspiring architecture. But first I snap a few photos and a couple of selfies and WhatsApp the girls, both sets, my sisters and my besties.

To ThreeAmigas: Hi girls, unexpected trip to Italy. Making the most of it. Isn't the architecture wonderful? You'd both love it here. Can we come back for my fiftieth?

To Sisters Like These: Afternoon! Well, I arrived at the hotel safe and sound, but no one was here to meet me. So I decided to go for a walk and look what I found.

I attach a couple of pics of the churches and the cobbled streets as well as the hotel, showing it being part of the castle, then add: *And it's warm too. Hope the rain has stopped over there and you can get back to the beach. Thanks for looking after the kids. Will bring you back something nice. Love you both xx*

Everywhere I look, or walk, history comes at me. It oozes out of the very framework of this ancient medieval city. Cappella Colleoni has the wow factor with its red and white Italian marble façade. It has so much detail, I could probably spend half a day drinking it all in. Talking of drink, I'm getting kind of thirsty. And another kick from the babies reminds me that I need to take care of myself and them. With so many quirky yet traditional cafés and eateries to choose from, it's difficult to know where to start. But start I must, so I head for Piazza Vecchia. I know it will be touristy, but I may only be here once, so I take a chance on Caffè del Tasso and order a sparkling water, a latte and a slice of polenta cake, whilst I peruse the menu for its savoury choices, only now realising it has been a long time since the croissant at the airport.

The menu tells me it's a historic café. Hardly surprising, given my companions are a marble statue of some clearly important person and the arch of what I soon learn from my map is the Palazzo della Ragione, the oldest municipal building in Bergamo. Who knew? Well, there's definitely been some fringe benefits to Lorenzo not picking me up on time today. I would never have had the opportunity to step back in time in the old town, which I'm learning is steeped in so much Venetian and Roman history. And as I squint to see whose statue is next to me, I can't help wishing I had a lot more time here. Maybe one day I'll come back with Ronnie. I wonder if Wendy and Jo would watch the kids, as this is really the place for adults to come and absorb the history, the culture and the atmosphere, as well as eat the amazing food, and drink the no doubt incredible wine, something I can't do at the moment, unfortunately. *That's your fault*, I tell the twins, stroking my belly.

I sip my latte and tilt my face to the sky, enjoying the sun's rays bathing my face in their warm glow. It's hard to remember it's October, particularly since when I left Arran, it was squalling rain, punctuated by the odd hailstone shower, and an inclement twelve degrees. I've just taken a bite of my polenta cake – to die for – when my phone rings. Unknown number.

'Hello, Louisa speaking.'

'Louisa, I am Lorenzo. I am so sorry I was not at the hotel to meet you. We had an unexpected delay and I had no way to contact you. I have your message from the hotel now.'

Somewhat mollified by his explanation, I say, 'No

problem. I'm in Piazza Vecchia right now. I figured there was no point hanging around the hotel when I can check my emails from this lovely piazza instead.'

'Oh, you are right. It would be a waste. I will come and meet you and then we can go to the *fiera*.'

I'm guessing he hasn't remembered the word for trade show, or exhibition. I only know because the name of the exhibition is Fiera Bergamo Sposi, effectively Bergamo exhibition for the bride and groom.

I haven't long finished my coffee and cake and am busy people-watching when a man of about six feet tall approaches. Crikey, he's George Clooney's double, well, George in his *ER* days. I was never a huge Clooney fan, I didn't see the attraction, but now I can appreciate why people found him so attractive.

'Louisa?' Lorenzo's sonorous tone startles me out of my reverie. He smiles and his gleaming white teeth dazzle, actually dazzle. I need a pair of sunglasses and fast.

'Yes,' I squeak. 'I'm Louisa.'

'*Piacere*.' He holds out his hand.

Ah, a word I know. That – pleasure to meet you – and *grazie* are some of the few Italian words in my repertoire, gleaned from a phrase book in the airport bookshop.

I grasp his hand. '*Piacere*.'

'Ah, you speak Italian. Wonderful.' His voice is so melodic and sing-songy, I could listen to it all day.

'Unfortunately, no, I only know a few words. And I mean a few,' I say self-deprecatingly.

'You are too modest.' He looks at my empty cup and plate. 'Are you finished? Are you ready to leave yet?'

I nod. 'Yes. I'm done.'

He goes to leave some money on the table, I have no

idea how he knows how much will cover it, but I'm touched he's offered. I raise a hand. 'Thanks, but I've already paid.'

He scrunches his eyes up slightly and shrugs. 'No problem. Anyway, let's go. We will take a taxi from the hotel to the show. We have a couple of hours and then we will come back and go for dinner. I'm not sure yet who else will come, but I will take you to a good place in the Città Alta, if that is OK for you.'

So not room service then. And I could do worse than sit opposite George Clooney's lookalike for a few hours whilst I eat. And it's not as if he's going to give me a second glance romantically, or cause me any trouble, so what harm is there in it?

As we walk back to the hotel, I struggle to keep pace with Lorenzo. It is pretty hilly, after all. Sweat beads my forehead and my blouse is sticking to my back. It's not that hot, it's clearly the exertion.

Lorenzo continues to talk, filling me in on the layout of the show and what's expected, what Charles has asked of us. He stops and turns round. 'Oh, Louisa, are you OK?' He looks at my stomach, where my blouse is straining over it. 'I'm so sorry, I hadn't realised you were pregnant. Had I known, I would have walked more slowly.'

I try to say, 'Don't worry about it,' but my breathing is laboured.

'Do you need to rest for a bit?' Lorenzo asks, concerned. He goes to put his arm around my shoulder, protectively I think, but must think better of it.

I shake my head. 'No, just let me catch my breath a

bit.' I pant. 'The heat, the lack of sleep and the babies are taking their toll.'

His eyes light up. 'Twins? You're having twins. How marvellous. I am a twin. My brother, Federico, is elder by seventeen minutes.'

There are two of them? Two George Clooney doppelgangers! The world is truly blessed.

'What a coincidence,' I say.

Lorenzo stands, hands on hips, smile as wide as an ocean, and tells me all about his brother, nonidentical, who is a heart surgeon and his parents' pride and joy. With glee he tells me he is the black sheep. Not that he's done anything wrong, more that he didn't excel as much as his brother. There and then I decide that neither of my twins will ever feel loved less than the other.

I have the sneaking suspicion that Lorenzo has stopped to have the twin chat rather than continue walking because he knows I do need a rest. How devious of him. I smile. We'll get along well.

In the cab, Lorenzo shows me a photo of him and his twin. His brother definitely doesn't look like George Clooney, but he has the air of someone who has the confidence of a Hollywood actor. He's still handsome, very, but his bearing gives the impression he knows it.

Even with traffic, it's not long before we arrive at the show. Immaculately coiffed and flawlessly made-up women hanging on the arms of beautifully turned-out men waltz up and down the aisles of the show. Are these the models? It doesn't take me long to realise they're actually brides- and grooms-to-be. I knew Italian women were beautiful and classy, but this is a different league altogether. Do none of them possess jeans or black leggings? Even before I had the kids I was never as well turned-out as them, even as a wedding guest. Do they nip in to Aldi dressed like that for their weekly groceries?

I'm not sure what I expected from the fair. The only thing I know about Italian exhibitions comes from car manufacturer or IT trade-show adverts where scantily clad beauties offer cups of espresso to everyone, or teeter around on impossibly high heels holding some promotional sign, kind of akin to a game show hostess on Italian TV.

The Cerulean stand towers above the majority. It's the only one I see, as we pass along the aisles, that deals with holidays, hotels and honeymoons, in particular. It's also one of the busier stands, with people jostling for attention. Or perhaps that's because it's currently undermanned, myself and Lorenzo having been missing in action.

'There is the cloakroom. Inside, there is a badge for you. I will try to help reduce the wait for people here and then come introduce you to everyone. Unless, of course, you feel happy to do that on your own.'

'I'll manage, but thank you, Lorenzo, that's very thoughtful.' I'm learning fast exactly how thoughtful he is.

I hang my cardigan in the cloakroom, smiling to a couple of girls on the stand, not scantily clad, I note. Ours is clearly one of the more sophisticated stands. My badge is sitting on the tabletop in the meeting room next to the cloakroom. I pin it to my blouse and pick up the exhibitor badge next to it and pop the lanyard over my head, then flick my hair out from under it and shake it into place.

Back out on the stand, I see it's still swarming with people, so I quickly introduce myself to the two girls I smiled at a moment earlier, and they tell me they are Lucia and Monica. I walk around the stand, smiling at the others, until I find the wedding stationery section. It's currently being manned by a guy whose badge reads Viggo. I hover in the background whilst he does the whole sales pitch on a couple who wouldn't look out of place gracing the cover of *Vogue* or *Grazia*.

The man's brows knit together and his wife-to-be purses her lips. Those signals don't bode well. The man interrupts my 'colleague' in full flow and says something I don't understand, then he and the woman flounce off. I wait until they've wandered off, to introduce myself, but not before I witness Viggo's posture stiffen. I don't think that conversation with the potential client went well.

'Viggo?'

He turns, fixing a smile on his face. I'm guessing from his looks as well as his name that he's Scandinavian, but I can't call it with regards to which country. 'Yes?' His eye contact is good, at least, although his eyes do flit to my chest to read my name off my badge.

'Louisa! Ah, welcome. Charles and Lorenzo told me you'd be arriving today, and not a moment too soon. The requests I have here are very specific, and I'm sure your products – which are stunning – fit the bill for many of these people, but I don't know the terminology.' He wrings his hands. 'And they seem very switched-on, in the know about these things, and I'm not. I'm used to selling high-end luxury hotel suites featuring grand pianos and peacock sculptures. This bespoke wedding stationery stuff is harder than I thought. I don't know one end of a letterpress-printed menu card from a foil-stamped day invite.'

I grin, and am smugly satisfied that my presence adds

value and that others see my product line as a quality offering.

'If it's any consolation, I'd be useless at selling high-end hotel suites. I'm much more at home with stationery suites.'

'Is that what they're actually called, or are you making that up?' Viggo narrows his eyes at me, suspiciously.

My shoulders shake with laughter. 'No, they're genuinely called that, when you sell them as the whole shebang.'

My phone beeps in my bag. 'Excuse me.'

Viggo waves my apology away with a flick of his hand, and returns his attention to the wedding suites as if seeing them for the first time. He takes out his phone and taps away, whilst looking at them, and I wonder if he's trying to rote learn the terminology.

I take my phone out. Jo. *Knock 'em dead*. With Jo that could mean literally. Take Lorenzo out with a single punch for daring to not be there when they said he would meet me at the hotel. I smile and put my phone away again.

'*Mi scusi*,' says a woman wearing an expensive-looking pale grey trouser suit with the pointiest shoes I've ever seen except on the Wicked Witch of the West in *The Wizard of Oz*.

'*Sì*,' I reply, then curse myself as she'll think I speak Italian. I was too busy taking in her outfit to think of my response.

Indeed, she rattles off a torrent of Italian, and I let her finish, only to say with a pained look, 'I'm sorry, I don't actually speak Italian. I'm from Scotland.'

'Ha ha. What a coincidence. I'm from Aberdeen, I just speak Italian.' She smiles and I see she doesn't have Italian genes after all.

'Your Italian's really good. I'm impressed. I can barely say thank you.'

She shrugs. 'I've had an Italian boyfriend for years. Now it's time to tie the knot. Ah, there you are, darling.'

A guy who could easily be a model joins her. He has a killer smile, whiter teeth than a baby's, exactly the right amount of facial hair, expertly trimmed, and eyes you could drown in. No wonder this sensible girl has bagged this one, although I'm sure his personality comes in to it somewhat, too.

'*Cara, siamo pronti?*' He glances at his girlfriend then me and beams.

'I'll be ready in a sec. Matteo, this is–' she stoops to see my badge '–Louisa. I was about to ask her about the stationery suites for the wedding, but I've just found out she's Scottish too. What are the chances?' She turns to me again. 'Sorry, I'm Angela.' She shakes my hand.

Then I really get the full benefit of Matteo's smile, which broadens.

'Really? And where are you from, Louisa? We haven't been back to Scotland for quite a while, but we will go before the wedding.'

His English is heavily accented, but he speaks it well. How wonderful to be able to speak more than one language fluently, and I curse myself for never doing more than that Spanish conversation class years ago.

I exchange a glance with Viggo over their heads. He's making faces at me, and then he gives me the thumbs-up.

I tell them I'm from Ferniehall, just outside Glasgow, in the direction of Loch Lomond, and Angela bats Matteo lightly on the arm. 'I told you we should visit Loch Lomond on our trip. This is an omen. Louisa, do you mind if we sit down? I'd like to–' she gazes at Matteo '–we'd like to discuss stationery suites with you.'

The next few hours fly past and I'm amazed at how much interest there is, as well as the volume of foot traffic at the exhibition. Is everyone getting married this year? However, I feel both professionally validated and proud of myself, of what I've achieved and at how well my designs and ideas have been received by clients. I already have a number of firm orders. Fabien will be pleased, and Charles can't fail to be either.

'Louisa, is half an hour enough for you to prepare for dinner? Change of plan. If it's OK with you, I thought tonight we could eat here as it's such a beautiful setting. You've missed the sun setting, unfortunately, but that can't be helped. You'll need to return earlier in the year for that, but it is truly remarkable from here,' Lorenzo says.

The enthusiasm shining out from him makes me smile. 'I don't doubt it. Yes, half an hour will give me time to have a quick shower and change.'

'Good, I will ask reception to reserve us a table. See you soon. Viggo will be joining us as he is also staying in the hotel.'

'The more, the merrier,' I say. Seriously? What a platitude. Anyway, dinner should be fun if I can stay awake, and I'm sure the food will be amazing. If I wasn't pregnant, a can of Red Bull would do the job, but I'm reducing my caffeine intake dramatically, so that's a no.

Oh my God, this shower feels amazing. I must sigh about a hundred times as the water cascades over my skin and releases the tension in my muscles. It's tempting to stay in longer, but I do need to dry my hair, and even though I can blast it with the hairdryer as it's curly, and looks the same whatever I do, it still takes time. Ugh, time to get out.

Fifteen minutes later, I'm ready. I venture downstairs and spot Viggo in reception.

'Viggo, hi. Glad to be out of your suit?' I grin. He's wearing faded denims, a Hard Rock Café T-shirt and a pair of Converse.

'I hate wearing suits,' he confides in me. 'I feel so constrained in them. And the ties, don't get me started.'

I laugh then see Lorenzo approach.

'Ready?' he says.

'Absolutely, I'm starving.' As if in confirmation my stomach growls and all three of us laugh.

'OK, OK, hold your horses, stomach,' Viggo says. 'We're going.'

The maître d' shows us to our table. 'Is this OK for you?' he asks.

'Perfect,' we reply in unison.

The mouth-watering menu makes it difficult to choose, although there are certain foods I have to avoid since I'm pregnant. Eventually, I ask the waiter to recommend something and he suggests the black quinoa with smoked trout and the hazelnut and bacon risotto. Both are combinations I wouldn't have thought of, and can apparently eat safely, so I smile and nod that that's what I'll have.

I have only one word for the food once it arrives: orgasmic. I'm not joking. I'm channelling Meg Ryan in *When Harry Met Sally*. Perhaps my hormones being all over the place heightens the sensations for me, but when people say something is better than sex, I now know what they mean. This food is celestial, from a different planet perhaps. It's so incredible I really have to concentrate to not let inappropriate noises pass my lips.

Conversation flows and although Viggo and Lorenzo are very different to each other, they're both excellent company, and I'm enjoying spending time with them.

'And what about you, Lorenzo, do you have a girlfriend?' Viggo asks.

I take a sharp intake of breath at the change of subject. It's rather personal. As far as I know, these two haven't met before this week.

'No, I don't,' Lorenzo says, his eyes moving uneasily around the table as if he's desperate for the topic to move on.

'Oh well, never mind. We have a few days left of the show, and did you see those girls on the welcome desk at the stand? Lucia and Monica, was it? Lorenzo, come on, Monica must be 36DD and as for Lucia, well, I bet she's not so innocent. She has that glint in her eyes. I'd do her no problem.'

Silence falls over the table. Nausea rises in my throat and it's nothing to do with my pregnancy. Did I slip into a parallel universe just then? Surely Viggo didn't really say all those crass things.

I glance at Lorenzo. His face is crimson and I can't tell if it's with discomfort or anger. He still hasn't spoken. I decide it has to be me who saves him from this situation, and reining my temper in, I say quietly, 'I don't think that's very respectful of the girls, Viggo, or appropriate.'

'Oh, c'mon, it's only a bit of fun,' he scoffs. 'Look at Lorenzo's face. He's blushing. He knows they're up for it.

He is too. Look at him.'

My eyes meet Lorenzo's and I try to convey sympathy for him in my look. I'm not sure how Viggo could possibly consider his loutish, laddish behaviour as being well received, but the man sitting beside me has his fist clenched down by his side, and from the set of his jaw, I can sense his teeth are gritted.

Finally, Lorenzo speaks. Like me he does so quietly, but his words couldn't carry more weight. 'Viggo, that was out of order, particularly in front of Louisa. She doesn't need to witness that disgusting talk. Apologise.'

Viggo stares at us both as if seeing us for the first time. 'Disgusting talk? She's hardly the Virgin Mary. If you haven't noticed, she's knocked up at the minute, so she knows all about S E X.' He whispers the final three letters.

'Excuse me.' I've heard enough. I rise from the table, but not before I see Lorenzo's eyes glitter with anger.

His voice dangerously low, he says, 'Apologise now, Louisa's home life is none of your business. She is your colleague and you have no right to speak about her in that way, or the girls.'

With a huge sigh, and not meaning it one bit, sounding every inch the petulant teenager, Viggo says, 'Sorry, Dad. Sorry, Mom,' then pushes his chair back from the table with a screech and storms out of the room.

I release a breath and all the air whooshes out of my lungs. 'What on earth–?'

'I am so sorry, Louisa. I had no idea he would behave like that. He can't go around speaking like that. I'll have a word with Fabien about him.'

'Small-man syndrome, we call it, in the UK.'

Lorenzo looks confused. Viggo isn't small. It's too hard

to translate and I'm too tired.

'If you don't mind, Lorenzo, I'm very tired. I think I'll go to bed.'

'I understand. I'm sorry that imbecile caused our evening to be cut short. Will you be OK?'

'I'll be fine, thank you, Lorenzo.'

'Is breakfast at seven OK for you? So we beat the traffic.'

I nod, deflated, then pick up my things, wish Lorenzo goodnight and return to my room. Thanks, Viggo. What a horrible end to an otherwise fabulous day.

Chapter Nine

Tuesday 19 October

To-do list
Consider reporting Viggo to Fabien for being a sleazebag
Pick up presents for kids and sisters
Text everyone to thank them for stepping in
Phone Mum to check how meetings went
Buy pregnancy vitamins – have run out
Check school clothes – have the kids grown out of anything yet?
Ensure have enough of the juice boxes Hugo likes – Ronnie always buys the wrong brand – cheaper, but they go in the bin as Hugo says they taste too strong

I drag my trolley case through International Arrivals as I think ahead to all the things I need to do now I'm back. The past few days have been wonderful. I've met some amazing couples who've loved my designs and signed up there and then; Lorenzo has had me touring the Città Alta each evening for dinner; and the food has been incredible.

I did my best to stay away from that asshole Viggo – how could I ever have thought he was a decent person – and was glad when he was reassigned to a different role on the stand. He may have slightly tainted the trip, but at least he didn't ruin it. Now, all I want to do is get home, hug my kids and snuggle into Ronnie for a bit of reassurance and to remind me of the most important things in life.

I turn my phone on as I go through the Arrivals door. I'd best call home and give them an ETA. I'm on the fourth ring, when I hear, 'Mummy!' and Hugo launches himself at me.

'Oof!' I say, all the stuffing knocked out of me. 'Darling, what are you doing here?' I hug him to me, breathing in his little boy smell of apple blossom shampoo and sweat. God, I've missed him. It seems longer than a few days. Much longer, I think grimly. I grasp him tighter and he says, 'Mummy, you're squishing me.'

'Sorry. Where's everyone else?'

He points to where Aria and Gen are standing with Ronnie, who's watching me in amusement. I muss Hugo's hair then put my arm around him and walk with him towards the rest of my family. It strikes me now like a sucker punch to the gut exactly how much I've missed them. A lump forms in my throat and I fight back tears. I will not cry. I will not cry. Channel happy mum. The truth is, my emotions are all over the place. I hug Gen to me as Aria wraps herself around my legs, her preferred position when greeting me. It's good to be home. Well, Edinburgh Airport. My breath leaves me in a whoosh like a punchbag that's had the stuffing knocked out of it. Home.

I kiss Ronnie on the lips and linger a little longer than would usually be considered appropriate in front of the children, or indeed, in an airport. 'What a lovely surprise,' I mumble into his shoulder, loth to move away from his embrace as I know my face is wet with tears. He hugs me extra tight as if he senses something is up. That's a story for another day. He'd be furious, but today is all about reuniting with the kids and my husband. I haven't felt this in synch with Ronnie for a while. I check my memory banks. More than a while, about a decade. I close my eyes and only when Hugo says, 'Mum, can we go? Dad said we could go for McDonald's on the way home,' do I raise my head from Ronnie's shoulder.

I smile down at Hugo. 'Of course, let's hit the road.'

'I'll take your case, Mum,' Hugo says gallantly, and my emotions almost tip me over the edge. I love these kids.

On the car journey home, after Ronnie fills me in on Martha's progress – she's improving, if slowly – everyone is vying for position to tell me what they've been up to in my absence.

'Mummy, Daddy helped us make the scarecrow. Wait until you see it, it's amazing!' Hugo boasts.

'Hugo, we agreed we wouldn't tell Mum, so she would get a surprise!' Gen shakes her head.

'Well, I wanted to tell her now,' Hugo says then sticks his tongue out at her. Ah, it's good to be home, bar the constant bickering.

'Mummy, the scarecrow is really cool. I helped Daddy stuff him,' Aria says.

'And I chose his clothes,' adds Hugo. 'I used some of Daddy's old ones, but they were a bit big, so we cut them to make them fit.'

I can only imagine. No, really, I can only imagine.

Gen has remained resolutely quiet about the scarecrow, apart from to blast her brother for not keeping to their agreement, and I wonder if she is becoming too old for the village's scarecrow festival. She's participated in it every year since she could stand. For some reason, I find the idea she's too old, unbearable, and again I tear up. Oh, c'mon, enough with the tears already. I've shed enough tears in this pregnancy to last me several lifetimes. Thank goodness I will never be pregnant again.

I've barely had that thought when the babies kick. Ow! I flinch and Ronnie lifts his chin, a question in his eyes.

'Babies. Kicking.'

His eyebrows shoot into his hairline. 'Already? Isn't it a bit early?'

'Daad. No, it's not. Are you sure you've had three children?' Gen says either disparagingly or in despair, it's hard to tell which.

He shrugs at Gen and throws me a 'How am I supposed to know?' look. I smile.

Gen rolls her eyes at Ronnie. 'Babies can kick from around twenty-two weeks. Isn't that right, Mum?'

'Maybe even before that.'

'Dad, haven't you been reading the parenting books?' Gen asks, a look of outrage on her face. 'You'd never pass Parenting 101.'

'What have I done to deserve all this abuse?' Ronnie asks.

I laugh and then Aria giggles, followed by Gen and Hugo.

The banter flows all the way home where I finally meet Humphrey, the scarecrow.

As I cross the drive to reach the front garden, I see Humphrey's stayed remarkably intact despite the recent run of extreme weather – I was lucky to escape it in Italy. So my trip had something going for it. Oh, it wasn't all bad, I suppose, I got the commissions, it was just that idiot Viggo who left a sour taste in my mouth.

Humphrey cuts an impressive figure, dapper in one of Ronnie's old navy and red checked shirts. He's a bit portlier than the scarecrow from *The Wizard of Oz* and appears to have sideburns. When he sees me looking, Hugo says, 'Black felt.'

'Ah.' He has ripped jeans and is a curious blend of a lumberjack, the Hulk and Elvis. Not sure whose brainchild this incarnation was, but it's certainly different.

My eyes meet Ronnie's and I suppress a giggle. If we don't win some sort of prize for this scarecrow, it will be a travesty.

'He's unbelievable,' I say to Hugo, who's looking earnestly at me.

'Thanks, Mum.' He trots off, happy with my comment as I explode in laughter. Gen sidles up. 'Hideous, right? Has to be seen to be believed, but it's sure to win a prize, if not least for ugliest and least likely to exist scarecrow.' Her thoughts echo my own and on impulse, I say, 'Well, if he's winning a prize, I want a photo with him before he knows stardom. He might ditch me after.' I hand her my phone and she willingly obliges, snorting with laughter as she does so. I adopt various over-the-top poses and then say, 'Your turn.'

She shakes her head. 'No way. I wouldn't be seen dead with that thing.'

'Just as well I want a photo of you alive with it then, isn't it?' I deadpan. When she continues to shake her head, I say, 'Please, for posterity. We won't ever have a scarecrow festival at this house again.' I give her my best puppy eyes.

'Mum,' she says, 'I'll do it, but only if you promise never to try to do puppy eyes again. That was embarrassing.'

I grin and take snap after snap, then I put my arm around my girl and together we walk into the house. Boy, it's good to be home.

Once I've settled in, and the kids have had their McDonald's – which Ronnie had to head back out for because we were having such fun on the way home we forgot all about it – I make a point of catching up with everyone: Wendy, Jo, Sam, Nicky. I fire out messages to them all then call Mum and Dad. It seems like ages since I spoke to Mum properly.

'Hi, Mum, it's me. How are you and Dad?'

'Oh, hello, darling. How was your trip?'

I gloss over the bad parts and highlight the good then she fills me in on what I've missed at Wedded Bliss. My company's beginning to feel like Mum's now, and although I appreciate her help, more than she'll ever know, she is supposed to be retired. I know she'll support me even more with the company when the twins are born, and I can't help feeling guilty that she's not taking up new hobbies and meeting up with friends more.

When I hang up, I'm more tired than I thought and I stifle a yawn just as Ronnie comes in and drops a kiss on my head. 'Dinner in fifteen minutes.'

'Dinner?'

'Yeah. I'm cooking.'

It's as well I'm sitting down. Ronnie doesn't generally cook. Maybe there's some advantages to be had from being pregnant after all. Hopefully he has remembered the many things I'm not currently permitted to eat.

'Quails' eggs then shellfish linguine,' he says as if he's read my mind.

I open my mouth to protest then realise he's joking. 'Ha bloody ha! What are we having though?'

'Breaded chicken with potato dauphinoise and petit pois, then banoffee pie to follow.'

That doesn't sound too bad actually. More homely than the fayre I've been eating the past few days, although that was amazing.

'How long did it take you to make the banoffee?' I ask, deadpan.

He scrunches his eyebrows and with a flourish of his hand says, 'Oh, it was but a matter of moments.'

'Icing on the Cake?' I say.

'Where else.' He grins.

I should have known. I'd have to file a police report for alien abduction of my husband if I genuinely thought he'd made the banoffee himself.

'How's Martha?' I ask. My thoughts are a jumble and I don't appear to be able to organise them or my questions into order of priority at the moment. Guilt stabs at me for not having asked after her earlier.

'She's doing a lot better. Should hopefully be home within the week.'

I frown. 'I thought she needed a care plan in place first. Has that happened?'

'Not exactly.' Ronnie dries a glass with the dishtowel as he meets my eyes. 'Brett's decided to stay on a bit, until she's steadier on her feet.'

This is news. I didn't think he'd be able to get more

than a few weeks off work.

'Well, that's great.' I realise the feeling that's washed over me is relief. 'She'll love having him around, and he'll sleep more easily knowing he's on hand.' As will I.

'Yeah. He's been round for a few beers and we went to The Crooked Chimney a few times for dinner. You can get fed up with takeaways.'

I raise an eyebrow. 'I'm sure.' But I'm smiling.

Wednesday 20 October

To-do list

Buy maternity swimming costume – not sure what size I was when I had Aria, but the old one isn't cutting it and I'm back at aquanatal with Sam

Check hoover still in warranty

Call about warranty repair for hoover – not sucking as it should

Renew Bear's pet plan – I'm sure it renews around now – maybe shop around – getting really expensive

Give Aria £2 for Grow Your Own Winter Garden project as per pre-holiday school letter

'Mummy,' Aria says as we walk to school in a slight drizzle. It's walk to school week, or we'd be taking the car. Why is walk to school week never in June?

'Yes, Aria?'

'Have you bought my zombie princess costume yet?'

'Not yet. And remember I said I don't think they have those types of costumes in your size.'

Aria pulls at my hand to make me stop. 'Yes, Mummy,

and remember I said you could make it if they didn't sell them in my size.'

I bite my tongue, literally. 'Aria, Mummy doesn't have time to make a zombie princess outfit. We'll have to see what's available in the supermarket.'

'OK, can we go after school?'

Damn. I'm not getting out of this, am I? Note to self: check which supermarkets are doing which costumes before I take her. Possibly bribe them to hide them for a day or so.

'We'll see. Now, have you got your lunch box? The bell will be going in five minutes.'

'Yes, Mummy. Hugo, you could go as a zombie prince.'

Hugo mumbles something incoherent, but which I'm pretty sure conveys his disinterest or perhaps even horror at the mere thought. Last year he went as Harry Potter. So far this year he's expressed interest in going as one of the Justice League, or Drac from *Hotel Transylvania*. Very specific. Can't just be the age-old Dracula. I think a girl he likes is going as Drac's daughter. That might have something to do with it. The sooner Halloween is over, the better. Although, that will mean the beginning of all the Christmas decorations and gift aisles. Ha! Who am I kidding? These days the retailers force those upon us in August.

'Bye, darling,' I say to Aria as she heads off into the playground having spotted her friends. 'Bye, my little zombie prince.'

Hugo glares at me. 'Mum! Don't.'

'I was kidding.' I hold out my hands, palms up in a gesture of peace.

'It's not funny. And Mum, please do something about Aria. I am not going to the Halloween disco as a zombie prince.'

'OK, I will. Have a good day.' I kiss him on the top of his head, and he doesn't pull away. Result. I thought he was too cool for that now, but since he was distracted, I thought I'd try it, and it worked.

Back home, I'm fielding calls, messages and emails, waiting for Mum to arrive for our summit meeting. I've done my report for Fabien and Charles and have started following up on the leads from the show. I'm feeling energised and productive. Long may it continue. Mum's later than I expected, so I take Bear and Patch for a short walk then resume my proactive streak. Soon my living room is awash with packages and envelopes with samples and packing materials, and I'm halfway through creating a new design for the Flahertys whom I met with before I went to Arran, when Mum breezes in.

'Morning! Oh, it's so good to have you back.'

I rise from my chair and go over to give her a hug. 'Thanks, Mum. You too. Coffee?'

'I'd love one.'

I put the kettle on and as we wait for it to boil, she says, 'Sorry I was late. I nipped to the supermarket in Lymeburn for a few things. I also bought some Halloween costumes for the kids. I hope you don't mind. They were doing three for two. I've left them in a bag in the hall.'

'Oh, Mum, you shouldn't have, you're always spoiling us.'

She waves my protestations away. 'They're my grandchildren. If I can't spoil them, who can I spoil?'

True. 'Well, thanks. It's appreciated.' Privately, I thank the heavens. At least now I can tell Aria her nana bought her costume, so hopefully she'll feel obliged to wear it – she loves her nana – and no more talk of zombie bloomin' princesses. A band of tension releases inside me. Thanks, Mum.

We go into the living room for our debrief. 'When did Fedex move in?' Mum asks.

'I had a lot of stuff to catch up on,' I say.

Her brow creases. 'From the show?'

'Mostly, but also some Wedded Bliss stuff. I emailed you the details this morning so you know what I've done.'

She frowns. 'You didn't need to do all this by yourself. I could have taken care of it.'

'Mum, you're already doing too much. You're supposed to be retired.'

'Yes, and you're nearly six months pregnant.'

'Touché. Shall we crack on?'

As we sip our drinks, we bring each other up to speed. Mum is meticulous and has really grasped the ins and outs of the wedding stationery business very quickly. I honestly have no idea what I'd do without her. I'm so glad we're a team.

A few hours later, we're having a break and I tell Mum I'm meeting Sam at aquanatal tonight. I've missed a few sessions and I feel as if I'm letting her down. I'm supposed to be her wingman there.

'I wish we'd had something like that back when you were born,' Mum says. 'Sounds very relaxing.'

'It's more fun than anything else. Fifteen women flopping about in water, moving like they can't do on land at the moment. The weightlessness is the main benefit.'

'How's Sam doing anyway?'

Do I tell her about the names debacle? I hesitate then

decide not to. Hopefully, Nicky's right and it will sort itself out. 'Really well. She and Erik and the girls are really looking forward to having another little girl.'

'Did Erik hanker after a wee boy this time, do you know?'

I screw up my face, trying to recall if Sam mentioned anything like that, but I come up blank. 'I don't think so. He's too laid-back to care if his dynasty continues.'

Mum chuckles. 'I think secretly all men would like a wee boy, but Erik will have his work cut out when they're teenagers. Three girls.'

'Eh, I have two, and we don't know what these–' I point to my stomach '–two will be. I could end up with four.'

'I know. I pray for you every night,' Mum jokes, or at least I hope she's joking.

It's a bit of a scramble later, once the kids are home, trying to feed them and check the homework's done. Aria is always a nightmare. She floats around the house doing anything but her homework, whereas Hugo does his, the moment he comes in, so he can go out to play, or as is the case today, with the now torrential rain, so he can play his Xbox. But finally I hand over to Ronnie, who has just come in from work, having been in the office today. We pass like ships in the night as I hand over the reins and reverse down the drive, off to Hamwell to the pool.

Fifteen minutes later, I meet Sam in the foyer. She looks huge, or rather, huge for someone carrying one baby. I look at least the same size as her, but then I do have double trouble.

'Sam. Wow, how we've grown!' I gesture between our stomachs and laugh. Fortunately, she hasn't lost her sense of humour. I know some people can be touchy about their size and shape when they're pregnant, but we've always bantered about it.

'Yeah, you'd almost think you had twins in there.'

I laugh and give her a hug. 'Looking forward to this?'

She smiles. 'I am. It's nice once a week to be on our own and focus on the fact that soon we'll be meeting our babies.'

'Not too soon, I hope. My house is a pigsty. I need the nesting instinct to kick in first.'

'You're not due for months yet, though.'

'Yeah, and it'd take me that long to tidy my house,' I say dryly.

We swim-walk our way through the class. A couple of women look ready for their babies to put in an appearance by the end of the class. Do we really look and walk like that towards the end of the third trimester? It's funny how you forget. They're huge. They eclipse both me and Sam. The one in front of me concerns me that she may be about to have a water birth. Maybe she's having triplets. If the instructor makes us do one more squat, we may need a midwife.

I tread water until we're told to grab a noodle and do some reverse crunches. Sounds painful, but is wonderful and relaxing. Do you think they'd take me in the class once I'm no longer pregnant? This kind of exercise I can do.

After the class, Sam and I do a few breadths of breaststroke. Meant to be the easiest stroke during pregnancy, but I don't trust myself to do lengths in case I lose momentum halfway.

We're both too tired to talk whilst we swim so we have a quick drink in the pool café afterwards to catch up.

'How's Erik doing?'

Sam moves a damp piece of hair away from her face. 'He's good. You know the Swedish, they take childbirth in their stride, even the men.'

'Yeah, but they're not giving birth.'

'No, I mean the looking after the baby part. Erik will be the one who comes to hospital, picks up his daughter with one giant hand, pops her in the baby carrier he's fastened to his chest, and off they'll go. Most men would be faffing about with the car seat straps and bringing five blankets to keep her warm. He's so chilled, and he was like that with the first one too.'

'It's not a bad way to be. Ronnie wasn't too much of a Mother Hen, but then I did rather make up for that, with Gen at least, as I was terrified. The other two not so much. Have you seen Nicky?'

Sam nods. 'We met up when you were in Italy. Nightmare about her insurance claim, isn't it?'

I shake my head. 'I can't understand it. How can they pay us but not her? I know she said because it was a personal injury claim versus possessions, but even so. World has gone mad.'

Sam sighs. 'It really has. Right, I best be going. I promised Ava I'd be back for bedtime.'

'Ditto. See you next week?'

'Wouldn't miss it. At least here I get some peace!'

'I know what you mean. Nobody can come disturb me when I'm in the loo to tell me the internet has gone off.'

Sam laughs. 'Oh yeah, although with me it's that Peppa Pig has finished, or they're fighting over a toy, or they want a biscuit. I could go on.'

'Yep, been there. Anyway, onwards and upwards. I'll text you in the week. Might see you at the scarecrow festival too.'

'We're going for the parade.'

'Well, if it's not too busy, I'm sure we'll bump into you. Right, I really must go now. You're a bad influence! I'll be late.'

'Look who's talking! Bye!'

I'm looking forward to reading with Hugo before he goes to bed. Aria should already be sound asleep and Gen will either be doing homework or watching Netflix or YouTube on her iPad in her room, unless she's availing herself of some Daddy–girl time in my absence. I'm visualising popcorn and a High School Musical fest. Hugo loves that franchise of films too. So when relatively loud music assaults my ears when I get out of the car and I see limbs being thrown around in the living room through the bay window as I walk up the drive, I could be forgiven for thinking I've parked outside the wrong house.

What the–? And when I go inside it's worse. I get a flashback to primary school discos as the 'Time Warp' is playing at full blast. Hugo bounds out dressed as The Flash and Gen follows doing the conga with Aria's arms wrapped around her waist. They look like evil twins, then I apologise to my twins still to be born for the thought by patting my stomach protectively. But they are the epitome of evil, Gen and Aria. Their hair is backcombed – that will be a nightmare unless they shower it out tonight – and they're dressed in layers of black, grey and dusty pink chiffon, mainly black though. What the actual–?

'Mummy!' Aria says, coming up to me. Her face is caked in thick stage make-up and her eyes are ringed with black, her mouth stained red above and below her lips as if she has somehow got a hold of a sacrifice.

I momentarily recoil before I remember this is my baby and instead I hold her at arm's length to avoid greasy make-up getting on me.

'Aria? Where did you–?' No! No, no, no, no, no. Mum? Really? She thought this was appropriate. Gah! Why didn't I check the costumes? I exhale noisily as I try not to wail, freak out or take my daughter by the hand straight to the bathroom and scrub it all off. My daughter is five years old, too sweet to be dressed like some zombie princess. Fleetingly, I think how Mum got Hugo's outfit spot-on.

I count to ten, trying to find inner peace but only find external chaos. Without realising it, I'd closed my eyes. When I open them, Aria is staring at me.

'So, Mummy, what do you think?' She gives a twirl.

She really doesn't want to know what I think. And nor does my mum. Thank goodness she's not here, or I'd be giving her a piece of…

'Louisa, darling, what do you think?' My mother floats out of my living room, dressed as Elvira. Am I having an out-of-body experience? What is Mum even doing here?

It doesn't often happen, but I'm rendered speechless.

'Don't they look great? I brought a cake round for Ronnie. You know how he loves my carrot cake. And I happened to mention to the kids about their costumes, and they couldn't wait to try them on.'

If steam isn't actually coming out of my ears, it's because there's no outlet for it, because believe me I'm about to blow.

'Mum, help me make tea,' I say through gritted teeth.

'Hey, Mum, pretty cool, eh?' says Gen. 'This'll totally rock Heidi's party.'

I give a tight smile and turn back to Mum, who finally heeds my warning signs and heads for the kitchen. I close the door.

'Is everything OK?' Mum asks, patting her Elvira hair. Wonder who did that for her. Gen?

'No, Mum,' I hiss. 'Everything is most definitely not OK. What were you thinking getting Aria a zombie princess costume? I've been having a battle of wills with her over it, and I had no intention of giving in.'

Mum's face falls, and I regret losing it with her, almost instantly.

'Oh, Louisa, I'm so sorry. I had no idea. All the little girls are wearing them at the moment. It was the same last year. It's very "in", you know,' she says as if imparting secret knowledge to me.

I sigh. 'No, I'm sorry for snapping. I just–' I huff out a breath '–Aria's at that wilful stage, and I really didn't want her wearing anything so freaky so young. It's bad enough when the P7s do it, but she's P1.'

'Sorry, darling. I didn't think. She was jabbering on last time I saw her, about Halloween, and she was so excited, it never even crossed my mind that you'd vetoed her costume.'

I sigh. 'Look, there's nothing we can do about it now.' I pause for a minute. 'And she was very convincing in that costume. She almost scared me out my wits.'

Mum laughs. 'She's a right little actress in the making.'

I raise my eyebrows. 'You're telling me.'

The door opens and Gen comes in. 'Hey, Mum, Nana. Everything OK?'

I glance at Mum then turn to Gen and say, 'Everything's fine. Hot chocolate?'

'Yes, please,' Gen says. She sits down on the seat I vacate and she and Mum discuss the finer points of Halloween whilst I prepare the drinks and dream of the halcyon days when Aria wanted a costume to match Cornie, her unicorn teddy. If only.

Saturday 23 October

To-do list

Remember hats

Loose change for stalls for the kids

Take wipes with me – they always get filthy

Take money out of the ATM

Find bumbag – scarecrows don't carry handbags

Today's the day. The main scarecrow festival events, starting with the parade at eleven o'clock then the judging of the best village scarecrow at three. The judges start judging the entries after the parade and make their final decision in time for the prize-giving at four, when they will also announce the best-dressed human scarecrow from the parade.

All day, stalls in the main street, which is pedestrianised for the event, will ply their trade in hot and cold food, cakes, ice creams, festival-themed gifts: knitted scarecrows, scarecrow sketches and prints, and there will be games of a scarecrow nature. It's lots of fun and the kids are really looking forward to it. This year, we're all dressing up. We try to get right into the spirit of it. These are the kinds of events that make villages what they are, and they're worth embracing. I smile at the thought that next year there will be two more little scarecrows to dress.

Each of us has a different colour floppy hat. I'm wearing denim dungarees and All-Star Converse, with a blue floppy hat and a cheesecloth shirt; Ronnie's wearing brown dungarees with one side undone. He has fake grass to chew and a red floppy hat; Aria has a yellow floppy hat and dark sunglasses and has chosen a matching yellow dress printed with daisies; Hugo has red dungarees and is emulating Ronnie's style of scarecrow but he's sporting a green hat instead of red; and Gen has a pink floppy hat, pink denim dungarees and has made her face up to look like a scarecrow. It's kind of freaky. She has a real talent for applying stage make-up though. The other day when she and Aria were dressed as zombie princesses, I'd assumed Mum had done the honours, but no, it was all Gen. Who knew?

If I say so myself, we look pretty cracking as a scarecrow family. Even Patch and Bear have tiny scarecrow details on their collars in a show of allegiance.

'Can we go yet, Mummy?' Hugo asks. He has already asked about fifteen times in the last half hour.

'Ten minutes, Hugo. Why don't you go tidy your room whilst you're waiting?'

The scathing look he casts me indicates that's a no.

Finally we're ready, and as we walk down to the main street, where we'll meet the others who'll take part in the parade, it seems everyone is at their front doors, eager to watch the parade. Toddlers on parents' shoulders, elderly people sitting on chairs in their front gardens, visitors to the area or those who happen to be passing through, who've stopped to see what's going on in the main street. We have to walk to the far end, near our partially reconstructed house, as the parade starts there and marches through the village.

The noise level starts to increase and the marching band comes along, heralding the start of the festival events. The organiser has a loudspeaker and they spend five minutes welcoming us to this year's festival and telling us the order of today's events, and then it's parade time. We line up in our spot. There must be several hundred scarecrows taking part today, many of them families.

Whilst we're milling around, I note a scarecrow which looks like Donald Trump, another resembles Boris Johnson – I wonder if they're friends. Harry Potter stands side by side with the Gruffalo, and Elton John meets Freddie Mercury. Did someone forget to tell me it was celeb-themed this year? I make a note to ask. We're never going to win the competition now. Not that winning is everything…but it is important.

And we're off, strutting our stuff down Main Street where everyone's cheering. Out of the corner of my eye, I spy Brett who is waving out of Martha's window. I'm not sure if he recognised us, or if he's just waving at the crowd, but I wave back anyway. A scarecrow in front of me does a cartwheel. Another passes me on a unicycle whilst juggling. We're seriously going to have to up our game next year. Maybe Ronnie could ride a motorbike with me in the sidecar juggling the twins. Of course, I jest, but that's what it might take to win! The scarecrows are incredible, and the kids are loving it. Even Gen, whose face has lit up so much that when it gets dark, we won't need street lights.

The music is pumping out, and there's a nod to a police presence. What we'd have called back in the olden days, bobbies on the beat.

The atmosphere is wonderful. A woman scarecrow jogs past me with a double buggy with two teeny scarecrows inside – it's a little freaky actually, but the toddlers seem to be having fun, although they have straw everywhere. They'll be deconstructed scarecrows shortly.

A couple of scarecrows dressed as sweets, a jelly bean and a liquorice allsort, throw sweets to the children lining the street – hope they go back and clear those up later.

All too soon the parade comes to an end, although I'm glad in a way as it was so exciting I'm exhausted, and the kids are too. Possibly a little cold too. Thankfully, it isn't raining.

'And now the judging of the static scarecrows will begin,' says the organiser, as four representatives peel off and head in different directions within the village, armed with clipboards. I wonder what the criteria are. I squint to see who is likely to be covering our street, but I can't work it out.

'Mum, can we get candy floss?' Hugo tugs my arm. 'Can we, can we?'

Hugo doesn't usually ask for sweet treats, and they don't come much sweeter than candy floss, so I nod and he directs me to the candy floss stall.

The organisers really have outdone themselves this year. There are so many stalls.

Hot drinks, hot food, crafts, artwork, handmade soaps,

candles. There's even a pet food supply stand. And a local author is standing signing copies of her latest book. I swell with pride at being part of this community.

As I ask the author to sign a copy of their latest thriller for my dad, someone taps my shoulder.

'Benedict! How are you? I thought you were in the States.'

'I was, but…unforeseen circumstances.' He looks down. A little girl is holding his hand.

'And what's your name?' I ask.

'Tiziana,' she replies, half-hiding behind Benedict's legs. She must be about four.

'That's a beautiful name,' I tell her, and she blushes.

'It's Italian, after my *nonna*.'

I smile at her and say, 'Well, your nonna must be a very important lady.'

She smiles sadly. 'She is. But she's in heaven now. Like my mamma.'

My eyes widen with concern.

Benedict shakes his head. 'She's my goddaughter. Actually, I've been meaning to call you. Can we talk later?'

'Sure. Is everything OK?'

He glances at Tiziana. 'Not exactly. Let me know when suits, yeah?'

'You can come by after the judging tonight if you want.'

He nods. 'That would be great. Thanks.'

I say goodbye to Tiziana as she and Benedict melt into the crowd. A band of pressure circles my chest. Something's up, and only now do I realise how grey Benedict looked, not the way he should do if he's living the good life in the US.

I try to put Benedict to the back of my mind so as not to spoil the kids' enjoyment of the day. Aria plays pin the carrot on the scarecrow and is the closest so wins a hand-knitted scarecrow as a prize. Hugo plays ten-pin scarecrow bowling and comes second, so he wins a voucher to spend at several of the other stalls, and Gen, with a little gentle coaxing creates a scarecrow rap and performs it on the makeshift stage and wins. The fact only three people participated in the 'talent show' doesn't matter. She wins iTunes vouchers and is delighted.

'I'm hungry,' Hugo announces.

'Hugo, you've been eating all day long. Grazing constantly. How can you be hungry?' I ask, incredulous even though I know what he's like.

'I'm a growing boy, Mother,' he says in a withering tone.

Honestly. 'Fine. There's a hot dog stand at the back. Do you want one?'

A chorus of yeses greet me, including from Ronnie, who has been remarkably absent this afternoon whenever anyone's making requests. I think he's been enjoying wandering around the stalls. The pop-up market really enhances the village.

Hot dogs in hand, we stand in front of the stage, where the organiser is about to declare the winners of this year's competition.

He waits for a hush. 'For the category of best-dressed human scarecrow in the parade, in third place, is Freddie Mercury.' A cheer goes up and the man goes up to claim his prize. Once he has shaken hands with the organiser, he retreats and quiet descends.

'In second place is Aria Halliday. Come on up, Aria.

He looks around for her. I raise my hand and point to her. 'Up you go. Go collect your prize.'

'Don't want to go by my own,' she says, burying her head into my legs, and I melt with love for her. My little extrovert having stage fright.

'I'll take her,' Ronnie says. 'C'mon, angel.'

Aria sashays to the stage, and the organiser hands her a little silver trophy of a scarecrow and a gift bag. She shakes his hand solemnly and Ronnie ruffles her hair as she stands holding her trophy aloft for a photograph for the local paper. Not that idiot, Justin Barnes, I had the run-in with, fortunately.

'And in first place, Boris Johnson.'

The crowd cheer as Scarecrow Boris takes the stage. He beams at everyone and laughs as someone shouts, 'Can't tell the difference. It's uncanny.'

Then the static scarecrow prizes are awarded. Third prize goes to the man who took Patch to the vet the night of the crash. I can't believe I've forgotten his name again. Icing on the Cake wins second prize, and Barney the Builder – who? – wins first prize: for the scarecrow on the site of the crash. What? I didn't even know there was one.

'Barney has managed to add a little levity where a tragedy happened earlier this year. I'm sure the Hallidays won't mind.' The screen behind the stage flares to life and I note the presence of not one, not two, not three, but four scarecrows, each about two feet tall: a policeman, a fireman, a doctor and a builder.

Tears fill my eyes. How thoughtful. A deserving winner. He truly has managed to turn the site from an empty shell into something positive. Barney takes the stage and asks to take the mike.

'Could the Hallidays please come up?'

A lump forms in my throat. Ronnie looks at me and silently we glide one after the other towards the stage and up the couple of steps to join Barney.

Once we're there, Barney beams at us and speaks into the microphone. 'The whole team who has worked and will continue to work on your house has been affected by what happened to you all earlier this year. We hope this team of scarecrows will make you smile.'

A tear plops onto my cheek and I watch Ronnie gulp. Gen's eyes are bright. Hugo says, 'Cool!' and Aria says, 'Can we keep them, Mummy?'

I choke-laugh. 'I think so, but it'll be up to Barney.'

Aria approaches him. 'Mr Barney, can we keep them? They're really special.'

Barney bends down to Aria's level and says, 'Of course you can.'

As Barney descends the steps a few minutes later, I squeeze his arm and say, 'Thank you. That made such a positive thing come out of a negative one. And the kids love it.' My voice cracks. 'I do too.'

'You're welcome.'

We've been home about fifteen minutes when the doorbell goes. Who's that at…? Oh God, I totally forgot about meeting Benedict, what with the emergency service and builder scarecrow surprise.

'Ronnie,' I say as I pass the living room on my way to answer the front door. 'I met Benedict earlier. He said he had something to speak to us about and I told him to come round after the festival.'

He frowns and lifts his chin. Yeah, he's as bamboozled as I am.

'Benedict, hi. In you come.' I shepherd him indoors to the living room, where Ronnie is diplomatically telling Hugo that Aria needs his help in the playroom.

'Benedict.' Ronnie nods to him. 'Have a seat.'

'Thanks.' He sits on the armchair opposite then glances up at me.

'Would you like a drink?' I ask.

Relief washes over his face. 'Yes, please. A glass of water. Thanks.'

I return a moment later with the water, and Benedict still looks a little on edge. I wonder what's going on.

'Here you go.' I hand him the water.

'Thanks, Louisa.' He drains half of it in one go. Just as well it wasn't vodka.

Ronnie and I exchange a look and Benedict notices.

'OK, I'll cut to the chase. My circumstances have changed…dramatically, and I need to be back in Scotland.' A shadow clouds his face and he shudders, his eyes closing for a fraction of a second. He seems to be composing himself. 'Tiziana's mother and grandmother were killed in a car crash two weeks ago. Tiziana's mother was my best friend growing up and I'm Tizi's godfather.' His eyes darken. 'Her father's not on the scene. Not even now.' He smooths a hand over his forehead as if trying to relieve pressure there, or as if he may find some inspiration. 'I have to find somewhere for Tiziana to live, permanently. Her mum was renting, and with her death, the rental returns to the council. She doesn't have any other relatives, so it's down to me to look after her. And I'm happy to do it, obviously.' He says this almost as if he thinks we're judging him. We're not.

'Sorry, I didn't mean to take so long to get to the point.' He blows out a breath. 'I need to either move back in here with my son and Tizi, or sell this place and find us something smaller.'

'Oh my God, Benedict, that's awful. That poor little girl.' I don't say it, but I think poor him too. He's had this responsibility thrust upon him, his own life ripped away from him, although I suppose not like Tiziana's with the loss of her mother and grandmother.

'I'm really sorry, Benedict, that's terrible,' Ronnie says, his voice heavy with sincerity.

Benedict puts his head in his hands. 'I'm so sorry to do this to you guys. You're such nice people, and obviously, I'll observe the lease. However, when the three-month lease period is up, I either have to sell or move in.'

'We understand,' Ronnie says. 'Don't worry about that. Apart from anything else, the insurance company reckon our house may be ready by the end of the year.'

All the air seems to leave Benedict's body at once. 'Well, that is a relief. We're staying in a tiny flat at the minute, but it's not ideal. She needs somewhere to play. And I'm sharing a room with my teenage son.'

My eyes stray to our garden. Benedict's garden. I remember Tiziana today and my heart goes out to her. She's lost everything. Well, almost. She still has Benedict, and I think how lucky she is to have him.

'Anyway, I wanted to drop by and tell you. I'll be in touch soon with more details.' He stands and puts down his water.

'Do you want to stay for dinner?' I ask.

'No, no, thank you.' He points to the door. 'My son's

looking after Tizi in the car.'

'Ah, OK. No problem.' Ronnie and I both see him out.

'Take care, Benedict, and if we can help with anything, just let us know.'

'I will,' he says, blinking furiously. 'Thank you.'

'Poor guy,' Ronnie says when we return to the living room.

'And poor Tiziana,' I add.

When something like this happens it really puts things into perspective. Even so, I can't help the little voice at the back of my mind which says, 'And what if our house isn't ready by New Year?'

Chapter Ten

Friday 29 October

To-do list

Buy more stage make-up – Aria and Gen have been going to town with the existing kit

Remember to be at the disco for 5.45 to help the PTA sell tickets

Bring the boxes of crisps and sweets and trays of cakes picked up from cash and carry for disco

Remind Ronnie he needs to bring Aria and Hugo separately as 2 different discos. He also needs to pick Aria up.

Sign flu jab permission slips for Hugo and Aria

We've had a whirlwind of activities at school this week. Some free, some which require me to part with a pound or two. Hugo's favourite was creeping cauldrons, a version of hide and seek, where you hide and try to get back to the cauldron and climb inside without anyone from the other team catching you. Aria loved everything. Colouring in the witches' hats, the broomsticks, the window decorations they made with witches' cats and pumpkins; the stick the tail on the witch's cat game – they really do milk the pin the tail on the donkey trope, don't they? Now there's every permutation possible. She made a mini pumpkin out of papier mâché; they wrapped each other in toilet roll and pretended to be Egyptian mummies and they enacted *The Little Vampire* after watching a movie of it in class.

But tonight is what she's really been waiting for – where she can unleash her zombie princess. God help us. Apparently, she's been practising some special zombie dance moves. I dread to think. Anyway, hopefully, I'll be too busy doling out drinks and treats as a parent helper to notice what havoc she wreaks.

Hugo is also very excited. He was talking to Nicky's son Xander on the phone earlier. Xander's disco is tonight too and he's going as Thor. Hugo doesn't know I heard him talking to himself earlier, in the mirror, I'm guessing, but he was talking to some nemesis as if he was actually The Flash. Cute.

'Mummy, Mummy, can we go now, please?' Aria grabs my hand and pulls me towards the door.

'No, I'm going. You're staying with Dad. You'll be coming soon. I'm going early to help the other mummies and daddies lay out the snacks.'

Aria crosses her arms. She looks like she's about to stage a sit-in. Well, have at it, love.

'Bye, Ronnie,' I call through to the living room as I grab my bag and go. 'Good luck,' I whisper sotto voce.

When I arrive at the school, it's the usual chaos that ensues when there are too many helpers, too many directions and not enough people doing anything constructive. There appear to be enough people sitting at the ticket tables – cushy number. I could be doing with that, I'm pregnant. I decide to do something constructive and return to the car to bring out the crisps and treats. I meet one of the other mums in the car park and she offers to bring in the juice boxes, which I'm relieved at as the trays are rather heavy.

We've set everything up in the hall and the rising chatter of high-pitched voices heralds the arrival of our offspring. Soon the gym hall fills up with primary one to three children. Some of the costumes are incredible. Maleficent, a triceratops – not sure what that has to do with Halloween, but since Hugo's going as The Flash, I can hardly judge. Wednesday Addams and my personal favourite, Cruella de Vil. Amazingly the little girl pulls it off so well. Full of attitude.

Soon the dance floor is awash with tiny bodies bopping along to the music, chattering and bumping into each other, falling over then being righted by a parent helper.

And then it's over, and the children are being shepherded out one door, whilst the older children are at the front door champing at the bit to be let in for their disco, Hugo included, I imagine.

My eyes catch Ronnie's over the sea of heads in the car park, snaking their way to the front door of the school to the makeshift ticket desk at the entrance.

He nods and I take Aria firmly by the hand and head over to where he and Hugo are standing in the queue.

'Daddy, Daddy, it was amazing, and I won a prize!' She holds up her goodie bag with glee.

'Will I get one, Mummy?' Hugo asks, eyeing up Aria's with longing, probably wondering what delights lie within.

I nod yes.

'Hugo, it was amazing.' Aria starts to tell her brother all about the disco as I say to Ronnie, 'I need to head back inside. See you at home.'

He smiles and I return to the fray, via the other door. P4 through P7 children are already in the gym hall, dancing to the strains of Rihanna. There are plenty of parent helpers on the floor, so I return to the makeshift kitchen to replenish snacks and refill goodie bags for later.

'I thought we had loads of stuff,' says one of the mums, 'but these kids are going through it all as if they haven't seen treats for months.'

I laugh. 'I know. The school decided to do it this way to make it fairer for those who don't have a great deal of money, but it does seem a bit like Armageddon out there once the kids lay their hands on the snacks.'

She smiles as she walks off carrying a tray of twenty treat boxes. 'Back into the fray.'

When I return, Hugo is standing shyly to one side, whilst a few girls dance beside him. None of his friends seem to be there yet. My heart drops. He can be somewhat withdrawn in this type of social setting, but once he gets going, he enjoys himself.

As I watch, a girl dressed as the Queen of Hearts from *Alice in Wonderland* approaches him. I don't know her, but she says something to him and then he's on the dance floor. Hurrah. Wonders will never cease. And I relax a little more knowing my son is enjoying the disco.

It's lovely to see the kids having fun, letting loose. This will be their last big event until the Christmas parties. Some of the parents seem to have gone all out with the costumes. It's easy to tell which ones have been made and which bought. I'm always in the bought camp. I wouldn't want to embarrass my children with their having to go to a disco in something I'd cobbled together. Although I can happily design a wedding invitation, my artistic flair definitely doesn't extend to costumes.

I gaze around the room, taking a good look at all the outfits. One child has a costume where they actually seem to glide then I realise they're on a hoverboard. Really? Which parent thought that was a good idea and how did they get past the ticket stall? I hate to be the party pooper, but that's way too dangerous. With a sigh, I head over to bring the boy back to Earth, literally. Can't have him mowing down any of his fellow students.

As the party ends, Hugo comes up to me as the other children filter out into the car park to be met by their parents. 'Can I help tidy, Mum?' I smile at him. I love my boy.

'Grab a bag and let's get this done double speed. Maybe we can watch half a movie when we get back.'

'Yay!' says Hugo, and with a ruffle of his hair, we set to it.

Saturday 30 October

To-do list
Pick up more Halloween sweets – with the vultures round here, they're usually gone in 10 minutes
Buy a couple more buckets for Halloween sweets
Pick up the prescription from the chemist before 1 – shuts early on Saturday
Repair Aria's Halloween costume – the zombie princess has ripped an arm of her dress

I slump on the sofa, spent. What a day! I've just dropped Gen off at a house party in Hamwell. The house was super posh. Electric gates, three storeys, they even had a swimming pool and an ornamental Japanese garden. The drive was filled with BMWs, Audis, Jaguars. My car was definitely the poor cousin. There were waiters for goodness' sake. Mind-boggling. For a kids', well, teenagers', Halloween party?

Today has been a whirl of pumpkin carving, adding decorations – at Aria's insistence – to the copious skeletons, witches, pumpkins and zombies that already adorn the house, and baking Halloween treats. I have barely drawn breath. In fact, I was glad to take the dogs for a walk in order to get away from all the spooky activities. I love Halloween but it is possible to go overboard, and Aria has gone overboard.

I popped over to see Martha today as Brett told Ronnie last night when I was manning the Halloween discos that she was getting out today. It was so lovely to see her back in her own surroundings and she definitely seems to have perked up, although how much of that is to do with Brett being around, I don't know.

Wendy dropped in with her lot earlier too, en route to a party in Glasgow, which one of her friends was hosting. And Jo arrived with Mum and Dad for a while, as, since Travis has a Halloween event on at the restaurant, she's on her own with the kids, but Mum and Dad said they would take them trick or treating, and my younger two chirped up that they'd like to go too, so Ronnie nodded a 'hell yes' and off they went. Meanwhile, muggins here, designated driver and all, took Gen to the house party. I've to pick up her and her friend Freya at ten. I'm sure they'll have a great time, but right now I'm aiming to have a little lie-down.

Shortly after I fall asleep, my subconscious is alerted to

noise downstairs. That'll be the kids coming back with Mum and Dad. Ronnie can see to them, I'm exhausted. My eyes drift closed again. I wake up with a start. What a terrible dream. I hear a noise against the window and my mind goes into overdrive. Just a bad dream, I tell myself. God, it really is Halloween. The wind is howling and the rain is battering against the windowpane. Was it even raining when I came back earlier?

Is that someone crying? I lever myself out of bed and slip my jeans on. That's definitely someone crying. What…? That's Gen. I force myself not to sprint along the landing and down the stairs in case I fall, but I'm still there pretty quickly.

Ronnie is standing in the hall with Freya – it's her I see first, soaked to the skin – and Gen, who's in at least as pitiful a state. Their zombie make-up has washed off, or rather some is over their dark clothing, white mingling with the black. They are both shivering and crying. What the hell…?

'Gen, Freya.' I move towards them then hug them both to me. Ronnie catches my eye above their heads, as they both stand sobbing into my chest and neck.

'Ronnie, can you get some towels, please?'

I lead the girls into the living room and tell them to sit on the sofa, then I turn on the living flame fire. I'd rather have a log burner, but it's not great from a pollution perspective.

'Shh,' I say into Gen's hair when I sit back down. 'It's OK now.' I rub Freya's back and arm. Both girls are freezing and sodden. Why are they here? I glance at the clock. It's nine o'clock. I dropped them off at seven. I was supposed to pick them up in an hour's time. Yet here they are, in our living room, like drowned rats. I need to wait for them to calm down so we can get the story out of them.

Ronnie returns with the towels and I pass one to Freya and the other to Gen.

'Girls, dry yourselves as best you can for now. We'll get you into the shower shortly.' I turn to Ronnie. 'Can you rustle up some hot chocolate for them?'

Ronnie nods and leaves the room.

'Gen, what happened? Why are you both here?' My eyes flick from Gen to Freya and back again.

At first, neither says anything, they just look at each other. Fear lances through my body as I consider all the possibilities. If anyone has harmed a hair on my daughter's head, I swear…

'She wouldn't let us in,' Gen sobs.

I frown. 'Who wouldn't?'

Gen bursts into tears, and it's Freya who pipes up, 'Heidi.'

'Heidi Courtenay?'

Freya nods.

'But wasn't it Heidi who invited you?'

Freya nods again.

I turn to Gen. 'Heidi wouldn't let you in, even though she invited you?'

Gen nods and says through tears, 'It was all a big joke to her. Get us there and then refuse us entry. She pretended to be so excited to see us and then…'

My stomach muscles clench. 'Then what?' I ask, my voice dangerously soft.

Gen breaks down again, and once again Freya finishes: 'Then she asked for selfies with us, and wanted to take them on our phones too, so we gave her our phones so she could snap some pics, then her friends grabbed our bags and together they shoved us through the gates onto the street and she closed the gates with the electronic beeper.'

'Wait a minute,' says Ronnie as he re-enters the room. 'So these girls left you out in the cold, the dark and the rain without your phones and without any money?'

Gen starts to cry again. 'Ye-e-es. And we-e-e were so scared. It was so dark and we couldn't even phone you or ask you to come get us. We did ask a few people outside if we could borrow their phones, but they were too interested in getting to the party.'

'Either that or they thought we were phone-jackers too,' says Freya, tears coursing down her face.

'So what did you do then?'

'We wa-alked,' says Gen.

'Walked!' I think I'm going to be sick. Walked, in the dark, in the rain and howling wind, just the two of them. Oh my God, anything could have happened. Ronnie puts his hand on my shoulder. He senses the storm brewing, and so he should. This is nothing to how I'm going to be when I get a hold of those little shits.

I try to calm myself enough so as not to make the girls any more afraid than they already are. But once I've sorted them out, and called Freya's mum, I am going round there.

The girls drink their hot chocolate whilst Ronnie and I have a quick conflab in the kitchen.

'Ronnie, what they did was downright dangerous as well as foolish. What if they'd been hit by a car as it was dark and they were walking, dressed in black? What if someone had mugged them? Or rather, someone else, as let's face it, that's what that little bitch did. Spoilt little rich girl indeed.'

'I know, Lou, but you can't go in there all guns blazing, especially in the middle of a kids' Halloween party.'

'All guns blazing? She's lucky I don't get the police involved. Theft of her phone, her bag, her purse. Freya's too.' I pause for breath. 'But it's the danger they put them in.'

Ronnie appears to be mulling this over. 'OK. I'll stay here with the kids, but ask Freya's mum to go with you. I don't want you going alone.'

I call Freya's mum, Felicity, and fill her in as best I can. Like me, she is both appalled and outraged. Once she's spoken to Freya to ensure she's all right, she tells me she'll drive straight over and pick me up.

The strain on Felicity's face is plain to see when she arrives and she's clearly been crying, although whether from fear or anger it's hard to tell.

'Louisa, hi, where is she?'

I invite her in and she heads straight for the living room where Freya is curled up on the sofa in a dressing gown, hair damp this time from the shower and not from over an hour of walking in torrential rain.

Felicity hugs her daughter to her, her body shaking as she comforts Freya. Once she's ascertained she is indeed all right and Ronnie will look after her and Gen, I suggest we go.

As we head for Heidi's, I beat myself up about letting her go to the party. The only reason I said yes was because Heidi recently started at Gen's gymnastics class, so even though I've never met her parents, I thought it was fine to let her go. And everyone in their class was going. I didn't want Gen to be the only one left out, plus she had been so looking forward to it. So had Freya. They'd done nothing but talk about it for weeks.

The rain is still pelting down. It hasn't let up all night. We pull up to the gates just as some people are leaving. It's hard to park in the street as there are cars double-parked, up on pavements, parked across people's driveways. It must have been quite the party, just not for my daughter or Felicity's, I think bitterly.

I jump out of the car and ring the bell next to the gates. No one answers at first, nor the second time, nor the third. A crackle comes out of the intercom as if someone is there. So I take the chance someone's listening and say, 'This is Louisa Halliday, Gen Halliday's mum, and if you don't open this gate and let me in, I'm calling the police to report Heidi for theft.'

There's a pause before the gates slide open and I hurriedly jump back in the car and tell Felicity to drive through them. At the moment, I'd gladly ram them, but I don't want to get done for criminal damage.

We pull up to the main entrance, which is flanked by a pair of white columns. It seems too grand to call it a front door. I ring the bell and see out of the corner of my eye a twitching of a curtain off to the far side of the house. The party seems to be coming to its natural conclusion, but there are still plenty of stragglers, many of whom are a lot older than twelve. I frown. Had I known that, Gen wouldn't have been allowed to go.

'Yes? Can I help you?' a surly-looking girl asks as she opens the front door. She looks at my bump and then back at my face.

'Heidi?'

'That's right,' she says, chin tilted upwards.

Oh dear, this little madam has messed with the wrong mum. 'I'd like to speak to your parents, please.' It's difficult staying calm when all I want to do is rip her head off and feed it to a couple of passing Rottweilers but I resist.

She smiles. 'They're not here, I'm afraid. I'm kind of having a party.' She flicks her thumb back indoors.

'That's a pity they're not here. And yes, I'm aware of your party. I do wonder what the police will think of someone stealing from two girls, leaving them with no phones or money to call home, putting them in the situation of having to walk three miles home in this weather in the dark.'

'I-I don't know anything about that.'

'Oh, really? Well, I had been hoping, as had Freya's mum here–' I glance at Felicity standing beside me '–to sort this out without going to the police, but since your parents have left you unsupervised, I don't see we have any other choice.'

'I don't think you need to do that.'

I frown. 'Why not? Because it would get you in trouble? Do you have any idea of the danger you put the girls in? Anything could have happened to them. They could have been hit by a car, walking that road, or attacked. As it is, they've had a horrible Halloween because you invited them to a party, then didn't let them in, but that wasn't enough for you. You stole their phones and their bags so they had nothing, and no one to help them. Yes, I think your parents, and the police, might be very interested indeed in that.'

A car's headlights come up the drive. A sleek silver Jaguar. A man and a woman step out and march towards the house.

'What's going on here?' asks the man. 'Who are you and why are you haranguing our daughter?'

'I'm not haranguing anyone, Mr Courtenay.' I glance to his side where his wife is standing with her arms folded, her eyes narrowed on me. 'In fact, I'm delighted you're here. It was you and your wife I wanted to speak to. I'm Louisa Halliday and my daughter Gen, and Felicity's daughter Freya were guests at your daughter's party this evening.'

'Yes?' Mr Courtenay asks, a flicker of irritation crossing his features. Obviously I'm taking up too much of his valuable time.

'Or rather, they should have been guests. Your daughter–'

'Daddy, let me explain,' Heidi interrupts.

'Quiet, Heidi,' he says, without even looking at her. 'I have things to do, so I'd like to get this over with quickly, and let Mrs Halliday and her friend be on their way.' He moves under the porch to be out of the worst of the weather presumably – we're not invited inside, I note – and I follow suit.

'As I was saying,' I continue, 'your daughter stole my daughter Gen's phone and her bag, did the same to Felicity's daughter, Freya and shoved them out the gates.'

Mr Courtenay's eyes take on a flinty quality. He whips round to Heidi. 'Is this true?'

Heidi's silence answers that question.

'Heidi, what did you do?' her father says. 'What exactly did you do?'

Heidi blushes furiously, not such a little madam now, but reverting to the tween she is.

'I didn't let them in,' she mumbles.

'And?' he prods.

After a brief pause, she mutters, 'I pretended I wanted to take a photo of them and then took their phones.'

'But why?' I can't help asking. 'I understand you might not have wanted them at your party, although I don't get why you'd invite them then, but why take their phones and bags?'

Mr Courtenay looks as if he'd very much like an answer to that too. He stares at Heidi, only a quick glance to his wife, who stands there resolute, her hands now dropped to her sides. Yes, we're not haranguing Heidi, we're trying to understand her actions.

'Because Quinn likes her more than me,' she whispers.

'What? Who what?' her father says, bending down to her level as if that will help him hear her more clearly.

'Quinn likes her better,' she finally spits out.

Her father's jaw clenches. 'Do you mean to tell me that this–' he throws his hands out expansively to encompass our little group '–is all because some boy likes one of their daughters more than he does you?'

Heidi nods mutely, tears coursing down her face. I almost feel sorry for her, but I don't. Not after what she's done.

He glances at me and Felicity for a second. 'Apologise to these ladies immediately, then go and fetch their daughters' belongings. And there had better be nothing missing.'

Heidi shrinks back from him as if the very prospect of apologising is anathema to her.

'Do it,' he repeats, 'and on Monday at school, you will apologise to their daughters, in the headmistress' presence.'

Heidi's face falls. 'Dad, Dad, please don't make me do

that. I don't want Mrs Bristol to know.'

'Tough! If you behave appallingly, you can take the consequences. Now apologise.'

Heidi turns to Felicity and me. 'S-sorry.'

I nod, and Felicity gives a tight smile. Neither of us says thank you or don't worry, or that's all right, because it's not. And Heidi has to learn that. I'm glad her father has been tough on her. I wasn't sure he would be. It's easy to tar all these toffs with their multi-million pound houses and their Jaguars the same, but actually although he initially seemed a tad brusque, he has dealt with it much as I would have done, minus the headteacher part.

'Now go retrieve their things,' her father says.

When she hesitates he says, 'Now!'

Heidi scurries off whilst the four adults stand watching each other.

'I'd like to add my apology to that. We were keeping an eye on things from my sister's house down the road, checking the CCTV at the house. I must have missed the episode at the gate. We wanted to give Heidi a little freedom and her cousin is here with her. Somewhere inside. She's sixteen, so we thought it would be OK. Clearly not.'

'Thank you,' I say. Felicity, beside me, adds her thanks too.

'How are your girls?' Heidi's mother asks.

I blow out a breath. 'Shaken, but they'll be OK.'

'How on earth did they get home without any phone or money?' her husband asks.

I look at him sadly. 'They walked.'

His eyebrows shoot up. 'Jesus H Christ, in that weather? In the dark?'

'Oh my God, anything could have happened to them.'

Heidi's mother lays a hand on her husband's arm as if for support.

'Quite,' I say.

'We are so sorry, so incredibly sorry.' Mr Courtenay shakes his head. 'I dread to think what…'

He doesn't need to say anything else. We all know what could have happened.

'They're safe now, that's what matters.' I glance to the door just as Heidi walks through it carrying the girls' bags.

'I put their phones inside the bags.' She holds them out to us. Her eyes are rimmed red from crying. 'I'm sorry, for everything.' She bursts into tears and stands there, hands covering her face, wretched, until eventually her mother takes pity on her and goes to comfort her.

'I think we'll leave you to it,' I say.

'Apologies again. We'll ensure nothing like this ever happens again, so thanks for bringing it to our attention.'

We return to the car, and once inside, my breath whooshes out of me like a balloon deflating.

'Phew. Thank God that's over. I'm no good at confrontation. You were brilliant there,' Felicity says.

'They were decent sorts in the end. I wouldn't like to be in Heidi's shoes right now though.'

'Nor me,' agrees Felicity. 'Jeez, I thought I had a few more years before I'd need to worry about bullying on this level.'

'You and me both. Why don't we go back to mine and have some of that hot chocolate the girls were having?'

Felicity smiles. 'One day, when neither of us is driving or pregnant, we can have something stronger, but for tonight that sounds wonderful.'

Chapter Eleven

Friday 5 November

To-do list – today I'm trialling the Kanban system. It's Post-it central here. Let's hope this works. Nothing else has so far.

Look out hats, scarves, gloves – temp forecast to be 4°C for tonight's bonfire event

Divest fridge of all the kids' drawings – need to make way for the inevitable Bonfire Night ones

Remember to put TV on for dogs when we're out

Check time to pick Xander up – he's coming for a sleepover to give Nicky and Valentin some time together

Remind my parents not to buy any last-minute fireworks – I have a pathological fear of those being set off at home – organised displays fine, own gardens no

Arrange for Benedict to come round again with an update – check if we can do anything to help

I'm on my way to meet Fabien at Garfield Grange, to discuss the upcoming wedding show in Hertfordshire. We haven't met in person for a while. It's all been Zoom calls, phone calls and emails. He's been travelling quite a bit too. It's been wedding show season for quite a while now, but

I'm really looking forward to the Luxury Wedding Fair at Hatfield House. It'll be considerably different from that in Bergamo, but amazing. Certainly the location is, and it has two distinct venues – the fifteenth-century palace, and the riding stables for smaller events. I'm hoping to have a little time to explore. This may also be the last time I am able to travel before the babies come. I think it will definitely be the last time Ronnie's happy for me to travel. He's been becoming more and more protective, particularly after Gen's ordeal at Halloween. He's lectured me on not walking down dark alleys – as if I would anyway – and telling me not to stop my car if I see someone injured or help drunk people stand up in the street, in case they're scammers and rob or injure me. He's a lot more anxious than he was with the others, perhaps because there are two of them, or maybe because I'm a 'geriatric mother'.

It feels like it will soon be Christmas. Already rows and rows of present ideas line the aisles in the supermarket and when I do watch regular TV, as opposed to Netflix or Sky, I notice the bombardment of toy ads has already begun. That said, I'm also getting those on Facebook. It's impossible to escape it, but it's Bonfire Night, and the kids are excited about the display in the park near Hamwell. The village park isn't ideal for a display of that size, and I guess the council have only enough money to provide displays for the larger towns, but it's usually good. I quite enjoy it too, particularly as I'm a total scaredy-cat when it comes to lighting fireworks.

Valentin's been travelling too recently, over to see his son Mario in Italy, and then to Latin America on business, so since he's only just back, I've told Nicky we'll take Xander to the fireworks with us so they can have a nice romantic meal, in or out, as they prefer. Nicky's still a bit on edge about her insurance claim, and whenever I see her, the signs of the strain it's putting on her are all too visible. I also think subconsciously it's impeding her recovery.

As I pull into Garfield Grange, I experience a twinge of longing, and I realise I've missed this place. If I didn't feel I knew almost every inch of its common areas by heart, I'd want to book in for a spa day. The grounds are impressive, and with the late autumn sun beating down and sending shafts of light across the lawns that lead up to it, it's simply stunning.

Fabien is waiting for me in reception. 'Louisa!' He stands and kisses me on both cheeks then gestures for me to follow him to a table at a window overlooking the grounds. 'This is such a nice view. Shame not to take advantage when the sun's out. Drink?'

'Hot chocolate. I'm already fed up with decaff coffee.' I pull a face.

Fabien chuckles. 'I can only imagine. How long now?'

'Still too long. I feel enormous yet I have another three months to go.'

Fabien's eyes widen and I laugh. 'Don't worry, I know I'm huge. You're worrying I might explode before then.'

His eyes crinkle and I see why, apart from his manners, women might go for him, even though he's not conventionally handsome. 'Not at all.' He claps his hands together. 'Let me just arrange for someone to bring our drinks and we can catch up and talk about the Luxury Wedding Fair.'

I return his smile and sit back in the leather chesterfield.

A few moments later, he returns. 'So, how have you been?'

'Good, thanks. Lots going on, as always.'

He nods. 'And the family?'

'Yep, they're the "lots going on".'

He laughs and it's a melodious sound, and his face lights up. 'They're quite the scamps.'

Given what happened when we were living here, I can only agree, so I encourage a change of subject.

'So, the Luxury Wedding Fair, beautiful setting for it.'

'Yes, indeed.' He goes on to explain in depth what our part in the show will be, how the layout will be very different to others they've done, how their focus will be on honeymoon hotel sales, since the wedding destination is Hatfield House, as a given, although there may be a small percentage of patrons who decide not to hold it there in the end, and go abroad instead. He smiles, as if he's produced a rabbit from a hat.

'…and of course some of our European colleagues will be coming for this show. To learn. To help. To sell!'

I manage a laugh but it comes out as more of a cough, as well it might, given that Viggo is the first person who comes to mind. Or Vile Viggo as I've nicknamed him. Viggo Mortensen he is not!

'Is Lorenzo coming?' I ask. He was great company and he'll be an ally if I have to deal with Viggo again.

'Yes, Lorenzo is always here for our UK show, but I'm not sure who else Charles has requested from his side.'

'Will we know prior to the event?' I ask as nonchalantly as I can pull off.

Fabien screws up his face. 'I'm not entirely sure. I usually leave that side of things to Lorenzo and Charles. You'll definitely have enough cover, if that's what you're concerned about.'

'No, no, not at all.'

'You're not still upset over Viggo's actions in Bergamo, are you?'

When I don't reply immediately, he goes on, 'Because I spoke to him. Lorenzo told me exactly what happened. Didn't Viggo call you to apologise?'

I shake my head.

Fabien throws up his hands. 'For goodness' sake. I specifically told him to call and apologise. He's a great worker, but he really is the limit sometimes. I'll have a quiet word at the show. And if he doesn't toe the line then, I'll make myself crystal clear.'

Thanks, Fabien. I appreciate that. Now, I really need to go, if there's nothing else.'

'That's it. I'll send you the itinerary and documents on email.'

'Excellent. See you soon.'

He stands and kisses me on both cheeks again and I head back to my car, heart thumping. Please don't let Viggo be there.

As I drive up into our street, I see a familiar figure getting out of a Mercedes. Oh no! Annabelle. What does she want? I had a whole afternoon planned out: phone calls, messages, parcel packaging, a little design, a bit of tidying. How will I manage that now? And more to the point, what does she flamin' well want?

'Annabelle. What are *you* doing here?' I ask as I step out of my car onto the drive.

'I came to see how Martha was, so it made sense to come and see you since you're so close by, but you were out.'

'Yes, I had a meeting with Fabien.'

She peers at me in that way she has, as if she has found me lacking. Clearly she has forgotten who Fabien is, despite the fact he put us up all-expenses paid in a luxury hotel for two months.

'Oh yes, I forgot you occasionally have meetings.'

I bristle and my jaw clenches. It's not just occasionally, I meet with clients for Wedded Bliss pretty darned regularly. 'Yes, it has been known, particularly when we have a trade event coming up, such as the one at Hatfield House next week.'

'In England? Didn't Elizabeth I grow up there or something?'

Ha! That'll sort Annabelle for yet again dismissing my job. 'Yes, Elizabeth I spent a lot of time there.' I've been checking the history as I love all these stately homes. Bring it on, Annabelle. Ask me another. But when she doesn't ask any further questions, I say, 'So, how is Martha?'

'She'll be fine. You know Martha.'

I do, far better than her. I'd like to say I'm not sure what it is about my mother-in-law that rubs me up the wrong way, but I can't. The truth is, she has never thought I'm good enough for Ronnie.

She waves a hand airily. 'Now, about that tea?' She stands to the side to let me open the door. What tea? I wasn't offering her tea. I'm trying to get rid of her, not encourage her to stay.

Wearily, I open the door, begging the dogs by osmosis to bite her, so she'll sod off and leave me in peace. OK, that may be a tad much, but I'm pregnant, tired, busy and in no mood for her petty jibes, or indeed her.

As I make her tea, I make a point of glancing at my

watch and wait for her to start conversation. Damn it! The woman's a menace. She makes it so hard to like her, then comes round uninvited and doesn't even have the wherewithal to chat. And, what also sticks in my craw is I work from home. How many times? Working from home doesn't mean 'I'm not working, you can pop in when you feel like it as you're passing', it simply means I don't commute, and in fact, I work more, because as well as working my two jobs, I throw washing in the machine, hang it up, run a mop over the floor, refill the air fresheners, hoover, dust, and all that fabulously exciting stuff when I take a five-minute break from my job.

How I wish I had the courage to say that to her. Instead, I sigh inwardly and pass her her tea. Here we go, small talk time.

'How's Phillip?'

'Oh, fine, fine, you know Phillip.'

Yes, I think, I do. He's my father-in-law, but since I'm trying to make conversation, you could at least give me more than that to work with.

'I went into the church earlier,' she finally says.

'Oh yes?' I say, wondering where she's going with this.

'Yes, there was no service on, but I absorbed the ambience.'

Is she for real? I wish I had time to absorb ambience. 'Mmm,' I manage.

'Looked like the flowers needed changed though. Who does the church flowers here?'

What's it to her? Is she going to find out their address and go reprimand them? Demand they be sacked from their volunteer position? Anything's possible with Annabelle.

'No idea,' I say truthfully.

'And I told the woman in Icing on the Cake that their carrot cake was actually quite passable.'

'I'm sure she'd be delighted to hear that.' Passable? Marjorie's a genius. I'd have thrown a bowl of frosting at her, had it been me.

The conversation continues in much the same vein, for over an hour, with me periodically glancing at my watch, the kitchen clock, the one on the microwave and the one on the cooker. She's not taking the hint.

Why is she here?

My phone rings. The school. Saved by…the school.

'Louisa Halliday?'

I listen to the member of office staff on the other end. 'PE kit? She doesn't have PE today.'

The explanation comes and I say, 'Yes, that's fine. I'll bring her PE kit up now. Bye.'

'Sorry, Annabelle. I have to go. Aria's class is having an extra PE session for some reason today, and then I have a few errands to run before the display tonight.' I wait until she takes the hint, because for a long moment I think she isn't going to, then she gathers up her jacket, bag and keys and we head out.

'I'll let Ronnie know you dropped by.'

I can't get out of the driveway fast enough. Has she literally nothing better to do? She was here for more than an hour and I have no idea why.

I will never understand my mother-in-law.

Fortunately, when I return from the school, Annabelle isn't skulking anywhere, so I'm finally rid of her. I set to dealing with all the tasks I had planned for this afternoon and just about manage to finish them before the school run. The others I'll catch up with tomorrow.

Nicky's messaged me back to say not to bother picking Xander up, as she'll drop him off around six, so he can have dinner at home first. That works for me. Gives me a little more time to arrange stuff for the show next week and organise the family for tonight.

When the kids are ensconced post-supper in the playroom, playing Minecraft or some other game they agree on, I cobble together a ratatouille for myself and Ronnie for later, and put it in the oven. Feeling quite proud of myself at the moment. Have produced a tasty, nutritious meal and haven't had a meltdown in the process, despite Annabelle having rattled me with her presence earlier.

'Mummy, is it time yet?' Aria asks ten minutes after consuming her lasagne.

'No, honey. Daddy's not home yet, is he? And Xander's not here.'

'Aw.' Her face falls. 'But I want it to be now.'

We're in dangerous territory here. Is she going to be sad, or is she about to launch into a full-blown tantrum? It's hard to tell.

'Me too, but it will be soon enough, and Daddy and Xander are so looking forward to it too,' I tell her.

Her eyes go wide. 'They are? I didn't think Daddy cared about Bonfire Night.'

'Oh yeah,' I say, overegging it. 'Daddy loves Bonfire Night.'

'Good, because next year I want us to have fireworks in the garden, and if Daddy loves Bonfire Night, he'll want that too.'

Great, I walked right into that. Being outsmarted by a

five-year-old does not a happy mummy make.

The door goes. Ronnie. 'Evening,' he calls from the hall.

'Evening,' I say.

'Look who I found outside.' He shepherds Xander in ahead of him.

'Hi, Xander.' I smile at him. 'Hugo's in the playroom. We'll be leaving in about an hour.'

'Are we all ready for the fireworks display?' Ronnie asks as he comes into the kitchen and spots Aria. I try to make throat-cutting gestures to him, urging him to change topic, but he doesn't notice.

'I am, Daddy, but it's not time yet, so I wanted to talk to you about next year's fireworks.'

Ronnie's face falls. He realises that he's been ambushed. I catch his eye and smirk. Oh well, he only has himself to blame. He needs to think before he speaks. Glad I'm not the only one who can put their foot in it.

Gen comes downstairs, where she's mostly been since she came in, on her phone and iPad, doing homework and chatting with her friends.

'What time are we leaving at?' she asks as she heads for the fridge.

'About seven. It starts at half past, but it'll be busy.'

She nods and pours herself a glass of orange juice. She's almost the same height as me. How is that possible? She's thirteen. I'm sure I wasn't the same height as Mum when I was her age. But then I wasn't all willowy and gazelle legs like Gen.

We're finally ready to leave. A sliver of moon hangs in the sky, lighting our way. Some of our fellow villagers have been a little impatient and have been setting fireworks off since the minute darkness fell.

Ronnie's locking the door when I put my hand up to stop him. 'Wait! I need to put the TV on for the boys.'

'Of course. God, Bear hates fireworks. Patch seemed OK earlier,' Ronnie says.

'He wasn't too bad, but I think that was because we were all there, making noise. Now, with the house quiet, those bangs will be so much worse.'

Ronnie tilts his head to one side as he does when he's reflecting on something. 'Fair point.'

I nudge past him to the living room and put the TV on.

'Come on, Mummy. We'll miss the show,' shouts Aria.

Where was Aria when God was handing out patience?

I lock the door behind me and soon we're whizzing along towards Hamwell.

A fabulous display of Catherine wheels and other assorted fireworks accompanies us on our route to Hamwell Park. I spot some Roman candles, but I'm not really good at the names. They look pretty, and that's all I need to know.

What I do know is the organisers will be using those bad boys, the not-safe-for-customers-to-use types, those with the highest hazard levels, which is why they're only supposed to be handled by specialists. I wonder what those guys are called – pyrotechnicians? Sounds plausible, right. I make a mental note to google it later to see if it exists. If it doesn't, it should.

When we arrive, I'm glad we left early. The place is packed. There must be over a thousand people here. I grab tight onto Aria with one hand and Gen takes my other, whilst Hugo and Xander slip a hand each into Ronnie's at my insistence.

The kids meet a few of their friends from school and we bump into some villagers as well as some people from the surrounding towns, whom we don't see as often. There's very much a carnival atmosphere and the dry weather, for November, is in part, I expect, responsible for the larger than usual crowd.

Some of the food stalls which were present at the scarecrow festival are here tonight, too, and my stomach rumbles and reminds me Ronnie and I haven't eaten yet. I lick my lips and hanker after a hot dog. Maybe after the fireworks display.

Ten minutes later and some official, or perhaps some Z-list celebrity – I wouldn't know as I don't follow all that stuff – takes to the stage and declares it's time for us 'to light up the sky'.

Everyone stands entranced as firework after firework shoots up into the air, and the excitement is almost palpable. Gen jumps when a particularly loud squeal sounds directly overhead, but it's simply the whistle of a firework. She clutches her chest and we giggle at each other.

A woman walks past with a Scotty dog, and my heart goes out to it. What on earth is she thinking? The poor thing must be terrified. I wonder how Patch and Bear are, and a stab of guilt lances through me. Should I have left Patch at all on his first Bonfire Night? Should one of us have stayed? But no, we need some family time, to be able to mark occasions like this together, go to some of these events. Next year, it won't be possible and probably the year after that too, not with babies then toddlers.

I'm impressed by just how amazing the show is. The

organisers have set it to pop music and the kids are soon dancing away, necks craned to the sky, and for once, I stay in the moment. It's mesmerising to watch the colours light up the night sky, and despite my woollens, I rub my hands together for warmth.

'Look, Mummy, I can see my breath,' Aria says.

Hugo notices and tries to outdo his sister, then Xander follows suit, and eventually even Gen caves and blows out a plume of breath. I smile affectionately. We come all this way on a freezing cold night, to see these spectacular fireworks, and the kids derive as much enjoyment simply from watching each other's breath leave their mouths as they do from witnessing the fireworks display.

The event lasts longer than expected and we browse the food stalls for a little while afterwards. The first bite I take of that hot dog is heaven. A trickle of mustard runs down my chin and I squeak. Ronnie stops me, takes a napkin from his pocket and wipes it away, his eyes on me. I think we're going to be OK. The past month or so has been so much better, as Ronnie has been there for me; even if he doesn't get my apprehension over becoming mum to twins in three months' time, he's upped his game in every other department, for which I'm truly grateful. I honestly don't know how I'd be coping otherwise.

'Mummy, can I have churros? Please, please?' Aria asks when she spots the churros van.

The last thing I need is Aria high on chocolate before she goes to bed, but a pleading look from the other three children too melts my resolve and Ronnie hands Gen some money to go get them all churros.

At nine thirty, we tumble into the house, happy. The kids are still discussing their favourite fireworks and munching on churros. Bear comes running up to greet us. I bend down to rub his ears and he rewards me with a tail wag.

'Hey, buddy, you OK?' I fold him in a hug. 'Good boy.'

'Mum, where's Patch?' Hugo asks.

'Kitchen?' I suggest.

I continue having a moment with Bear, thinking either Ronnie or I will have to take him and Patch for a short walk before bed.

'Mummy, I can't find Patch,' Hugo says.

I frown. 'He's not in the kitchen? Have you tried on top of your bed?'

'Yep, I've looked everywhere. He's not here.'

Gen's face registers alarm.

'Gen, can you and Xander help Hugo look upstairs? Maybe he's under one of the beds or hiding. Perhaps the fireworks scared him.'

'Sure. C'mon Hugo. You know what he's like, and he's so little, he can fit almost anywhere.'

They lope out of the room and Ronnie and I have a look downstairs. 'Bear, where's Patch?' I ask, but all he does is whine. That's odd. Usually, he would bark and show me. Unease swirls in my gut. I cast my mind back to when I last saw him. He was here when Ronnie came home, for sure, as Xander fussed over him as he always does. Did I see him before we left? I remember having to come back in to put the TV on for them, but did I actually see the dogs, and Patch in particular? I'm not sure that I did. Oh no! Could he have somehow got out before we left and not be indoors at all? Could he have been outside all this time? Please, no.

'Ronnie,' I say as he comes into the playroom where

I'm currently looking in cupboards, calling Patch's name. 'I have an awful feeling he's outside somewhere.'

Ronnie straightens up from where he's looking behind the playroom couch. 'Seriously?'

I nod. 'Technically, he might have shot past us when I was back in putting the TV on for them before we left, or indeed at some other point. If we can't find him in the house, we'll have to search for him outdoors.'

Tears sting my eyes, and I swipe at my face to dry it. Ronnie comes over and hugs me. 'Don't panic just yet. He's probably fine, and indoors. You know how good he is at hiding.'

I do, but I have this terrible sense of foreboding and it won't go away.

'Mu-u-um, we can't find him.' Hugo's voice wobbles and he must see my face as he starts to bawl. 'Something's happened to him. I know it. I want Patch.'

Xander stands beside him, patting Hugo's back. 'H, we'll find him.' He looks at me. 'Right, Louisa.'

A lump forms in my throat. 'Right, Xander.' I keep my fingers and everything else crossed, hoping I haven't promised something I can't deliver.

'Ronnie, you take the girls and the boys can come with me. We'll take Bear too,' I say. 'He can't have gone far.' I hope I'm right. He's only been out of the village a couple of times.

'At least it's a dry, clear night,' Ronnie says. 'Why don't you take the car and start at the other end of the village?'

'That's a good idea. C'mon, boys. C'mon, Bear. Car.' Bear's ears perk up. He loves going in the car.

'Mum, we could put it on the village Facebook group,' Gen suggests. 'Maybe other people could help look for him, too, or at least check he's not hiding in their shed or something, or under a tree in their garden.'

'That's a brilliant idea, Gen. Well done.' I take my phone out and quickly post to Ferniehall Village Facebook Group: *Hi everyone. Our Beagle pup Patch has gone missing. It's his first year of fireworks, so he's probably holed up somewhere scared. We've checked our house, but definitely not there. Could you possibly check your sheds and anywhere he could have sheltered at your houses/gardens? Please can you DM me if you hear or see him? Thanks.*

'Right, let's go, everyone.'

We split into our teams and head out into the cold night. Poor Patch. He's a dote, but too young to be out on his own. Plus, he's never been allowed off the leash except when with us. He's not a street dog. The world will pose lots of threats for him. We need to find him and fast.

As I park at the far end of the village, I can't help but notice that work is really coming on with our house. Even since I last visited Martha, progress has moved on considerably. However, I have more pressing things to think about at the minute. I'm instantly heartened to see lots of responses to my Facebook message. *Give me 2 minutes, I'll come help you look in the street after I check mine*; *Aw, poor wee thing. I'll check ours now and our neighbour's as they're on holiday*; *Let me know where you need help looking. I can take the car out to cover more ground*; *I've checked ours, he isn't there, but I'll check over at the church for you, and my husband will check the park*; *Poor Patch. Is someone checking the roads to Hamwell or Lymeburn, or are we just staying in the village for now? I can go in either direction, and my daughter will go the other. Let's find him*. The messages go on and on, and once again, I'm glad we chose to live in such a tight-knit community. It gives me hope we'll find him.

Twenty minutes later and that hope is fading fast. We've met many of the volunteers in the street and Ronnie has phoned a few times to ask if there are any updates. Gen has been replying to all the messages on Facebook and I've been trying to coordinate the search efforts by telling her what to reply. She types so much faster than me.

I'm beginning to really worry now. I thought we'd have found him by this time. My heart almost stops as I consider the possibility he has been hit by a car. No, I can't think like that. The boys are starting to shiver. I'm just about to tell them to head back to the car, we'll drive for a bit to see if we can find him when Gen Facetimes me. 'Someone's found him. He was in Martha's garden.'

'But that was one of the first places we looked,' I say, readying the lead I've brought with me so the poor little scamp doesn't scarper.

'Maybe he wasn't there then, but he is now. We're on our way.'

The boys race back down Main Street towards Martha's. A teenage boy is holding Patch, who is trembling violently. The boy has taken off his jacket and wrapped Patch in it. If anyone criticises the youth of today again, they'll have me to deal with. I could kiss this boy, but that wouldn't be appropriate, so I settle for a thank you.

'Patch!' He almost jumps out of the boy's jacket towards me, but I cradle my arms and the boy passes him to me instead.

'He's a sweet wee thing,' the boy says.

'Patch!' Hugo rushes forward and Patch rewards him with a lick on the face. 'Yuck, same old Patch.' Hugo and

Xander giggle. I attach the lead to Patch, then pass Hugo the lead, just as Ronnie and the girls arrive and soon everyone is fawning over Patch.

Ronnie lays his head against mine. 'Thank God. I hadn't realised how much I doted on that wee thing.'

'Oh, I did.' I smile at him. 'Right, I best message the Facebook group and let them know he's safe. Everyone has been so wonderful.'

'Community spirit,' says Ronnie. 'One of the many reasons I love living here.' He turns to the young boy who found him. 'Thanks. We really appreciate it. Here.' He takes out his wallet and the boy shakes his head. 'No, thanks, but no, I just love dogs. I don't need money for finding him. Knowing he's safe is enough.'

Ronnie nods his head in acceptance, thanks the boy again and puts his wallet away. The boy disappears down the street. We didn't even get his name. In fact, how come I don't know who he is?

I smile then fire off the message. Ronnie and I stand, arms around each other, watching our children and Xander fuss over Patch – the dog of the moment. Even Bear is getting in on the action.

My eyes meet Ronnie's and he lowers his lips to mine. When we pull apart, he entwines his fingers in mine and says, 'Let's go home.'

'What a great idea.'

Chapter Twelve

Friday 12 November

To-do list

Remember flyers that came from printers for the Luxury Wedding Fair

Leave strict instructions for Ronnie about bedtimes and treats allowed

Run through class times with Ronnie – Aria has drama club at five thirty

Diesel, plus check oil level – was dangerously low last time

'Bye, darling.' I hug Hugo to me as Aria sprints off into the playground to join her friends. I was almost tearful seeing Gen off to the bus this morning. I'm only going away for two days, and I am technically in the same country. Yes, yes, it's England, but even so, it's not 'abroad'. I have the car and I could be home post haste if necessary, so why am I so jumpy about it?

Ronnie's picking the kids up later and I'm basically hopping in the car and driving the six hours from Ferniehall to Hatfield. I don't mind driving, it's almost all motorway, and as long as the weather remains as it is, cold but dry, a touch of cloud, I'll be happy. I'm quite looking forward to listening to my new audio book in the car. I rarely get time to read, and I might get through half an audio book on this drive. Yay!

I stop halfway at Wetherby services as I need the loo and my eyes are tired. I grab a coffee and a bacon sandwich. That'll keep me going for now. I'm surprised I didn't have to stop before now as this pregnancy lark has me running to the toilet all the time. The twins have stopped pressing on my bladder, giving me a little respite.

Unfortunately the fine weather didn't last. But despite the driving rain and gusting wind, I drive down the motorway, singing along to the local radio. I've turned off my audio book as I fancied a change for a bit. My brain's still whirling with the few days that lie ahead. If it's anything like the Bergamo show, it will be very good for business. Fabien has already talked to me about a bonus. Woo hoo. That will come in handy with two new babies arriving soon. I haven't really thought much about the financial impact until now, apart from the nursery costs.

I think I've finally reached the point where I'm at peace with the thought of the babies. Just as well, since there's not that long to go. As ever, and as I'm sure is the case for many, if not all mums, we worry over whether we will be good enough, whether we can give them everything they need. I know it's only natural, but I felt so overwhelmed at the start of this pregnancy. It was such a shock. Now I can start looking forward to it. Once I get back, I'll start preparing. First on the list is a new buggy – I've never had a double stroller before. The variety is eye-watering. I had a quick look and I've been on Mumsnet looking for advice. I could arrange to have everything delivered to our house when we move back in. Maybe Mum would like to…

What the hell was that? A clunking noise comes from the front of the car. Oh no, please tell me I don't have a puncture. I scream and physically shrink back as something huge flies up in the air and comes back down, about to come through my windscreen when I brake sharply, pulling the car off onto the hard shoulder. Thank God I was in the inside lane still. My heart is racing and I honestly feel like I'm about to have a heart attack. Did something fall off a lorry? I shake my head to dismiss that thought. But there weren't any lorries in front of me. I slam on my hazards, realising I haven't done so previously. Cars swerve around the lane I've just left and eventually, tentatively, after grabbing my waterproof jacket, I manoeuvre myself across the passenger seat, not easy at six months pregnant, and get out of the car that way.

And that's when I see it. My bonnet. The bonnet of my car is lying on the road behind me. Oh my God, my car! Then it occurs to me how dangerous that is, lying there, for anyone driving along, for me, if they hit it and it flies up again. Do I have one of those road triangles in the boot? I have no idea. Are you meant to put those on a motorway or only a dual carriageway? Eventually, I decide I can't risk it, so from the verge I call 999 and explain what's happened. Within five minutes, a police car roars up, lights flashing, then it slams its hazards on too, immediately before the bonnet, to prevent anyone driving into it, I assume. I let out a huge sigh of relief. Others are safe, but what about my bonnet? How am I going to get to Hatfield now? What about my car? My heart is palpitating.

'Hello, Madam. Are you all right?' His eyes sweep over me, lingering on my stomach.

I nod. 'Just very shaken.'

'Because of the nature of the incident, and the danger to other road users, we have to clear the road, so even if you've already called a breakdown service, unless it gets here quicker than the police one, it'll have to remove your vehicle and your bonnet to the nearest garage.'

My heart sinks. How will I get to Hatfield now?

'What do I do then?'

'We'll arrange for you to accompany your car, with the breakdown driver. At that point, if you have breakdown cover, I'd suggest you call them.'

I let out another sigh.

'You were very lucky.'

It suddenly occurs to me exactly how lucky I was, the bonnet could have crashed through the windscreen as it nearly did, and tears cloud my vision. I nod.

'I've got some biscuits and a flask of tea if you'd like some for the shock,' he says.

I stare at him. Who would have thought in this day and age, when everyone's racing here, there and everywhere, and everybody's always on a tight schedule, that a policeman would be offering me a cuppa.

'That would be great, thanks.'

'C'mon. Sit in the patrol car whilst we wait for the breakdown truck. I don't imagine they'll be long.'

Eleven minutes later, the police breakdown truck arrives, by which time I've eaten three custard creams, a Kit Kat and downed a cup of fairly weak, sweet tea. However, in present circumstances it tasted as good as the gourmet fayre I ate at Garfield Grange most nights.

'What's been happening here then?' asks the

breakdown man.

'The bonnet flew clean off, no warning,' I say. 'Well, apart from a clunking noise a few seconds before.'

'Doesn't happen that often, but you had a lucky escape, I reckon. Especially with these gusts,' He struggles to stand upright as one hits him. 'Let's get you into the cab, whilst I deal with this.'

I nod and tiredness overwhelms me. It's all been too much. I was having a great start to my morning, leisurely drive down to Yorkshire, then heading on to Hertfordshire. What now?

Whilst the breakdown guy takes care of my poor car, and bonnet, I make some calls. First to Ronnie.

'Jesus, Lou, you could have been killed. When was the car in for its service? Surely they should have noticed if anything was wrong with the catch. Your bonnet doesn't just up and decide to fly off one day.' Fear and concern more than anger lace his voice. He's good at deflecting to cover up how scared he is. But I know him too well.

'I know, but I wasn't, and I appreciate how lucky I was, more than you know.'

'Do you think–' he pauses '–you should get the babies checked over?'

I frown, not having thought of that. 'No, I don't think that's necessary. I feel fine, I didn't have any whiplash or anything, and apart from the initial shock, I'm completely fine.'

Ronnie exhales noisily. 'OK, as long as you're sure. So what are you going to do now?'

I glance at the breakdown man as he winches my car up onto the lorry. 'Honestly? I don't know. I'm pretty sure my car won't be driveable anytime soon. I need to call Fabien and also our breakdown service to see if they can offer me onward travel. We do pay for that, but obviously I've never been recovered off a motorway by police before, so I'm not sure how that affects the policy, or what service they can provide now.'

'Well, let me know later. Hopefully, they'll take you there, but they might give you a hire car.'

'Yes, quite frankly I'd rather they drove me there too.' I'm exhausted and I'm only halfway to the show. Thank goodness it starts tomorrow.

'Love you,' says Ronnie. 'Stay safe.'

'I love you too. Give the kids a hug for me. I'll call you later.'

When I hang up, I call Fabien.

'Oh my goodness, Louisa, are you all right? You must have been terrified.'

'Yes, I'm fine, just shaken. And yes, it was scary. I'm waiting for the breakdown truck driver to get us underway and when I get back to the garage, I can find out what my options are. The car won't be driveable though.'

'Don't worry about a thing. Worse-case scenario, we'll cope, but obviously we hope to see you here for dinner tonight. Take care.'

'Thanks, Fabien.'

Whilst I'm waiting, and it does seem to be taking an interminably long time to attach everything, although no doubt there's paperwork for the man to fill out too, I message Wendy and Jo, as well as Sam and Nicky. A barrage of messages comes back at me.

Oh my God, are you all right? Sam.

Holy Jesus, it could only happen to you. Jo.

Oh, Lou, how awful. Hope you're OK. Is there anything we

can do to help? Nicky.

No response from Wendy yet, but she's probably in a meeting or something. I decide not to tell Mum and Dad.

'That's us. Let's get going so you can hopefully continue your journey shortly,' says the breakdown man.

'Thanks.' I sit back and close my eyes for a few minutes.

'Here we are.'

My eyes fly open. I'm parked outside a garage, Wetherby Autos. The truck has stopped opposite the workshop, where another car is on the ramp with a boiler-suited mechanic standing underneath banging away at something.

'What happens now?' I ask.

'I'll give the paperwork to the office and they'll let you know of any costs involved. Might be something you need to pay for then claim back off your insurance. Did you say you had breakdown cover?' When I nod, he goes on, 'I'd give them a call now to explain the situation.'

After waiting twenty-two minutes to get through, my breakdown service informs me they can't arrange for me to be driven, although I can take public transport. Not possible, not with all the luggage, the time it would take and the fact I'm six months pregnant and shouldn't be lugging stuff around, so I go for the other option which is for them to provide me with a courtesy car. They tell me it will be delivered to Wetherby Autos within the hour. It isn't.

Fortunately, the receptionist at the garage takes pity on me. 'I'm just back off mat leave. I know what it's like. I remember all too well how I felt at that stage of my pregnancy. What are you, seven, eight months?' she asks as she sips from her Diet Coke.

'Six.' I try not to yawn. I am dead beat.

Her eyes widen. 'Wow, you're having a big baby then.'

'Two babies,' I mutter.

If possible, her eyes widen even further. 'Oh my goodness, twins, that's so sweet. They always say twins look after each other, they're hardly any trouble at all as a result.'

Distractedly, I wonder who 'they' are.

'I'm nipping out to get a sandwich. Do you want one?'

'Yes, please. Tuna mayo if they have it, otherwise ham or cheese is fine.'

'No problem. Back in ten minutes.'

Unlike my breakdown company with my courtesy car, she returns when she says she will. I devour my sandwich like a lion chomping on a gazelle. It's not a pretty sight but I am ravenous. Must be the stress.

My phone beeps. Wendy. *Are you all right? Jeez, Lou, what a fright you must have got. Ring me.*

I finish my sandwich and then call her.

'Lou, thank God, what the hell happened?'

I relay the details to her and she says, 'But these things don't just come off on their own. Was there any indication anything was wrong?'

'Not until a few seconds before. I heard a noise, and whilst I was wondering what on earth it was and where it was coming from, the bonnet flew up and nearly crashed down on top of me. If I hadn't pulled onto the hard shoulder at the last minute, it would have hit me.'

'That's horrifying. I've never heard of that happening before. But you're OK, you're sure?' she asks.

'Yeah, I was a bit wobbly for a while, but I'm fine now. I didn't even know initially that it was my bonnet. I thought it was part of a load fallen off a lorry. Just wishing I could get underway as I still have a three-hour drive once I get back in the car.'

Wendy's voice ratchets up a few octaves. 'You're not driving it today, are you?'

'No, I'm waiting for a courtesy car to be delivered. I imagine they'll need to weld the bonnet back on, if it's fixable, or get me a new bonnet before I can drive it. God knows how I'll get back from the show. Maybe I should check train routes and times from Hatfield and have one of the others send me on any work materials. I don't even know if it has a station. I just know it's relatively near London but above.'

'Are you sure you're OK to drive?' Wendy presses.

'I'll be fine. Don't worry. And I'll phone when I get there, I promise.'

About fifteen minutes after my call with Wendy finishes a brand-new Fiat Uno arrives at the garage. An Uno, really? I hope I can fit my bump behind the wheel.

I sign the paperwork and transfer the contents of my boot – since my car is finally about to go on the ramp, but is currently sitting in the car park – into the back seat and the boot of the Uno.

Soon, I'm on the road again, and I put my audio book on to listen to; it's too much like hard work to sing along to the radio.

I finally reach Hatfield at around six fifteen. I hit rush-hour traffic, so that delayed me somewhat. I take the key to my room in Melbourne Lodge gratefully. All I want is a shower and to lie down on what I expect, and hope, is an obscenely large bed. I don't even have the energy to take in the beautiful surroundings and in any case, it's pitch dark, so I miss out on seeing the grounds altogether. I lie down on the extremely comfortable canopied bed after my shower. I reckon I've earned a little nap.

Raised voices wake me. What time is it? I fling out an arm, reaching for my phone. Half past midnight. Damn it! I've missed dinner, and then some. I have some messages. Lorenzo. *Hi Louisa. I heard what happened. Reception told me you had checked in. I convinced Fabien not to wake you for dinner. I imagine you need the rest. See you at breakfast. Lorenzo x*

What a sweetheart. He's right. I was shattered. I slept nearly six hours straight. It's surprising the babies didn't wake me. Usually, the moment I lie down, they decide it's party time and start wriggling around. Not that there can be that much space in there with two of them.

My stomach rumbles. Oh great, now I'm starving. I haven't checked yet, but surely my room must have a minibar. It's bound to have water, juices, maybe even some crisps and chocolate. I cast around for any sign of a fridge. Ah, inside the wardrobe, next to the safe. I open it and it's like an Aladdin's cave. Perfect. It has sea salt crisps, sweet popcorn, nuts in a tube and cans of orangina and Appletiser. A veritable feast. A midnight feast. Literally.

Once I've had my fill of fridge goodies, I check my messages and emails. There's a message from Ronnie asking me to call him as he's worried I haven't been in touch. Oh no, of course he'll be worried. I had an incident with the car, had to wait ages, then drove another three hours and disappeared without a trace. I bash out a text. *Sorry, hon, just woke up. Slept almost 6 hours. I'm fine but clearly needed that sleep. Hope you weren't worried.*

Flippin' typical. Now I'm wide awake, and so are the babies, since I'm not moving much. So, I settle down in bed in as comfortable a position as I can and read my romance novel until my eyes drift closed.

Saturday 13 November

To-do list

Very little as my husband is looking after the children and the only person I have to look after is myself.

'Good morning, Louisa.' Lorenzo almost bounces into the dining room. I'm already sitting at the table drinking a cup of real coffee from my weekly rations.

'Lorenzo, lovely to see you. How are you?'

'Never mind me. How are you after your ordeal?'

I raise my hand to wave away the 'ordeal'. 'I'm fine, or rather I'm fine after that really long sleep. Thanks for telling Fabien not to wake me. I was sleeping like a baby.'

'Ha ha, very funny, since you have two babies inside you at the moment.' Lorenzo smiles.

I give a wan smile. It wasn't that funny, but I like him, so I pretend it was.

'And how have you been, Lorenzo? Fabien was telling me you travel to all the European events.'

'Yes, I do. I love it. And I'm good. Busy, but good.'

A shadow falls over the table and I look up into Viggo's eyes. Oh God, I truly detest that man after what he said at dinner in Bergamo. He turns my stomach.

'Louisa, I heard you had quite the scare yesterday. How are you today?'

'I'm good, thanks, Viggo. You?'

'Oh, I'm all the better for seeing you.' His perfect smile which I'd noticed the first time I met him I now see as wolfish, almost as if he's eyeing up prey. He goes to sit beside me, but just as he's about to pull out the chair, Fabien appears. I could kiss him.

'Louisa. So glad to see you're fine. You had me worried. So tell me everything.' He sits down in the seat Viggo was about to, and I note Viggo's huff as he moves along a chair. Tough. I'm glad the sexist pig isn't right beside me. I'd have difficulty not telling him what I think of him.

As I fill Fabien in, the others dig into breakfast and a few of the other members of staff join us, and I note with relief that they engage Viggo in conversation.

After breakfast we have a twenty-minute window before we need to leave to prepare the stand for the show. The hard work has been done, but there are some cosmetic details that need attending to. Since I didn't have the chance the night before, I take the opportunity to explore the grounds and actually appreciate the beauty of the hotel itself. Melbourne Lodge was one of the closest hotels to the stately home where the show takes place, so, again in the absence of a Cerulean hotel in the area, we're still staying in style in the eighteenth-century coach house. I don't have a great deal of time to fit everything in, but I do see the lakes and the golf courses on my walk of the Brocket Hall Estate, the grounds the lodge stands in. It's very pretty and would be the perfect place for a romantic weekend with Ronnie, if the six-hour journey each way weren't so off-putting.

When I return to reception, Lorenzo and Fabien are already waiting

'I'll nip out to grab the flyers from the car and I'll be with you,' I say.

Five minutes later, we set off for Hatfield Hall, which is only a fifteen-minute drive.

On arrival, Fabien gives us each instructions then he and I head directly to the stand, as he doesn't want me doing any lifting. It's sweet how protective of me he is.

Hatfield House really is quite something, and so much more impressive than I'd imagined. Set in parkland, it has, if I've counted correctly, four exquisite gardens, including one with a mini-maze. I'd quite like to see that. There's something magical about mazes, even for adults. Our stand is inside the old palace itself, and I'm dying to see inside.

From the moment I cross the threshold, I wonder if any woman could visit this palace as a wedding venue and find it lacking. It is breathtaking: vaulted ceilings, elaborate ornamentation, perfection in every way, and it's an actual palace. It looks every inch fit for a royal wedding, never mind a layman's.

It's all so beautiful and pristine, picture-perfect. I'm almost afraid to touch anything, but I go where directed and Fabien relays his instructions for the day again. The others bring in the remainder of what's required for the show, and then we're all set. The show may begin.

And begin it does, in earnest.

What's lunch? I don't know because we don't have time for one. From the moment the doors open to the public, until the moment the tannoy announces in delicate tones that the fair will close in five minutes, we are inundated with questions, bombarded with requests for full brochures and further details and take dozens of commissions and bookings.

'Phew, I'm glad that's over for the day,' says Lorenzo, loosening his tie as we stroll through the West Garden. Fabien and Viggo have taken a car back together, whereas Lorenzo and I both want a chance to see the fabulous surroundings.

'You and me both. It was non-stop. But good for business.' I look up at the cloudless sky, where the sun is beginning to sink behind the horizon, and I consider how lucky I am. I'm with a good friend, a new friend, in a lovely setting, chatting happily, doing a job I love and carrying twins. Yesterday's car incident is but a blip to be overcome.

'Can I tell you a secret, Louisa?'

My face must fall before I mask it, because he quickly reassures me, 'Nothing bad, I promise. It's good, for me, at least, and for Cerulean, I hope.'

I smile. 'Don't worry, it just makes me nervous when people ask me to keep secrets, although I wasn't really expecting you to confess to being a closet serial killer.'

'Far too much planning involved for me, I'm afraid.' His eyes twinkle. 'No, Fabien will announce it at dinner tonight, but I'm very excited about it, and I wanted to tell someone, a friend. And I consider you a friend, Louisa.' He looks at me a little shyly.

'And I do too, Lorenzo. 'I gesture with my glass. 'Go on. Hit me with your secret.'

He bursts out laughing. 'You'll probably think mc silly, but for me it is very important.' He takes a deep breath. 'Fabien has asked me to be the European Events Manager.'

'Oh my goodness, Lorenzo, that's wonderful.' I hug

him and say, 'Well done. No wonder you're pleased.'

'Yes, well, I was bursting to tell someone as you probably noticed.'

I laugh and pat him on the arm. 'I did, and very well deserved it is. I can't imagine anyone better placed to run the events for Cerulean.'

'Hmm, not everyone will be so happy, though.'

I scrunch my brow. 'Oh?'

'Viggo also wanted to be Events Manager. In fact, I think he may have assumed, wrongly, that Fabien would give him the role automatically.'

My mouth downturns. 'Bit of an assumption, wasn't it?'

He sighs. 'Yes, but I'm not sure he'll see it that way. I only hope he accepts my appointment with good grace.'

I hope the same thing. I don't know Viggo well enough to comment, but if his attitude towards women is anything to go by, I wouldn't count on it.

'Shall we head for the Old Palace Garden?' I ask.

'Sounds like a plan,' Lorenzo says with a smile.

We eat dinner at the Auberge du Lac restaurant within the coach house. The restaurant overlooks the lake, which is softly floodlit, given night has already fallen. The menu, which uses mainly locally sourced produce is worthy of a Michelin-starred restaurant. I opt for the pumpkin soup and the fillet of beef with chanterelles, although had I not been pregnant I'd have been keen to try the duck egg with quinoa. The food is sublime. I wouldn't be surprised if a moan escapes my lips as I savour every morsel.

The others are pairing wines with their food, although

I'm rather enjoying my mint mocktail, the mint, I'm reliably informed, freshly grown on the estate.

Soon it's time for coffees and petits fours, and I turn when Fabien clinks his spoon gently against his glass.

'Can I have your attention, please? I have an announcement to make.'

Everyone gives him their full attention, some with quizzical expressions, others with amused ones.

'It gives me great pleasure to announce that I have promoted Lorenzo to European Events Manager. So, everyone, can you raise your glasses to Lorenzo, please?'

Cheers go round and glasses are raised. Congratulations and thanks pass back and forward across the table from all the team members, with the exception of one: Viggo. Finally, his jaw clenched, he grinds out, 'Congratulations, Lorenzo.'

'Thank you, Viggo.'

I let out a silent exhalation of relief. Drama averted. But as I turn to speak to Fabien, I catch Viggo glaring daggers at him. Oh dear, as I suspected, he isn't taking it well.

The evening progresses as we continue discussing the day's success and the expectation of the business we will land as a consequence of the numerous enquiries today.

I feel a little tired, so I decide to go outside for some fresh air. It's colder than I thought, and I wish I'd grabbed a jacket or a scarf. I shiver.

'Here, you can have my jacket,' a voice that turns my blood to ice says.

'Oh, hi, Viggo. Actually, I think I'm going to go in. It's a lot colder than I thought.'

'Stay, keep me company. I could be doing with it

today.' He mutters the last under his breath.

'Just a few minutes then,' I concede.

He holds his jacket out to me and it seems rude and churlish to refuse, plus it's freezing, so it's more practical to accept.

'Thanks.'

'No problem.' He takes a vape out of his pocket and puffs on it. 'Sorry, I should have asked. Is this OK?'

'Why wouldn't it be?' I ask.

'The babies.' He points to my stomach.

'Ah. No, it's fine, we're outside.' Perhaps I misjudged him as that was very sweet of him to check, considerate too.

'So, have you enjoyed the show?' he asks.

'Yes, and this restaurant, the hotel itself as well as Hatfield House are lovely.'

'They are,' he agrees. 'Will you be at the next event at the end of the month?'

I frown. 'I don't know. Fabien hasn't mentioned anything. Where is it?'

'It's in Biarritz.'

'Very swish. No, I doubt I'll be there, especially not at such short notice. Plus, I won't be able to fly for much longer.'

He looks at my stomach. 'No, I don't suppose you will. So, this will be adieu for some time.'

'Looks like it,' I say. 'Right, I really do need to go back inside. Even with your cosy jacket, the rest of me is freezing.'

He leans towards me. 'I could fix that.'

I bristle and step back, appalled. But, I breathe a sigh of relief when he pulls off his jumper. How many layers is he wearing? I mean, I know he's from one of the Nordic countries, but even so. My heart rate returns to normal. For a moment, I thought he was going to make a pass at me. Ha, deluded middle-aged woman, pregnant with twins. Who on earth is going to make a pass at me? That ship has sailed. Not that I want anyone to make a pass at me, but…oh, I'm digging a bigger hole here for myself, aren't I?

'No, it's OK, I'm feeling a bit thirsty again, anyway. Plus, I need the loo.' I point to my stomach. 'Pregnancy does that.'

He gives me a strange look. 'As you wish.'

When I return from the ladies' room, the wine is flowing, or if not wine, whisky and gin. Looks like the boys are intent on having a good time to celebrate the show's success or possibly Lorenzo's promotion, or maybe even both.

The team are good company and we spend a pleasant couple of hours exchanging anecdotes, and Fabien regales everyone with the tale of what happened to my car. On that note, I wonder what's happening with it. I'd left word for them to call Ronnie, since it should be recovered to our house. I haven't heard from him yet. To be honest, I should probably phone him anyway, if not least to speak to the kids. Guilt spears me as I realise I haven't spoken to them since I left. Even with the extenuating circumstances, my bad mummy alert comes on. As I go to rise from the table, Viggo does too, so I wait a few moments. I don't want any more sticky moments where he peels off his jumper.

Eventually, I decide to call Ronnie or it will be too late to talk to Hugo. As it is, Aria's probably already in bed. As I walk out the main door, Viggo is vaping, leaning against the wall.

'We meet again.' A smile crosses his face.

'Just going to get my charger from the car,' I say. 'A fleeting meeting.'

He gives a humourless laugh as I walk past him.

I decide for privacy's sake to call Ronnie from the car.

'Hi. It's me. How are things?'

'Hello, me. Good. You?'

'Yeah, show went well, place is lovely, my friend Lorenzo was promoted, just had a sensational meal. All in all a good day. How's the kids?'

'Good. This morning Aria was invited to a birthday party next week and this afternoon she was invited to another birthday party, although I can't remember exactly when.'

'Lucky girl. Popular.'

'Indeed.' Ronnie coughs.

'You OK?' I ask, concerned.

'Yeah, you know what it's like this time of year. Everyone's sick and our beloved children are little bug transporters.'

'You have such a nice turn of phrase,' I say, but I'm smiling.

'Can I talk to Hugo, if he's still up?'

'He is, but you've missed Aria.'

'I thought as much. Can you give her an extra hug in the morning and tell her I'll see her for dinner?'

'Sure. What time do you think you'll be back?'

I almost slap my hand against my forehead. 'I nearly forgot to ask, what's happening with the car?'

'No word yet. I thought they'd called you since I hadn't heard anything.'

'Oh no, I hope this isn't going to be a problem,

although I guess that means I'm driving a Fiat Uno home.'

Ronnie chuckles. 'Is that what they gave you? Hardly seems a good match for yours.'

'My thoughts exactly,' I say dryly. 'Can you put Hugo on, then I'll speak to Gen and get to bed. It's been a long day, and I'll freeze soon.'

'Oh? Where are you?'

'In the car. I came to get my charger. Thought I'd get peace to talk to you out here.'

'Eh, don't you have a bedroom?'

The mobile reception breaks up a little, then I say, 'Of course I do, but we were in the restaurant. Oh, anyway, it seemed easier, and I needed the charger from the car.'

'Fair point. Right, safe home tomorrow. I love you. And hugs to the babies.'

'Difficult, but I'll see what I can do.'

I speak to Hugo, who bombards me with info on the latest Xbox game he has been playing online with Xander and a few other friends. Honestly, it's as if my children arrived from another planet. I remember playing video games as a kid and enjoying them, but these days they're so advanced, even if I cared enough to play them, I still probably wouldn't have a clue what they were on about.

Gen tells me how gymnastics went and that Ronnie dropped her at Freya's for a bit and they borrowed Felicity's make-up and tried on some of her clothes, for fun, with her permission, and it was all a bit of a laugh, although she did think the make-up Felicity wears is a bit too subtle for her. Subtle. I didn't even wear make-up until I was in my mid-teens. She's only thirteen. I tell her I love her and to give Aria a kiss for me, in case Ronnie forgets, and that I'll see her tomorrow.

I'm oblivious to everything as I head across the car park to the main entrance. Then voices draw my attention and I see a young woman with Viggo. Oh God, he's trying to charm some other unsuspecting person. For a moment, I wonder if there's a way to avoid them, then unmistakably I hear the woman say, 'Get off me' then Viggo's mumbled voice, followed by her 'I swear I'll scream.'

I stride across the car park. 'Viggo!' My voice is shrill. 'What the hell is going on here?'

The woman looks at me and I see she is a little dishevelled. 'Is this your husband?'

'Nooo!' I say incredulously. 'My colleague. Are you OK?'

'Yes, just about, but that man's a menace. He's lucky I don't report him.' She throws him a look of pure disgust and mutters something which I don't entirely catch, but which sounds like 'Vile specimen of humanity' as she passes him and enters the reception area.

'What on earth, Viggo? What do you think you were doing? Did you attack that woman?'

'Me? Attack someone?' he scoffs. 'Yeah, like I would need to do that.'

'Well, Viggo, it doesn't look like she was particularly interested, does it?'

'Her loss,' he sneers. 'And what about you, Louisa, you're definitely interested. I can tell.'

I splutter and it takes all of my wherewithal not to choke. 'Do you hear yourself? Are you delusional? I wouldn't be interested in you if you were the last man on earth, Viggo.' I turn to walk away, but he catches my arm and pulls me up against his chest. I back away, but he's too strong. The cloying musk of his aftershave gets in my throat. 'Viggo, get off me!' I scream, mirroring the woman's words from not less than five minutes ago.

He presses his face into mine, his lips on mine, his hand on my spine preventing me from pulling back any further. Oh dear Lord, get him off me. I struggle, my arms beating against his to ensure the message is getting through, but it doesn't. I feel physically sick as if he has violated me. He has violated me.

And then I'm free. Hands. Hands pulling Viggo off me. A woman standing in the background, the woman who Viggo attacked earlier. Fabien. Lorenzo.

'Viggo,' Fabien says, his teeth gritted and his chest heaving. 'Go sleep it off, and tomorrow, find another job. You're fired.'

Lorenzo and the duty manager lead Viggo away. Fabien takes one look at me and shepherds me inside. 'Louisa, I'm so so sorry. I had no idea he was such a…such a…'

'Lech?'

He nods. 'If that woman hadn't come to warn us, I dread to think…'

So do I, but I don't allow us to dwell on that thought.

'She did, though, and that's what matters. He tried something with her and I stopped him.'

'Here, let's get you inside. Are you sure you're OK?' He looks at my stomach. 'And the babies. Would you like me to call a doctor?'

'Thanks, Fabien, but that won't be necessary. I think I might have a cup of tea, though, and then go to bed.'

'If you're sure. C'mon, let's get you that tea.' He leads me back into the dining room and summons a waiter, who takes his order and disappears, returning a few moments later with my tea.

As I sip my tea, I wonder how so much can happen in twenty-four hours.

Chapter Thirteen

Thursday 18 November

To-do list – I've gone back to my original system. None of the books on list-making have done any good. I've trialled several methods and I'm yet to see an improvement.
Check with Jo and Wendy what they're getting Mum
Get Mum's birthday present and card
Call the insurance about my car
Chase up remainder of leads from the show
Contact nurseries re places for the babies when they turn one – not all nurseries take one-year-olds, but some have waiting lists

I've had a much-needed quiet start to the week. Ronnie was incandescent when I told him what had happened. He had a few words with Fabien too about hiring such a 'disgusting piece of scum' and he talked about pressing charges, but I begged him to leave it. I don't need the drama, and hopefully Viggo will have learned his lesson: not only didn't he get the promotion Lorenzo won, but he lost his job altogether, given his own revolting behaviour.

I've caught up with my sisters, both of them, and it seems such a long time since that last happened. Our

October break was halted rather abruptly, after all, with Cerulean's urgent need for me in Bergamo. I apologised to Jo again for that, and Wendy. And Wendy admitted that she'd felt a little resentful about that, not for them keeping the kids, but because in her opinion it spoilt Jo's enjoyment of her rearranged birthday party. I apologised, again, for being so self-centred, even though all I was doing was trying to help out my new boss. God, I can't win.

Dad dropped round, unannounced. Not like him at all. He was on his own too, Mum apparently being at some self-defence class. Self-defence? She's showing me up. My sixty-eight-year-old mother is learning about headlocks and whatnot. Yep, that's the extent of my self-defence knowledge, although given what happened with Viggo, it might not be a bad idea for me to attend that class once these babies have been born.

Dad was so sweet. He brought me a gorgeous bouquet of flowers, a real riot of colour, from Blooming Marvellous. He spoke to Susan, who told him she knows all my favourite flowers, so she chose everything I liked that was in season.

He made me some tea, said he'd drop my Wedded Bliss parcels off at the post office for me and fussed over Patch and Bear like it was going out of fashion. Those dogs adore him, and he them. I really enjoyed his company, and it was so nice it just being the two of us. I see plenty of Mum, usually, especially as she's virtually running Wedded Bliss single-handedly half the time – something I still need to address – but I don't see so much of Dad. I worry about him sometimes. He doesn't seem to have many interests. He liked his cruising and he loves his grandchildren and the dogs, and the house on Arran, although they haven't been as often as I thought they'd go – and that's probably my fault since Mum's helping me so much with Wedded Bliss – but other than that, he doesn't seem to actually have anything for himself. And I'm realising how very important it is to have something for yourself.

Once the babies are born, I must try to eke out some me time, whatever happens. I realise that's a pie in the sky notion, but I need to make it happen, otherwise I'll be swallowed whole.

'Are you looking forward to the babies coming, Louisa?' Dad asks.

What kind of question is that? Do I answer honestly – yes, but I'm terrified, feel I won't be a good enough parent, even though these will be children number four and five, and I lie awake at night, still, wondering how I'll cope, or do I fudge – yes, it's going to be wonderful?

In the end, my hesitation means Dad speaks again first. 'You see, I've been thinking. Mum has Wedded Bliss to help you with, and I'm not very good at that sort of thing.'

'Dad, you and Mum do so much for me. You help with the school run, when I need the kids picked up or looked after last-minute if I have a meeting…'

He nods his head. 'I know that, love, and yes, we do, and we love it. But I can sense you're worried about having five children, and well, I'm good with the children, aren't I?'

I frown. Where's he going with this? 'Of course you are.'

'So, I was thinking,' he says, as if I haven't answered, 'that maybe I could help you with the babies.'

My brow creases. 'What do you mean?'

'Well, I could spend part of each day here, when

Ronnie's at work and the kids are at school, helping you with the feeding, or nappy changing or even the cleaning and tidying, as that will be so much harder to manage once the babies are here. And I love being with the dogs too, as you know. I could be here for a few hours each day, just to make it easier. Let you have a little nap during the day, that sort of thing.'

I swallow hard. My wee thoughtful dad, often eclipsed by the larger-than-life chatterbox that is Mum… He's a gem.

I go over to him and hug him. 'Dad, you're amazing, do you know that? Yes, that would be wonderful. Thank you so much.'

'Not a problem, love.'

'But you must promise to tell me if it becomes too much,' I say sternly.

'Oh, I will, but it won't. I'll be like a wee pig in muck.'

I don't think that's the analogy, and I'm not sure that's the best way to describe how he'll feel looking after my children, but I run with it. I love my parents. I really do.

And now it's only a week until Mum's birthday. She's been such a godsend to me, I want to do something extra special for her. But what to get her? She has everything.

A spa day? An overnight stay somewhere? She did say she fancied Garfield Grange. I could arrange that easily enough. A framed photo or selection of framed photos of her and the kids.

A photo shoot with her, Dad and the kids? God, this is so hard. Theatre tickets? Afternoon tea somewhere posh?

No, this is pointless, I'll call Wendy. She needs to tell

me if she has already bought something anyway, and what.

'Wendy, hi. You busy?' I've caught her on a break between meetings. 'Mum's birthday. Have you done anything about it?' I ask as I put her on speaker and put a load of washing in the machine.

'Nope, not yet. I was hoping you might have some ideas.'

I sigh. 'Well, I do, but I'm just not sure if they're any good. I wanted to get her something a bit special because of how much she has been helping me with Wedded Bliss.'

'Hmm,' Wendy says. 'How about…sorry, Lou, I have another call coming in. It's Brandon. I need to take this. Talk to you later? Bye.'

That was abrupt. What is going on with Wendy lately? Oh, maybe I'm being selfish. I'm not trying to be, but I'm so used to having Wendy as my sounding board, that when it's taken away, I really notice it.

I call Jo, but her phone goes to voicemail. 'Hi, Jo, only me. Wanted to pick your brains about Mum's birthday. Give me a ring.'

I'm not really getting far and I can't face the prospect yet of calling the insurance about my car. I have no desire to dent my half-decent mood by being kept on hold for half an hour only to be told my car isn't ready yet and they don't know when its new bonnet will be here.

Fresh air's what I need. I grab my bag and take a stroll down towards the shops. I pass the park, where the squeals of toddlers on the swings make me smile. That will be me again soon. Aria still goes on the swings, Hugo too, although he is getting a bit big. He's more interested in online games and the like now. Autumnal leaves tumble to the pavement as I walk on by, and I remember why I love autumn so much, well, the dry parts anyway.

Pine cones riddle the earthen floor, and acorns lie dormant beside them. I make a mental note to bring Aria here. She loves collecting pine cones to decorate and I'm sure I could engage Hugo's interest in having a conker fight with Xander. Well, for five minutes at least. Are kids happier these days with all the gadgets at their disposal, instead of the conkers and five stones we had?

I go in to see George at the butcher's, my lifelong friend and not only because he brought those steaks to our house the day I discovered Martha unconscious. Any shop owner who provides a service like that has my business for life.

'Afternoon, Louisa. How's the family?' George asks, a warm smile on his ruddy face.

'Can't complain. How's yours?'

'Oh grand, grand. What can I get you today?'

'Can we have four of those chicken kievs you had last time and perhaps two pounds of sausages. And is there any chance you have any bones going for Bear?'

'Oh, Louisa, you spoil that dog, but, yes, I think I might. Not for Patch, though. He's too little still.'

'Oh no, don't worry, Patch doesn't get anything like that. He'd choke.'

Once I've sorted dinner at the butcher's, I head to Icing on the Cake, where I buy an assortment of cakes for this evening.

I'm looking forward to seeing Sam and Nicky. Valentin's dropping Nicky off and going to pick her up afterwards. She can't drive yet, but hopefully it won't be too long. Her recuperation is slow but steady. Sometimes I still can't believe it has all happened, and sometimes I have the most hideous nightmares about the night of the crash.

'Marjorie, I know it's short notice, but do you think you could do me a birthday cake for Mum? It's next Friday, the twenty-sixth.'

'Louisa, for you, and indeed for Liv, I'll fit it in.'

'Thanks, Marjorie, you're a dote.'

Marjorie blushes. 'Oh, away with you. So, what would you like?'

I hem and haw, but eventually I settle on lemon drizzle cake, which my mum loves. And Marjorie's lemon drizzle is to die for. I had some at a wedding last year and it was incredible. If I could, I'd order one once a week, but then I'd be even heavier than I am now. I look down at my stomach ruefully. At least that's all baby. Or rather, babies.

Once the cake is taken care of, I make my way along the main street to check on Martha, see if she needs anything, since I'm down the town anyway. Maybe she can help me with ideas for Mum's birthday too.

Before I ring Martha's bell, I study our house, next door to it. It really is beginning to take shape. It now seems possible that it may be ready when the insurance company told us it will. It occurs to me that all I seem to do is deal with insurance companies, first the house, now the car. At least I'm not having to deal with them for personal injury. Poor Nicky. I wonder if she has any update to give us tonight.

'Louisa, what a wonderful surprise.' Martha ushers me inside. She looks amazing for someone who had a bad fall, entailing being in hospital, not six weeks ago.

'Lovely to see you, Martha. You're looking well. No Brett?'

'I feel great. Come in, sit down. Brett's away into

Hamwell. He has some business to conduct, whatever that means.'

I smile. 'Probably exactly that.'

'Tea?' Martha asks. 'It has to be better than that decaff coffee you've been drinking since you became pregnant. And I don't have any decaff anyway.'

I smile. 'Tea's fine. How've you been? Enjoying having Brett here?'

She puts the kettle on to boil and turns to me. 'I wish he'd never go home. I love having him here.'

'I'm not surprised.' I pass her the cups. 'I've felt so much better he's with you here too. At least soon we'll be back home and can look in on you too.'

A smile lights up her whole face. 'I can't wait until you're back home where you belong. I really miss the kids, and the dogs, and you, of course,' she says when I plant my hands on my hips in mock outrage.

I laugh. 'Well recovered.'

'Actually, Annabelle was here week before last. Did she mention it?' Martha takes two cups and reaches for the teabags.

'Yes, she said. I didn't realise you two were so friendly.'

Martha waves a hand through the air. 'Oh, we're not, but we have found common ground a few times over the years, and it was nice of her to visit. Have you seen how much work the builders have done at yours?' she asks, changing the subject. 'It really all seems to be coming together.' She hands me my tea.

'I know. I was pleasantly surprised, although since the insurance company has told us it's to be ready by the end of the year, perhaps not surprising. At least we'll be starting the new year in our own home. And the babies will be brought back there when they're born.' I pat my stomach fondly.

'So, how are you feeling about the new arrivals?' She nods towards my bump.

I pause to gather my thoughts. 'Better than I was. It's not that I don't want the babies, although clearly they weren't planned, I was just so overwhelmed by…well…everything, wondering how I'd cope.'

She nods. 'I can see how that would frighten you, but Louisa, mothers have been doing this from the beginning of time. Remember that only in the past generation or so have families been so much smaller.'

I make a noncommittal noise.

'Plus, you're an incredible mum, an incredible woman, actually. You're always looking out for everyone. You do too much, as mums often do, of course, but you cope and you get things done, as well.'

I bite my lower lip. She's right.

'And this will be no different. It will be a period of readjustment, but you'll embrace it wholeheartedly as you do everything else.'

I hug her frail birdlike frame to me. 'Thanks for that, Martha. That's really sweet of you, and I needed to hear it.'

'Well, as long as my pep talk works, that's all that matters.' She hugs me back then clasps my hands. 'You are a very special girl, Louisa, and you have a lovely family. Treasure it and stop beating yourself up.'

Wise words indeed.

We take our drinks through to the living room when Martha has put some biscuits on a plate, and I sit on the dusky pink armchair I've always favoured in her house. It's as if it's been moulded especially for me, and never more so than now. Bliss. Martha takes two coasters from the antique sideboard and I place one under my cup and rest it on top of the rose-patterned antimacassar.

'So, how are your folks?' Martha asks as she eases herself into the matching pink armchair opposite me.

'Good. Mum's still working away, helping me out with Wedded Bliss, and I've just seen Dad.'

I tell her all about his offer to help once the babies come.

'That's a great offer your dad has made. He'll be a fantastic help. And you'll have me on tap too. You know how much I love babies, yours in particular,' Martha says.

I grin. Martha has been like a third grandmother to my children and a saviour to me when they were little, in particular, often coming in to play with Gen when Hugo was feeding, or entertain Hugo when Aria had croup. A good part of my adult life is tied up with this wonderful woman's, and I count the days until we move back home, so we are close to her again.

'I do. Actually, I was meaning to ask your advice. When you mentioned Mum and Dad there, it reminded me.'

Martha leans forward in her chair, eyes wide. 'Oh yes?'

'I need a birthday present for Mum, something more special than usual. She has been amazing these past few months. I honestly don't know what I'd have done without her – probably exploded or sat in a corner bawling my eyes out.'

Martha laughs. 'As if. So, let's see.' She runs through a few ideas which are mainly along the same lines as what I've been thinking. Then she says, 'OK, so she loved the picture you did of all the kids and had framed for her, for Mother's Day.'

'That's right.'

'Isn't your friend Nicky a photographer?'

'Yes.'

'So, how about you have Nicky do a photo shoot with your mum, your dad and the kids? That's incredibly special and something she could look at every day when she's not with them.'

For a moment I say nothing, my brain thinking of some flaw in this idea. 'Martha, you're a genius.' I get up and kiss the top of her head. 'She'll love that. And I'm seeing Nicky tonight, so assuming she feels up to doing it, that could be the answer. Right, I'm going to make a move. You've spurred me into action. Thanks for the tea, and I'll see you again soon, real soon.'

She goes to stand up. 'Don't worry. I'll show myself out. You enjoy the rest of your tea, and say hi to Brett for me. Ronnie was intending to ask him out for a curry again soon. They seem to be enjoying their get-togethers.'

'Brett certainly does. Take care, Louisa, love. And hugs to the kids and Ronnie.'

'I will. Bye.'

I finally deal with the task I've been putting off for some time: calling the insurance. And the result is, I still don't have my car back. Unbelievable, but apparently the part has to come from Germany or something. It's a bonnet, for goodness' sake. I'm stuck with this teeny car for now, an Uno, for a family of five, well, seven nearly and two mutts. C'mon. Someone up there is having a laugh.

Hugo's doing his homework, supervised by Ronnie, who arrived home a little early, not long after I picked the kids up from school. Gen's upstairs in her room braiding Aria's hair, a challenge I imagine, given all the curls. The doorbell rings. That'll be Nicky, or Sam.

'I'll get it,' I say as I walk through the hall. Nicky. I can see her head through the glass panel at the top of the front door.

'Hello, you! You look amazing,' I hug her then stand back. 'Hey, Xan, how you doing?'

He gives me a roguish smile. 'Good. Hugo around?'

'In the playroom doing homework. I'm sure he won't mind you interrupting him.'

'I'll bet,' he mutters as he takes his shoes off then heads for the playroom.

Valentin stops the car as he passes the house again. He's obviously gone to the end of the cul-de-sac to turn. He rolls down the window. 'Hey, Louisa. How are you?'

'Good, thanks. You not coming in?'

He shakes his head. 'I have some things to do, but you have fun, and hopefully I can join you another time.'

Nicky and I wave him off, and as I look at my friend my heart expands with love for her. She is so happy, they are so happy, and it's so wonderful to witness it. She had such a terrible time with her ex, Xander's father, that she was long overdue meeting someone amazing like Valentin.

'In you come.' She follows me indoors and removes her shoes, as Xander did. 'Actually, don't let me forget, but I have something to ask you.' I usher her into the living room.

'Oh?' She tilts her head to the side.

'Wait till I get you a drink. What you having?'

'A glass of wine would be good if you have one.'

'Sure. Red? White?'

'White's good, thanks.' She fiddles with the charm bracelet on her wrist.

'Back in two ticks.'

Whilst I'm in the fridge trying to find a cold bottle of wine, the doorbell goes again. Sam.

I close the fridge and stride down the hall. As I pass the playroom, boys' voices flow out; Ronnie's obviously challenged them to Trivial Pursuit, the kids' version. I'm just amazed the Xbox hasn't been called into service yet.

Sam hands me a spray of what I think are orange carnations.

'Aw, you didn't need to do that. Those are gorgeous. Thanks.' I kiss her cheek, giggling as we try to manoeuvre into a position where our bumps aren't in the way.

'You're getting bigger,' she says, assessing my bump.

'That's generally the way these things go, but I'm glad you brought it up, as my eyes nearly popped out my head when I saw how big you were.'

'I know. I don't think I'll be able to go to aquanatal if I get much bigger, although it's wonderful when we get in the pool. I'm already struggling to get down the steps. They might need a crane to get me back out.'

I laugh. 'You're not that big, yet.'

She pretend-cuffs me round the ear. 'Oi, you! Nicky here yet? I thought I passed Valentin's car as I came into the village.'

'Yes, he dropped her off five minutes ago. Why don't you go through? I was just getting drinks. What would you like?'

She mulls the question over for a moment. 'Can I have sparkling water now and maybe a hot chocolate later? I don't want you to go to the hassle of making the hot chocolate now as I'm dying for us all to have a chat. It's been ages since the three of us have been together.'

I give a sad smile. 'I know. But we're rectifying that tonight.'

She waddles off to the living room whilst I balance the drinks on a tray and bring them through, together with some nibbles.

'Ooh, you're feeding me, I like it,' Sam says. 'I can't stop grazing, it's ridiculous. If I didn't feel like a cow already, I do now.'

Nicky laughs. 'Don't say anything like that when I'm drinking my wine, or I'll be spitting it everywhere.'

I sink down into the chair and sip my mint and lime mocktail. Aah.

As Nicky and Sam catch up, they haven't seen each other for even longer than I've not seen either of them, I sit back and absorb. This is the life. You can tell when you're in the company of good friends as it's so effortless.

'So, we're thinking of calling the baby Elodie,' Sam says. 'I really like it, and Erik does too.'

'Lovely name.' Nicky studiously ignores my coughing fit. She'd better not give Sam any push towards deciding definitively on the name or I'll kill her.

'Yes, there's something really elegant about it, and it's so unusual,' Sam agrees.

'More drinks anyone?' I ask.

Sam studies her glass. 'I've only just started mine. You haven't hoovered yours already, have you?' She looks at mine and sees that I have indeed drained it. 'In that case, can I have that hot chocolate now, please?'

'Sure.' I beat a retreat to the kitchen, placing my hands on the worktop. Please don't steal my favourite baby name.

Please, I will her.

Five minutes later, I've delivered the hot chocolate, a virgin mojito for me and another glass of white for Nicky, whether she wanted it or not. Hope she's no longer on strong painkillers, or we'll be carting her out of here later.

'So, Nicky, before I forget, I know you're not back at work yet, but I was wondering if you thought you'd be fit enough to do a photo shoot of Mum, Dad and the kids. It's for Mum's birthday next week.'

She leans forward, hands on her knees, rubbing them. 'Actually, that would be a great way to see what I'm fit to do. When would you want it done?'

I shrug. 'Sometime after her birthday. I'll try and encourage her to do it sooner rather than later, though, and I'm sure she'll want the kids' photos up as soon as.'

'True, she will. Yeah, that's great, thanks. I'll write you a voucher over the next couple of days. I don't have any with me.'

'No probs.'

We lapse into silence and then Sam and Nicky go to speak at the same time.

'You first, Sam,' Nicky says.

'No, you go, it was nothing important.'

'Sure?' Nicky checks.

Sam nods.

'Well, in that case, I do have something important to tell you. Or rather, Xander does. Let me go tell him to come in.'

Xander returns, a grin playing at his lips, his hands behind his back.

'Hey, Xander,' Sam says.

'Hi, Sam.' He clears his throat, then from behind his

back he whisks out a card, then another, then another. Sam and I tilt our heads and try to work out what the message is.

WILL. YOU. BE. MY. BRIDESMAIDS?

'Oh my God!' I turn to Nicky and grab her by the upper arms. 'Valentin asked you to marry him?'

She nods.

'Oh, that's a relief,' says Sam, 'as for a minute, I thought Xander was asking us if we wanted us to be his!'

All three of us roll our eyes at her.

She holds her hands up in defeat. 'OK, joking. That fell flat.' She stands. 'Congratulations, Nicky. I'm so happy for you both.' She hugs her and kisses her cheek, then I do the same.

I clap my hands. 'Well, this calls for some champagne. Xander, go tell Ronnie we need him in here.'

Ronnie strolls in. 'Evening, ladies. Looking b-beautiful, Sam.'

Ha ha. He nearly said big, but he's remembered most pregnant women don't like to be called big in the last trimester. That's fine in the first, when you want to be showing, but not when you're ready for the big push, pun intended, and you feel like a heifer already.

'Thanks, Ronnie.' Sam smirks.

'Ronnie,' I say innocently. 'Nicky wants to tell you something.'

He raises an eyebrow, but turns to Nicky expectantly.

'Valentin and I are engaged!' She holds out her hand where the most exquisite diamond solitaire has miraculously appeared on it in the last few minutes.

'Let's crack open that champagne then. I'll join you, Nicky, since the two pregnant women won't be able to, but

I do believe we have some non-alcoholic bubbles in the fridge too.'

'I was keeping them for a special occasion,' I confide to the girls, 'and I can't think of a better one than this.'

Ronnie goes off to tell the kids to come in so Nicky can tell them too, and then he organises all the drinks, pouring the children some sparkling grape juice too, so they can truly celebrate with us, whilst we gush over Nicky's ring.

'It's gorgeous, Nicky,' I say.

'It is,' she agrees, 'but I'm terrified to wear it daily as it must have cost the equivalent of the GDP of a small African nation.'

Sam and I laugh.

'Valentin's rich, but he's not that rich.' Sam smiles.

We raise our glasses. 'To Nicky and Valentin!'

I catch Xander's eye and see the happiness shining out of him. He adores his new stepdad-in-waiting. Then my gaze falls on Nicky, radiant with joy, and I thank the heavens she has finally found her soulmate.

Chapter Fourteen

Friday 26 November

To-do list
Pick up Mum's cake from Icing on the Cake
Collect book I ordered for Mum from the Book Nook
Take money out of bank – I'm lucky if I have £2 in my wallet
Call plumber – WC is leaking
Unsubscribe to at least 10 companies' emails today – the volume of emails is becoming ridiculous
Give Aria money for her drama group costume
Change the direct debit for drama group
Re-order flea and worming tablets for Patch

Mum's sixty-nine today. Can't believe she's almost seventy, although I'd best not mention that today or she'll string me up. Plus, I've just received a little, or rather, not so little piece of good news. I pat my pocket where I put the envelope earlier. It'll keep for now, until we're all together.

Since it's a Friday, Jo and Wendy have said they'll leave work early, collect their kids and meet us at Mum's for five to do the great birthday gift-giving ceremony. Travis has once again, kindly invited us all to lunch at his restaurant,

Solitude, and then we can have a lazy, leisurely Sunday afternoon together, but since today's Mum's actual birthday, us three children and the grandchildren will meet up to hand over her gifts, and Brandon, Ronnie and Travis can pitch in on Sunday.

Sometimes, it's nice it just being us: Mum, me, Wendy and Jo anyway. Although I'm used to spending holidays and birthday trips with my sisters and the kids, Mum doesn't come on those, appreciating that the topics of conversation aren't always for her ears. But she's very young for almost seventy. Oops, there I go again. I'd better watch and not be caught out saying it later.

Nicky gave me a lovely voucher for her and I think Martha's right, she'll love that. She doesn't have an enormous framed print of her and the kids, plenty of little ones, but nothing above A4 size. It'll be expensive, even Nicky doing it at mates' rates, but I wanted something truly individual to mark a truly unusual year.

This letter's burning a hole in my pocket. I have to tell someone. Maybe I could nip in and tell Martha. No! Louisa, exercise some restraint.

As if gleaning that something's unsettling me, the twins move. Ow. Was that a foot? I definitely felt some give against my tummy there. I have no idea if twins act the same way as single babies when it comes to timescale for movement and development. I really should read up on this more. And I still haven't bought anything. I'd promised myself I'd go look at prams, but I haven't had a chance yet, and I need to order cots, although first I need to sort out a couple of Moses baskets. Galling to think we had all this stuff and gave it all away. Oh well, can't be helped. Expensive business, babies.

Right, I'd best crack on. I'm going to head into town. I didn't want to just give Mum a voucher for the photo shoot, so I ordered her a special edition of *Anne of Green Gables*, a book she has always loved, and which she tried to interest Gen in, but to no avail. Geraldine at the Book Nook said it would be in today.

Since I'm in town, I might nip in and see Martha too. She did give me the birthday gift idea, after all.

It's been an unseasonably dry November, for the most part. Clouds hang above me in the sky but they're innocuous enough, no great storm clouds, which is just as well as I need to carry Mum's cake back to the house.

I nod to George as I pass the butcher's and pop in to see Marjorie about the cake.

'Afternoon, Louisa. It's all ready for you.'

'Marvellous. Can I have a peek? I'm going over to pick up a book from the Book Nook in a minute, and I'm heading over to see Martha. Thought I'd pick it up on the way back.'

The unwelcome parallel of my being in the butcher's less than two months ago and saying I was en route to Martha's and would pick my meat up on the way flows into my subconscious.

'Sure. What do you think?' She opens the box.

'Oh, Marjorie, that's gorgeous, thank you so much.' I bet you it tastes even better. I can't wait to try it later.

'You're welcome. Right, I'll see you later then, and remember to wish your mum a happy birthday from me.'

'I will.' I raise my hand in a wave and cross the road to the Book Nook.

'Hi, Geraldine. How are you?'

She's stacking books on the counter, and about a dozen

boxes of books surround her. 'Redoing the window displays. Christmas stock.'

'Ooh, let me have a look.'

'Don't you be mixing up all my stock before I've had a chance to log it in the system,' she says, but she's smiling.

'I won't. I promise.'

'You in for your *Anne of Green Gables* then?'

'Yep. It is in, isn't it?' I ask, worrying for a moment that it hasn't yet arrived.

'Yeah, came in this morning.'

'Excellent. I'll have a wee look through these whilst I'm here. Can you believe I haven't even started my Christmas shopping yet?'

'I never start my shopping until the week before. I enjoy the buzz,' Geraldine says.

My eyes widen. It's on the tip of my tongue to ask if she's mad, but I control myself. She may not take that comment well, despite us having a decent reader/bookseller relationship.

I nod and continue looking through her Christmas stock.

'Well, except books, of course. I always buy books before Christmas as presents. Perk of owning a bookshop.'

'I can imagine. Right, I'll take these.' I hand her six books, two for each child.

'Ronnie not getting any?'

I blush. My dirty mind, for a second, thought she was referring to s-e-x. Now I realise she means books. 'No-o-o, not from your Christmas section anyway.'

'You OK? You look a bit hot. Would you like some water?'

Hot? If only she knew. 'I think I just need some air.

How much do I owe you?'

Geraldine packages up all the books, her eyes narrowed on me. She knows she's missed something.

'See you later' I open the door. 'Actually, could I leave this here for now? I'm heading to Martha's.'

'No problem, give it here.' She holds out her hand for the bag.

Five minutes later, I'm at Martha's.

'Come on in. What a lovely surprise.'

'Thanks, Martha. Brett out again? I keep missing him.'

Her face falls. 'You'll be missing him for a lot longer, or rather you won't be.'

I screw my face up. 'Martha, you couldn't be more cryptic if you tried. What do you mean?'

She slumps down on her chair, and I sit opposite. 'Is everything OK?' I ask.

Martha passes a hand over her weary face. 'It's nothing, I'm just being a silly old fool, but Brett's booked his ticket home. He leaves next week.' Her eyes fill with tears and she pulls a handkerchief out of her cardigan and dabs at them.

'Oh, Martha, no wonder you're upset, but you knew he'd have to go back sometime. It was never going to be forever, him being here, and at least he's stayed for almost two months. When was the last time he was here for that long?'

She dries her eyes. 'Before he moved to Australia. It's just, I've got used to him being here, living here, and it's been…nice.'

'Of course it has, but he has to get on with his life too. I don't mean that to sound harsh, but…'

'Oh, Louisa, you don't have it in you to be harsh. I know exactly what you mean and you're right, but it doesn't make it any easier to deal with.'

I hug her to me and she lets out a little sob. 'I know it's not the same, but we'll be back here soon. In fact…' I pause then make an executive decision. Ronnie won't care that I told Martha first, given the state she's currently in. 'I have some good news. It won't make up for Brett going, but–' I remove the envelope from my pocket '–have a look at this.'

Martha takes it from me, then lifts her reading glasses from the sideboard and props them on her nose. 'It's from your insurance company.'

'That's right.' I beam at her.

'Oh my goodness, Louisa, that's marvellous,' she says, as she reaches the part where it tells me my home will be habitable from 18 December.

'It is. I haven't told anyone yet. I was intending to wait until after Mum's birthday lunch, but, well, I think you needed a piece of good news.' I hug her to me again.

'Oh, Louisa, you have no idea.' She hugs me back. 'It will be so good to have you all back home where you belong.'

'I second that. Tea? I'm making it.'

I close the car door as Hugo skips towards my parents' house. You'd think it was his birthday, he's so happy.

'Mum, can I give Nana her gift?' Aria asks. 'Please, please.'

Hugo turns to me, his eyes downcast. He adores Mum. 'Hugo, why don't you give Nana this one–' I hold out the envelope '–and Aria can give her the other one?' Under my breath, I murmur, 'The envelope has her main present in it.'

His eyes light up. Aria's watching, so he clears his throat. 'OK, I suppose.'

'Yay,' Aria says, holding her hand out for the gift bag containing Mum's book.

I ding the bell to announce chaos is imminent, open the door, then shepherd them in ahead of me. Gen's carrying some flowers I brought from Blooming Marvellous. Susan reliably told me it was called cyclamen. It's pretty, so I took her recommendation. I never go wrong with Susan's recommendations. I follow behind carrying the cake. I hope Mum lets us open it soon. I'm starving. I haven't eaten very much today. Bad mummy. Must remember to eat properly for the babies' health.

Soon the kids are falling all over their nana, and there are hugs and kisses and thanks for her gifts.

The kids and I traipse through to the living room where Jo, Aurora and Jackson are sitting obediently, gift-wrapped presents on the coffee table in front of them.

'Hi, gang. How you doing?' I accept the kisses and cuddles bestowed upon me. I can't believe the height of them. What on earth has Jo been feeding these kids? If this is what country living does to you, no thanks, otherwise my kids will all be taller than me in a few years.

'They've taken a stretch,' Jo says. 'Honestly, whenever I do any ironing, I constantly have to put some item of clothing to the side for the charity bag as they've outgrown it. It's ridiculous.'

'And expensive,' I say.

'That too,' she agrees.

The door goes – Wendy and the kids. Aurora and Jackson ask if they can leave the room to go play with their cousins.

'Be back here in five minutes so Nana can open all her presents,' Jo says firmly.

'Yes, Mum,' they chorus.

Who are these children? When did they become so well-behaved? Aurora's usually a tomboy scamp. Who is this child before me in the red velvet dress and immaculate white knee-high socks which wouldn't be out of place in a commercial for laundry detergent as the 'after' result?

'Hi, sis,' I say when Wendy comes into the room.

'Wow, you look huge.' She stares at my bump.

'Thanks, you look like you've gained a few pounds too,' I say deadpan.

'Ha bloody ha.' She checks no kids are around before delivering the expletive.

'How's things?' I ask after she and Jo hug.

'Tell you later. So, Jo, Travis busy with bookings for Christmas?'

That was an odd change of topic. I hope nothing's up. She's unlikely to tell me at Mum's birthday meet-up anyway if anything is. Did she mean later tonight, or later, as in, not now, but sometime before the next century starts? Hard to tell with Wendy sometimes, and lately she's been so…distant.

I shake my head as if to dispel the thoughts.

'Yeah, the bookings have gone off the chart in the past two weeks. Any gaps have been swallowed up. Great for business, not so great for seeing my other half.'

I smile. Travis and Jo are the perfect match. She's so independent, but doesn't give a toss about so many things which other mums worry about, and is a successful accountant, whereas Travis worked his guts out to open his own restaurant, Solitude, and he revels in the pressure. Thinking of Travis brings me back to thoughts of Caden, our kiss and the turmoil that ensued a few months previously. What a period of madness that was. Guilt stabs at me as I remember Dolores, his girlfriend. A real feisty Spanish woman. I hope they're still together and that they're happy.

I haven't thought of Caden for weeks, possibly more. Is this a symptom of Ronnie and I getting on so much better now, or simply that so much has been going on, I've barely had time to draw breath? I'd like to think the former. We *have* been getting on better: he's been more supportive, engaged, involved with the kids, doing things around the house, taking his turn, looking after me protectively in my pregnancy – so sweet. Maybe it took all that 'nonsense' with Caden for us to reach where we are now, and we're definitely in a better place.

Mum comes into the room, her grandchildren having stopped wishing her Happy Birthday. We each take our turn at hugging and kissing her.

'Where's Dad?' I ask, realising he hasn't joined us.

'Out. He went out about an hour ago and hasn't come back yet.'

'Maybe he's gone to pick up your birthday present, Mum.'

Mum shakes her head. 'I don't think so. He got me these lovely earrings–' she shows off a pair of tiny diamond earrings '–and a new Kindle.'

'Dunno what he's up to then. I'm sure he'll be back soon,' I say. 'In the meantime, how about we gather everyone together and you open your presents?'

Dad returns whilst Mum is opening her gifts, the grandchildren waiting patiently – some more patiently than others – to see their nana's reactions. This is the difficulty of having so many pre-schoolers and P1s in the same family. Aria tries to 'help' her nana to unwrap the paper as she's 'taking too long, Mummy' and Jackson blurts out that one parcel has gloves in it, and a hat. We all laugh, and the look of despair Jo gives Jackson has us creasing up.

She unwraps the book. 'Oh, Louisa, I love it.' *Anne of Green Gables* is my favourite book of all time.'

I smile. 'I know. So glad you like it.' I accept her kiss on the cheek before she turns to receive a gift from Wendy. A restaurant voucher for Two Fat Ladies.

'Thanks, Wendy.' She kisses her and says, 'Although where I'll find another fat lady to go with, I don't know.'

'Nana, enough of the Dad jokes, please. I get too many of those from Daddy as it is,' Hugo moans.

A chuckle goes around the room, then Mum opens her other presents, until finally she sees the envelope sitting on the table. She glances at the three of us. Wendy and Jo shrug. She looks at me and I smile. She opens it, reads what's printed on the voucher, gulps, and her voice thick with emotion, says, 'Thanks, Louisa. It's perfect.' She shows it to my sisters and they give me congratulatory looks.

'Look, kids, Auntie Lou has bought Nana a voucher to have a photo with you all.' She looks at the voucher again, frowns, then glances up at me. 'It is for all of us, isn't it, not just your three, although that would be fine too, obviously,' she hastens to add.

'Mum, it's whatever you want it to be. And it's Nicky, so tell her exactly what you want and she'll accommodate it.'

'Thanks so much for this.' She looks at my sisters then at her nine grandchildren. 'All of you. Thank you for your gifts and thank you for being here with me today to celebrate. It means the world.'

'Hear, hear,' chips in Dad. He was so quiet sitting there, I'd almost forgotten he was in the room.

'I just hope we can all fit in the one photo,' Mum says. 'There's so many of you now. Nine grandchildren.' They clamber over her, like newborn puppies. 'Soon to be eleven. Oh my goodness, how did I get to be this lucky?'

My sisters and I exchange glances, then I stand up. 'Who wants cake?'

I'm barely home before I have to grab my swimming stuff, kiss Ronnie hello and goodbye within the space of five minutes, and be out the door again for aquanatal. I've missed too many sessions already, I can't miss another.

I arrive puffing and panting, change into my costume, and in an ungainly fashion join the other mums-to-be in the pool. Sam's floating with a noodle.

'You cut it fine, we're just about to start. Helga was glaring daggers at the door every time it opened.'

'Her name's not Helga,' I say.

'I know, but I can't remember what it is, and Helga seems to suit her. She's very drill sergeant-ish. She'd have done well in the army.'

'Helga' blowing her whistle calls us all to attention and

the other mums exchange glances. Clearly we're not the only ones who think Helga's let power go to her head.

We spend a fun thirty minutes, quite frankly, making tits of ourselves in the pool, but it's enjoyable.

'Ooh, I don't feel so good.' Sam stands up in the water.

My brow furrows. 'What's wrong? The baby's not coming, is it?' I'm imagining the irony of being in a swimming pool when your baby decides to arrive, despite you not having planned for a water birth.

'No, nothing like that, but I feel as if I've strained something. Must have been those star jumps.'

'Do you want to get out?' I ask.

'I'm going to have to. Can you help me up those steps, though?'

I signal to the instructor. 'Sam's strained something, so we're going to get out.'

'Helga' ensures Sam's OK and not about to go into labour or anything, and between us, we manage to get her out of the pool, without causing Sam undue discomfort.

As we stand in the changing areas, Sam says, 'I think this will be my last class. That was so embarrassing, you and "Helga" having to manoeuvre me out of the pool.'

'Don't be silly, anyway, everyone knows every shred of modesty and reserve goes out the window once you're pregnant.'

She manages a chuckle. 'That's true.'

By the time, we've showered and changed, Sam is complaining of pains in her stomach.

'Labour pains?' Surely not, it's too early.

'No, it's probably indigestion. I had a tuna sandwich before I came out. It's probably that,' but I feel a bit weird. Can I ask a big favour?'

'Sure. What is it?'

'Would you mind dropping me off at mine? Mum's having Emily and Ava whilst Erik's with his family in Sweden this week. She's keeping them until tomorrow, so I can have a rest. I'll get her to drop me back tomorrow to pick up my car.'

'If you're sure. I'll text Ronnie to let him know I'll be home a bit later.'

'Sorry to be a pest,' she says.

'Stop it!' I bat her lightly on the arm. 'It's no problem. I just don't want him burning my dinner.'

'Ooh, he's making dinner now, is he?' she asks as we gather our things together.

'Yes, it's fabulous. He's become a regular Jamie Oliver, or whoever's the cool chef these days.'

'Lucky you, Erik only cooks Swedish food, and whilst I like Ikea meatballs as well as the next person, he can keep his rollmop herring.'

'Oh, Sam, you do make me laugh. Do you think our babies will be best friends too?'

'They will, I'm sure,' she says. 'Crikey, look at the size of us. We're like two bowling balls.'

'Speak for yourself,' I feign indignation. 'I'm more of a watermelon.'

In the car, I tell Sam I bought my first Christmas present today.

'God, I haven't even thought about it. I know I should, and we need to write their letters to Santa, I keep getting letters from those companies that send them out, but I simply don't have the energy.'

'I get those too. You'd think it would have reminded me to buy presents before now. And we haven't even talked about their Santa letters yet. I'm going to have to do that, aren't I?'

'Yep. Ooh, ouch, Jeesus!' Sam says.

'You OK?' I ask, panic threading through my voice.

'Yeah, that was just…uncomfortable.'

'Are you sure you're going to be OK home alone tonight?'

She waves a hand dismissively. 'Yeah, I'll be fine. Wow!'

I swerve the car. 'Sorry!'

Sam gives me a look. 'I'm the one who should be apologising. It's my baby girl who's causing all the hassle, getting more active than she…'

'Than she…?' I prompt.

'Oh my God!'

'Sam, what is it?' I ask, glancing at her as I keep my attention on the road in front.

'My waters have broken.'

'You're joking!'

'Do I look like I'm joking, Lou?' she almost shrieks at me.

'Sorry, Sam. I just wasn't expecting you to say that.'

'No, I'm sorry. Oh, Lou, your poor car. I'll pay for it to be cleaned, obviously.'

'Don't worry about that. And anyway, the car's had far worse happen to it recently.' I give her a wry grin. *I've only had it back two days, but who's counting?*

'Yes, losing its bonnet on a motorway…' she takes deep breaths '…has to be up there with the top three worst things to happen to it. Although a pregnant lady wetting herself in it has to be close.'

'You didn't wet yourself!'

'Feels like it,' she mumbles.

'Sam, I think we should call the hospital since your waters have broken. How many weeks are you?'

'Twenty-nine and a half,' she parrots.

My heart sinks. I'd thought she was a little further along. 'Listen, I'm pretty sure the hospital will want to check you out because your waters have broken and you're not due.'

'Jesus!' she says, and it takes all my resolve not to slam the brakes on. She keeps giving me heart attacks.

'You OK?'

'No, my waters have broken, my baby's only twenty-nine weeks and this is…ow, ow!'

'Sam, what is it?'

'Lou, pull over. We need to call the hospital.'

A bus lane appears out of the darkness. Thank God.

Sam is already wrestling with her seat belt when we stop.

'Sam, what are you doing?'

'I need room, I feel so constricted,' she moans.

I dial the hospital and explain the situation. They tell me to bring her in right away. It would be quicker than waiting for an ambulance, as that could be hours.

I hang up and tell Sam to put her seat belt back on. I'm taking her to hospital.

'Lou,' she pants. 'I can't.'

'Why not?' I ask.

'Because…Lou, I think the baby's coming.'

Chapter Fifteen

Friday 26 November

'What did you say?' I ask, shock rooting me to the spot.

'The baby's coming!'

'How can you be sure?' I ask, hoping she's wrong.

'Do you want me to draw you a bloody picture, Louisa? How do you think I know? I need to push.'

'No-o-o! No pushing,' I'm panicking the baby will be here in minutes.

Sam grits her teeth. 'Louisa, this isn't a joke. I don't have much choice in the matter. You're going to have to help me push this seat back, and take my trousers off.'

Oh my God, she's not kidding! How can she be so calm? She may be delivering her baby in a car, and it's only a mid-size.

I jump into practical mode, but first I dial 999. As I help Sam undress, I talk to the response handler. 'Hi, my friend's about to give birth in my car. She's twenty-nine weeks. We've pulled into a lay-by near the petrol station on the main street in Lymeburn. I need someone to tell me how to deliver the baby. It's not going to wait.'

The handler gives me instructions and then a nurse or a midwife or someone comes on the line, introduces herself as Sheryl and asks me a bunch of questions which I answer, with the help of Sam, as best I can.

'Is she pushing?'

'She has the urge to push.'

Sam shakes her head.

'Sorry, you don't feel the urge to push?' I ask.

'I'm pushing. I can't help it. Oh my God.' A powerful contraction seizes her and I hold her hand with my left. I may need the right shortly to intervene with this baby.

'We're despatching a paramedic now, but they're half an hour away.'

'This baby's not waiting half an hour!' screams Sam. 'It'll be here in minutes!'

'I guess you heard that,' I say to Sheryl.

'I did. Right, looks like this baby's really impatient, so here's what I need you to do, Louisa.'

I follow her instructions, which she provides coolly and calmly, and that helps me a little. I'm not sure it helps Sam one single bit, though. All our classes about breathing, the fact she's had two children already, none of it seems to matter, as her breaths come in short, sharp, herky-jerky movements.

My phone rings. Ronnie. Clearly I can't answer it, but he'll be worried sick.

Fifteen minutes later, I lift the teensiest baby girl I've ever seen to Sam, but not before I mutter to her, 'I don't care what your mummy calls you, just be well.'

I bundle her in my cardigan and hand her to her mum. 'Here, Sam, say hello to your daughter.'

'Louisa, thank you,' she tells me with tears in her eyes, as she looks down with such unbridled love at her daughter, oblivious to the harrowing events of the evening. I can't even begin to get my head around how she managed without gas and air at least, particularly in such a stressful situation. I guess it really does go to show what the human body is capable of.

Sheryl stays on the phone, briefing me on what to do with the afterbirth and other such fun things, until the paramedic arrives five minutes later and takes over much to my relief.

The paramedic stays with us until an ambulance arrives. I have no idea how much later that is, and although the paramedic's discussion with their colleagues on their radio is relatively whispered, she doesn't give any indication that we should be overly alarmed.

I glance at baby Elodie as Sam is put on a stretcher and the baby is put on her chest.

'Can my friend come in the ambulance with us?' she asks.

'Of course,' the driver says, 'but you might want to get someone to come collect your car.'

Whilst they settle Sam and Elodie in the ambulance, I quickly text Ronnie.

I delivered Sam's baby in the car, on way to hospital with her now. They're both fine. Can you have someone retrieve the car from the lay-by next to the petrol station in Lymeburn, pls? Not sure when I'll be back. Will phone as soon as can x

I don't receive a reply straightaway, which means he's probably settling the kids for bed.

I step up into the ambulance with Sam and see that they've attached her to a drip and some tubes I don't know the names of. I guess they're monitoring her. Elodie is red and wriggly, but seems perfectly happy with Sam, enjoying a bit of skin-to-skin contact. She's perfectly formed. I'm not sure if the paramedics have done anything with her yet, or if the doctors at the hospital will deal with that.

'Well done, Mama,' I whisper to Sam as I kiss her head. 'You did one helluva job.'

She gives a wan smile. 'You and me both. Isn't that right, Octavia?'

'Octavia? Is that the paramedic's name?' I try to recall if she'd told us.

Sam rolls her eyes. 'No, that's my daughter's name. Octavia.' She looks at the tiny bundle on her chest. 'Don't you think it suits her?'

Octavia. I gaze at the baby, her perfect eyelashes, long and dark, her mass of dark hair, and her teeny fingers and nails. My eyes flit to Sam's. 'I think it suits her perfectly. A regal name for a little princess.'

As we sit in the ambulance, heading for Glasgow Royal Infirmary, I think, 'All this bloody time I was worrying about us choosing the same name, and she ups and changes it at the last minute.' I shake my head in disbelief, at the whole evening, and rest as best I can until five minutes before we arrive at the maternity unit when I realise we haven't told Erik. Sam's husband's still in Sweden. I take my phone out and make the call.

'Erik, it's Louisa.'

'Louisa, is everything OK?' His voice has risen an octave and his accent sounds more Swedish than I've ever heard.

'Yes, everything's fine, but Erik, you may want to speak to Sam.' I pass the phone over.

Sam smiles as she speaks into the phone. 'Erik, I think you should come home and meet your daughter.'

Saturday 27 November

To-do list
Have car valeted
Sleep – a lot
Buy Sam a baby card and gift
Check if Nicky knows and tell Mum, Martha etc

The cab dropped me off sometime after midnight. Once we arrived at the hospital, everything happened really quickly. Doctors and nurses descended on Sam and Octavia and they were whisked away to be checked over.

Finally, a midwife came out to see me. 'Louisa?' She noticed my bump. 'Oh, you're pregnant, too.'

'Yep. I'm on trend.'

'Was it you who delivered your friend's baby?'

'Yeah.' I exhaled a noisy breath. 'Everything is OK, isn't it?'

She smiled. 'They're fine. But, I think we'd like you to be checked out too, just as a precaution.'

I tried to protest, but she was really insistent, and I was so tired that eventually I gave in.

Finally, they let me go home. I wasn't allowed to see Sam or baby Octavia. Because she was born so early she's in the neonatal unit which has severely restricted visiting. I'm not even sure Erik will be allowed in to see them. I hope he is though. He's on the first flight back from Stockholm in the morning.

When I arrived home, Ronnie was waiting up for me, and I fell into his arms exhausted. All I remember is him telling me how amazing I was, that I'd delivered a baby and that he was so proud of me. Superwoman featured in the conversation somewhere, but that's the last thing I recall.

I wake around eleven and I hear nothing. Not a thing. Strange. I pad downstairs to discover everyone sitting on devices with headphones on.

'Morning,' Ronnie says. 'I wanted to ensure you got peace to sleep. You were wiped out last night.'

'Thank you.' My eyes drift closed again momentarily and the events of the night before slam into my consciousness. Sam's had her baby! Octavia. Not Elodie. God, I must get over the name thing, although I can actually use it now. Shut up, brain! Oh man, I'm so muddled right now.

'How about some tea and toast?' Ronnie suggests.

I nod and the effort involved almost has me crumpling up with exhaustion. I feel like a punchbag that's been hit for ten hours straight by heavyweight boxers.

I'm thirsty too, so I pour myself a glass of water and down it in three gulps.

My brain starts to come into focus. 'Oh my God, I need to tell Nicky.'

'No you don't, I messaged her last night whilst you were on the way to the hospital.'

'Thank God.'

'Right, Lou, you've had a bit of an experience. Why don't you go chill for a bit and try and relax? We can let everyone know later.'

'That sounds like a great idea, but I need to at least call the hospital to see how they're doing.'

'I'm not sure they'll tell you.'

'But I delivered the baby!' My voice wobbles.

'Hey, hey.' Ronnie comes over to me and places his hands on my upper arms. 'We'll find out how they are one way or another. Don't fret. The main thing is you delivered the baby safely. You did that. Be proud. Be very proud. I know I am.'

I smile and close my eyes. Octavia's wriggling, crying. I'm holding the umbilical cord, me calmer than I've ever been, following the instructions from the call handler.

'I am, and relieved that they're OK, and that the paramedics came when they did. It was a bit hairy for a while.'

'I can only imagine,' Ronnie says, his fingers caressing my neck.

'You're right, you can!'

'Hey, guys, what do you think of Mummy delivering Sam's baby last night? Isn't she amazing?'

Gen slides up beside me. 'Mum, I've watched *Call the Midwife*. Serious kudos to you. That is so brave.'

'Sam was the brave one. No gas and air.'

'Yeah, but Mum, what a responsibility you took on. Not everyone could've done that.'

'Thanks, darling.' I hug her to me.

'Mummy, can our babies be born somewhere cool, like a car, or a double-decker bus, or on a train, maybe a plane?' Hugo asks.

'Absolutely not. And for the record, H, being born in a vehicle is not cool.' I make a mental note to tell Fabien I'm not travelling any further than a ten-mile radius from the house until after the birth, not that a short distance from home mattered in Sam's case.

The day's spent alternately resting and informing people. Erik stops by to give us an update. He looks exhausted so we invite him to stay for dinner. His mother-in-law has kept the kids. We've also offered to have them here tomorrow if it helps him or his mum-in-law out.

'Mummy, can we write our letter to Santa today?' Aria asks.

I glance at the calendar. Such a lot has happened in twenty-four hours. This time yesterday we hadn't even seen Mum for her birthday.

'Sure, go bring me some paper and an envelope from my office.'

She pads off obediently, one of the few times she does anything she's asked, first time.

'So, what do you want to write?' I ask.

'Well, Mummy, I was hoping you would write it, if I tell you the words.'

'OK, fair enough. Why don't you want to write it yourself?'

'Mummy–' she looks at me as if I'm really dim '–I'm five, and my writing is not very good, so I worry Santa won't know what it says, and I really want a Little Live Pets pig.'

'Ah, I see. OK, well, give me your paper and pen, and you tell me.'

'Thanks, Mummy.' She beams at me. 'Ready?'

I nod that I'm ready.

Dear Santa

How are you? I hope you are not too cold. Mummy told me the North Pole is as cold as inside our freezer. I've checked. You don't live in our freezer. I asked Hugo to check too, but he didn't find you either. Do you need new gloves? I was thinking about sending you a present. Maybe you could send me your list.

How is Mrs Claus? She always looks very happy

and jolly, but I think sometimes you annoy her, as sometimes you are late for dinner. Try to be on time.

For Christmas I would like a Little Live Pets pig; a Barbie Dreamhouse; a new tea set – I'm getting a bit old for the one I have; a new scooter (the one I have I got when I was three, and now I've grown and it doesn't fit); Princess Jasmine and Mulan Lego and some books about wizards and dragons.

Thank you Santa, and Merry Christmas.

I'll try to get Mummy and Daddy to leave the chocolate chip cookies like last year. I really liked those ones. And I'll leave three carrots for Rudolf.

Lots of love, Aria Halliday xx xx xx

I smile. She really is such a chatterbox, but her heart is in the right place, as is borne out with her checking on everyone's health and well-being. I think to the future. She is so going to mother these two babies. Good, if she can start bottle feeding one expressed milk, then I can feed the other one. Will save me some time. Chance would be a fine thing.

'So, what do you think, Mummy? Can I see the letter, please?'

I show it to her and she tries to read it.

'I think Santa will be delighted to receive such a lovely letter, although perhaps he will only be able to get some of the things on your list. He does have to keep some toys for other children.'

Aria frowns. 'But I didn't ask for half as much as Tatyana or Cleo.'

'What they ask for is up to them and their families, but I think we need to be realistic. If you have too many toys, someone in another country gets fewer toys and sometimes none.'

I'm trying to appeal to Aria's sense of fair play as she mulls this over and then says, 'Well, I don't want someone to have no toys, although it is OK if they have fewer toys, as at least they'll still have something to play with.'

I can't fault her argument, at least not to her face.

'Let's address the envelope later. Hugo, your turn. I know you won't need me to write it for you, but have you any idea what you might like?'

'Well,' he says shyly, 'I *would* like the new Minecraft and there are these really cool laser guns I saw. I thought maybe Xander and me, or Aria and me, could play with those. Maybe some new art stuff.'

'Great, sounds like you know what to put in your letter. Will you let me know when you're done and then we'll put it in an envelope and post it off to the North Pole?'

Hugo nods then I hear Aria ask Gen why she isn't writing to Santa.

'Oh, I email him,' Gen replies airily. I hide a smile. Well deflected, Gen.

I'm about to check over Hugo's letter when it hits me, I haven't told Ronnie the good news yet. With everything that's been going on, I haven't had a chance.

I walk into the kitchen where Ronnie is making dinner.

He looks up from the pot of ragú he's stirring. 'Hey.' He smiles and my heart skips.

'Hey. I forgot to tell you something last night.'

'I don't know if I can take any more revelations. Sam

wasn't having twins as well, was she?'

I chuckle. 'No, nothing like that, but I did get a letter yesterday before all the drama unfolded.'

'Oh?'

I pass it to him. As he reads, his lips curve upwards and his smile widens the further he reads. He glances up at me. 'The eighteenth.'

'Yep,' I say.

'In before Christmas?'

'Looks like it.'

He comes towards me and hugs me tight. 'It's all going in the right direction.'

I lay my head on his shoulder. 'It's about time.'

Chapter Sixteen

Sunday 28 November

To-do list
Iron kids' Sunday clothes
Ensure all homework is done for tomorrow
Catch up with Wedded Bliss correspondence
Send off new designs to Fabien
Order winter bulbs – pansies – for Aria for school
Start packing for the move
Call Benedict

'Are you sure, Mum?' I ask as we're having our coffee at Solitude. 'You don't mind us all rushing off?'

She raises her eyes to the heavens. 'You're hardly rushing off. We've been here nearly three hours.'

'I know, but it's your birthday celebration.'

'Lou, I'll have plenty more of them too. Now, are you taking my grandchildren to see the Christmas lights being switched on, or not? It's tradition.'

She's right. Ever since Ronnie and I moved into Ferniehall, we've always gone to the switching on of the lights. It's still a relatively quiet affair compared with some of the showier spectacles in some of the towns, but I think it suits our little village. Understated but classy. No Z-list celebrity cutting a ribbon for us. We have the local councillor, who's very well respected. We're lucky to have her, and we know it.

There are no stalls or anything in the streets like we had for the scarecrow festival, instead the whole of Main Street makes a huge effort. It's like a Christmas wonderland. Decorations hang from the street lights, criss-crossing bells, candy canes and gingerbread men, from one side to the other, but it's the non-council-provided decorations which win my, and the village's, approval.

Each shop window is dressed to perfection, and each year there's a new theme. The village shop owners' cooperative meet a couple of times a year and this is one of the items they discuss: the Christmas theme.

This year it's a snowman theme, so there are all sorts of snowmen in the windows, as well as other Christmas decorations, but snowmen have the edge, and are placed in the most prominent positions. There's also a snowman trail, where the children can pick up a leaflet in any of the participating shops and spot a particular snowman either in the shop or on the outside, as well as a few in the village itself. The kids love it. Last year it was a gingerbread-man trail, the year before a nutcracker trail. I quite enjoy it myself actually.

I can't wait to see what antics the snowmen get up to. It's a bit like Elf on the Shelf, but with a new theme each year, and it's the shops and businesses who create the chaos, not the parents, although obviously there's nothing to stop families decorating their homes in this way too.

One of the main outdoor locations is the park, just down from where we live now, since it's the biggest outdoor space in the village, and with its bandstand, it's the nearest we have to a village green, and it's the best focal point for villagers. The village Christmas tree is also erected right outside the park gates.

It doesn't take long for us to arrive back in Ferniehall, about forty minutes, so Wendy and I park the cars up at the house, our offspring nip to the loo, as do I, and then we head down to the park, where we can already hear the excited voices of dozens of children.

'How much longer, Mummy?' Aria asks.

'Aria, we just got here,' I say.

'I know, but I want to see the lights.'

I smile and Ronnie ruffles her curls. 'We all do, angel, but we have to be patient.'

Aria folds her arms. 'I don't want to wait.'

'Aria.' My warning tone must have some effect on her as she drops her arms by her sides and sneaks round beside Gen and starts whispering to her. I'm sure my ears would be burning if I could hear her. She has to learn that she can't assume everything will happen when she wants it to and she mustn't go in a strop if it doesn't fit in with her expectations.

'I hope they hurry up,' says Wendy. 'Lyla needs the toilet again. Honestly.' She rolls her eyes. 'Nothing is ever simple.'

I grin. 'Life would be boring if it were.'

'I like boring,' says Wendy. 'In fact, I aspire to boring.'

I laugh. 'Yeah, well, good luck with that, as you may be waiting some time.'

A cheer goes up and the councillor steps up to the mic.

'Good evening, everyone. Thank you for turning out in such numbers on this glorious November evening.'

'Is she having a laugh?' I ask Wendy. 'It's going to bucket at any minute.'

Wendy sniggers. 'I know. And what does she mean "glorious", it's pitch dark, it's not as if we can see the sunset, or the shops all lit up, because they aren't yet.'

Aria turns round and looks at us sharply. 'Shh.'

Wendy's eyes widen. Yeah, a five-year-old did just shush us. I'll need to remind her who's the adult once these lights go on.

The councillor thanks various members of the shop owners' cooperative, and then says, 'Drum roll, please!' Laughter ripples through the crowd, then after everyone's impromptu drum roll, the councillor proclaims, 'Let's light this village up. Happy festive season, everyone.'

'Wow!' Hugo is impressed.

The tree, which I haven't paid much attention to until now is fabulous. Soft cream lights adorn it, fake wooden and stone presents lie under it. Fairy lights are strung through it too. And there are a few little wooden messages hanging from its branches.

'You may notice that the schoolchildren of the village have written their Christmas wishes and thanks for everyone on the wooden heart ornaments – this isn't their list to Santa, but rather what we as villagers believe is good about our village and what possibly we could add to it to make it even better. The children have worked so hard on choosing the right words for theirs. Please join them in adding yours. There are boxes of hearts where you can write your wish sitting at the foot of the tree. Thank you.'

'Look at the angel at the top of the tree, Mummy. She looks like the one we have. Can we put our tree up when we get home?'

November's a bit early for me. I know it's only a few more days, but I think we've had an exciting enough weekend. Adding anything else to it may send me over the edge.

'Let's wait until next week, Aria, because I believe you're making decorations at school and I want yours to go on the tree.'

'Hmm.' She frowns and puts a finger to her lips. 'We could put the tree up today and add my decorations later.'

'Hmm.' I mirror her response. 'But yours will be special and I'd like them to be there from the moment the tree goes up,' I say, my lips downturned slightly.

She stands taller. 'You're right, Mummy, mine are special. OK, we'll wait until next week.'

I think it'd be easier negotiating a treaty than trying to get Aria to settle for something she didn't want to, so I'm enjoying my win here.

We walk along Main Street in the direction of our own house, so that Wendy and the kids can admire the shops lit up with their snowmen and so Wendy can see how close our house is to being ready. I'd broken the news at mum's birthday lunch about us being able to move back in soon, and everyone was delighted, not least the cousins. They love our house, although they've also come to love our new temporary home too, particularly the garden.

But I've been meaning to talk to Wendy ever since I made the announcement, as her reaction was a bit odd. She almost bristled, as if she was annoyed about it, which can't be right. So as we walk along the road, the younger kids with the dads, the slightly older ones walking ahead of us, peering in the windows to see which shops have which snowmen and what they're up to, I decide to try to figure out what's going on with her. I'm beginning to have a sense of foreboding. I cross my fingers and pray no one's ill. She wouldn't keep that from me surely.

'Wendy, this may not be the best time or place, but there never seems to be a good time or place,' I say as Mollie interrupts, 'Look, Mummy, this snowman has three snow babies.'

Wendy agrees with Mollie, giving the snowmen a quick smile then shoots me a quizzical look. 'OK?'

'Have I done something to upset you?'

Wendy's face falls. 'What?' she asks as her mask slips back into place. 'No, nothing.'

'Wendy, I've always known when you're lying, and now you're worrying me, because even though it's been a long time since you have, you're lying now. What's going on? You've been really distant lately, and less…supportive. Sorry, but I needed to say that.'

Wendy remains silent.

'Look,' I stress, 'I'm not trying to spoil the day.' She raises her eyebrows at that. 'But I don't feel as if we're as connected as usual, and if I'm honest, it's been like this for months. What is it? What's wrong?'

She pauses as if she's debating something with herself and then says, 'Not here,' like some gangland moll.

'Fine. Where then? When?' Now I'm the one who sounds like she's engaged in nefarious underworld activities, instead of just trying to get my sister to tell me the truth.

'We'll come back to yours for a bit, then you and I can say we need to nip out for something.'

'OK…' Now it's my turn to raise my eyebrows. I hope she doesn't have any meetings planned in supermarket car parks where dodgy parcels are exchanged.

Once the kids have oohed and aahed over the snowmen in all the shops, and those in the park, I say, 'Right, it's getting cold now. Who's for some hot chocolate?'

'Me! Me! Me!' come the replies.

'Right then, everyone back to the house.'

We quick march back to the house, Main Street notably emptier than at the switch-on. Most people have gone indoors out of the cold. The wind has picked up and the smell in the air tells me rain isn't far off. I should have been a weathergirl, I'm good at this stuff.

The kids gather round whilst I make the hot chocolate in the pan, their favourite way, and Wendy helps add marshmallows, cream and other accoutrements depending on everyone's personal tastes. Even Ronnie and Brandon have some, much to my surprise. In fact, it feels like a lovely family moment, and I'm loth to leave it, but I'm dying to know what Wendy's about to tell me, so I say, 'Oh, we're running out of marshmallows. Ronnie, can you take care of things here? I'm just nipping to Tesco.'

'No worries. Who wants more hot chocolate?' he asks as he starts to stir. Shouts of 'Me' abound and hands are raised, some of our offspring clearly more used to being at school or nursery and forgetting they don't need to do so at home.

'Oh, Wendy, didn't you say you forgot something in your Asda order?' I say pointedly.

'Yeah, that's right. I'll come with you.'

'What did you forget?' Brandon asks as we pass him.

Wendy starts, caught out for a second, then recovers well with 'Oven cleaner.' She smiles sweetly at him. 'Back in a tick.'

As we collect our coats in the hall, Brandon says to

Ronnie, 'Oven cleaner? I was sure we paid a company to come clean our oven.'

Wendy and I look at each other and edge out of the front door.

We do actually go to Tesco, as I don't want us to go home empty-handed, and we go in straightaway as they close soon. When we come out, we sit in the car, in the deserted car park like a couple of dodgy dealers.

'So, Wen, what's going on?'

Wendy's face is pinched and drawn, and her eyes fill with tears. 'Brandon's been offered a promotion.'

'But that's great news. Congratulations.'

She shakes her head. 'No, you don't understand, the company's merging with a bigger one, and they're moving him.'

'Where to?' Their head office is in Edinburgh, so he'd still be able to commute.

'Swindon. That's where the other company's head office is.'

'No! Oh no, Wen, you're not moving to Swindon, are you?' I clutch at straws. Of course she's moving to Swindon. She's hardly going to let her husband move and not go with him.

But the three of us, Wen, Jo and I have never been further than twenty or thirty miles from each other for more than a couple of weeks at a time, and that's when we go on holiday, and often we're together on those. No, they can't be moving to Swindon. It's so far away.

She looks utterly wretched.

'When?'

'March. I don't need to bother about putting the house up for sale yet as the company will deal with it all, as it's a relocation, but it will be sometime early next year.'

'I can't believe it. Oh, Wendy, I'll miss you so much.'

'And I you.' She leans across the gearstick and hugs me. 'And I can't believe I won't be here to see the twins grow up each week. I've tried to think of every way possible for us not to have to move, but there are no comparable jobs going in Brandon's line of work right now.'

'But what about your job? You worked so hard for that promotion.'

She sighs. 'I know, and I'm gutted, but frankly, you know I don't need to work, although I still will.' She adds rather sheepishly, 'Brandon's increase in salary for this move is more than my annual salary.'

'You're joking.'

She shakes her head. 'I wish I were. If I was, it would be easier to convince Brandon to turn this job down. But he'd basically be heading up a new and bigger division than he does right now, in the heart of the new company.'

'But what about the kids? School?'

'That's tearing me up, but Brandon's, as ever, more clinical and practical about these things. He says they'll adapt easily enough and it's just us who worry. By that he means me,' she says dryly.

'Oh Wendy, I don't know what I'll do without you.' I hug her and she hugs me back.

We pull apart and she says, 'You're sitting on the marshmallows.' We laugh, but we both know she's trying to make light of a sad situation.

As we drive home, I can't help but feel that a little part of my heart has been ripped from me, and I fear I'll never be completely whole again.

Chapter Seventeen

Saturday 4 December

To-do list
Write cards
Buy more cards for children to send to friends
Book to see Santa
Order Christmas food
Start buying presents
Ensure Aria's costume doesn't get damaged in the car and that we have all the bits for it
Check in with Sam to see if she has any news re when getting home

'Keep Hogmanay free,' Nicky says down the phone.

'Why?'

'Because Valentin and I are having an engagement party!' she squeals.

'Hurrah! I assume we can bring the kids.'

'Well, apart from the fact I want them there, you'll get arrested if you leave them at home,' she says mildly.

'Fair point. So, when did this all come about?'

'We were just talking the other night and Valentin said he'd really like to celebrate our engagement, shout it from the rooftops if he could, and asked if he could set it up. It's going to be at one of his posh but understated places. Luxurious but not poncy.'

'Like Hotel du Vin.'

'Yes, but not, as that isn't part of their restaurant group.'

'Indeed. Sounds fabulous. Wow, a real party with people who aren't family at New Year!'

'Oh no, I'm inviting your family too: your mum and dad, Wendy and the gang, Jo and her lot.'

'Please tell me you're not inviting Annabelle,' I say.

'Ha! Would I do that to you?' she asks.

'Depends what mood you're in,' I joke.

'Now for that comment, I just might. Anyway, that's my news. Are you all ready for Aria's big moment? Your little star.'

'My little star with a big attitude and a big head at the minute.'

'Aw, let her enjoy her fame.'

'Fame? She seems to think I'm her agent, or skivvy. She keeps telling me how she's going to be the best star there's ever been. Someone at drama club, one of the well-meaning adults, told her so.'

Nicky laughs. 'Make sure you're on hand to deal with any stalker fans, hold back those looking for a selfie with her and put her many buckets of flowers in water for her, will you?'

'Ha bloody ha. Honestly, with everything else Christmas entails, having this to deal with too is the icing on the cake.'

'Speaking of that, do you think Marjorie at Icing on the Cake would make me an engagement cake?'

'I'm sure she will. Do you want me to say something to her? I'm nipping along to Martha's shortly as Brett's leaving today. He and Ronnie are going for lunch whilst I do the matinee show with her ladyship, Hugo in tow, and then Ronnie's taking her to the evening show, with Gen for company.'

Nicky blows out a breath. 'Two shows in one day is quite a lot for a wee one that age. She'll be wrecked.'

'That's why I only wanted her to be the star at the weekends! Can you imagine her going to school the next day? She'd be like a deflated balloon.'

Nicky chuckles. 'Right, I'll see you later at the show. Best get ready. Don't forget to talk to Marjorie.'

I roll my eyes, even though she can't see me. 'I won't.'

'Of course I'll make her cake? For Hogmanay, you say? Aw, that's very romantic, isn't it?' Marjorie says, when I ask her if she can accept Nicky's commission.

'It might be quite grand,' I say. 'Her boyfriend's Valentin Pendragon.'

'Ooh! The Pendragon boy. Very easy on the eye. He's a keeper, one of the good ones.'

'I know. He's been wonderful for Nicky. They're totally loved up.'

'Aw, that's lovely. You tell her to message me anytime, with her requirements. And if she scans this–' she takes out a business card featuring a QR code '–it'll take her to my website with the cakes I've done recently.'

'Marjorie, when did you get all tech savvy? I don't even have a QR code on my website!'

'My nephew showed me. I was giving him odd jobs to

do to try to help him save up for a school trip to Italy. His mum said she'd pay half, but not all, so give him his due, he's been asking around to do odd jobs. Then I saw one of them QR things somewhere the other week and I asked him about it. I'm quite pleased with the results, actually.'

'And so you should be,' I say, as I scan through. 'He really has a knack for showing things off to maximise their potential.'

Marjorie narrows her eyes. 'I hope that's not your way of saying my product's not much cop and he's having to make it look good.'

'Oh, no, not at all,' I backtrack.

Marjorie wags a finger at me. 'Ha! Had you good and proper there. I'm only teasing. Now, can I get you anything else today?'

'Yes, I'll take two of your Sicilian lemon cheesecakes and a Belgian bun.'

'You're off to Martha's, aren't you?'

'Yeah, how'd you know?'

'Because Brett has been in here most days for a Belgian bun. Says they don't get them in Oz. Lovely boy. He told me yesterday he's flying back today.'

'Yeah. I'm going over to say cheerio. He's off out for lunch with Ronnie later, as he has a late flight.'

'I noticed they've become friendly. At least something positive came out of Martha's fall.'

'Indeed, and I can't wait until the eighteenth when we're back next door again. That way I'll always know she's OK, or at least I can check in on her.'

'You're not wrong there. We'll all sleep more easily. Hard when they get a bit older, isn't it? Not to worry about them, I mean.'

'Yep. Right, I'll see you in the week.'

'Don't forget–'

'I won't! I'm seeing Nicky this afternoon for Aria's theatre show. I'll tell her then.'

'Fair enough. Bye for now.'

I raise my hand to wave and then head down towards Martha's.

An air of dejection projects from the doorway the minute Martha opens the door, and I enfold her in my embrace.

'He'll be back soon,' I say.

'I know,' she says, 'but I'm an old woman. I won't be here forever.'

'Martha, you'll outlive almost everyone you grew up with, your spirit's so indomitable!'

'It doesn't always feel it though,' she says sadly. 'I'm going to miss him so much.'

'I know.' I rub her back. 'Listen, why don't I collect you later when I get back from the theatre? You can come to ours, and me, you and Gen can watch *It's a Wonderful Life*. Hugo too, if he wants, although I will warn you, he's likely only to come in for the snacks, then disappear to the playroom to play his Xbox.'

'If you're sure I wouldn't be imposing,' she says.

I give her an 'as if' expression.

'Well, that would be lovely, Louisa, thank you.'

A noise from upstairs has us pulling apart and Martha wipes her tears from her face just in time as Brett wanders in.

'Hey, Louisa, Aria all set to be the star of the show?' He grins.

I shake my head. 'Dad jokes. Honestly, if she were here

she'd be telling you so too. And yes, she is. Worryingly so.'

He tilts his head to the side. 'Oh?'

I exhale heavily. 'She's becoming quite the diva.'

'Ahh. Anyway–' he casts around as if for another subject, then rubs his hands together, smiling '–is Ronnie ready for the Last Supper?'

'Are you sure you aren't glad he's leaving, Martha? These jokes are awful.'

'That they are,' she says, glancing from me to Brett, 'and I love every one of them.'

'No, Martha, you're getting mixed up with every hair on his head.'

'Oh, so I am. Yes, Brett, you need to work on your patter. Your jokes are terrible.'

Martha and I burst out laughing and Brett holds his heart then his side as if we've mortally wounded him.

'Anyway, Brett, safe travels, lovely to see you again. Make sure it's not so long before the next trip.'

'Thanks, Louisa. It's been great being back here with Mum and all of you. You look after those little ones–' he gestures to my stomach '–and the other three. And please don't have any more, as you're making me look bad.'

Martha holds up a hand. 'I've said nothing.'

'Bye, Brett, see you later, Martha.'

'Aria, sit still so I can strap you in,' I say. We have plenty of time, I tell myself, but her star costume is so elaborate it takes up the entire boot of my car. She's absolutely hyper, as if she's found and eaten an entire packet of original Skittles.

Hugo is playing some noisy game on his iPad.

'Hugo, can you turn that down, please?' I ask.

'It's that loud, Mum.'

One, two, three, four, five, six.

'Turn it down,' I say at a marginally higher volume than usual, definitely not a shout.

'OK, OK,' he says sulkily.

Tough. I'd love to sulk, but no one would even notice.

Twenty minutes later, we arrive at the theatre car park to discover that not only are there no spaces, but people are double-parked all over the place. The traffic wardens will be sharpening their pencils with glee. Where the hell am I going to park though?

I glide down side street after side street, go into council car park after council car park. I'm so far away from the theatre, I'm in danger of being closer walking from home. Well, not quite, but I'm nearly half a mile away. This is ridiculous. Eventually, I decide, sod it, if I can't beat them, I'll have to join them. My girl's the star of the show, literally, she has the five points to prove it, so I pull the car up onto a kerb and leave it there.

We make it to the stage door with five minutes to spare, to much clucking by the owner of the drama school, as I chivvy Aria into her costume, amidst apologies and explanations about being unable to park.

Hugo and I barely have time to take our seats before the curtain raises and out come the performers in the first act.

I'm not really sure what the story's meant to be. I mean, it's not as bad as the nativity in *Love Actually*, with octopuses. In fact, this isn't a nativity, but it does have three wise men, a couple of donkeys – and that's me being polite – a few angels, and Aria the star. In addition, it has a young boy, doing some sort of feel-good gangsta rap, someone playing the part of a YouTuber, another playing an influencer, and Green Lantern and Thanos from the superhero movies have roles too. The mind boggles.

Aria's set isn't until near the end, but when she comes on stage, in her all blonde-curled glory, she literally lights up the stage. I say literally because they've put a spotlight behind her to outline her.

And she glows, not aided by light, but with happiness. My youngest, my angel, well, star, at the moment. She's fabulous. When she sings, it brings tears to my eyes, tears of pride, not those of frustration that she won't stop as is often the case at home when she's humming or singing some dirge off YouTube. The difficulty of having older kids is your younger kids are exposed to so much more tripe, so much sooner.

I glance across at Hugo, who is clapping away as if he's being paid a pound for every clap. I guess he's enjoying his wee sister's show. The twins have been active during the show. They must like the music, or perhaps it's because I've been sitting on my butt doing nothing for a while. That doesn't happen very often. It's the same as in bed, at night, when I try to go to sleep – that's when they wake up and party.

When the show finishes and the lights go up, Hugo says, 'That was really cool. Aria was fantastic.'

I smile. 'She was, wasn't she? Make sure you tell her.' Then I wish for a sec, I hadn't said that, as we'll never hear the end of it. And she still has another three shows to go, including another tonight. I wonder if she'll manage a nap in the car whilst I take her home for dinner.

'Mummy, Mummy, what did you think?' Aria runs up

to us the moment I walk into the backstage area.

I bend down and wrap my arms around her. 'I thought you were wonderful.'

'Really?' Her eyes shine.

'Really.'

'Yeah, like really wonderful,' says Hugo, coming up behind me then hugging her. 'But wasn't the rapper sick?'

I leave them to chat whilst my eyes seek out Nicky and Xander. They were a few rows behind us, I think, but with us arriving later than planned, I didn't have a chance to look for them.

I text Nicky. *We're backstage, if you want to come join us, or if you're free for a bit after and not doing anything with Valentin, come over. I've asked Martha to come watch* It's a Wonderful Life.

A few seconds later, my phone rings. 'We're in the foyer,' says Nicky. 'Will we meet you back at yours? Valentin's up at his grandfather's at the moment.'

'Cool. See you there. I'm picking Martha up on the way. Ronnie was running Brett to the airport after they had lunch, so I thought tonight might be tough for Martha.'

'Yeah, poor thing. Right, see you in a bit.'

'How come we've never watched this film before, Mum?' asks Hugo. 'It's really good.'

'I've seen it before,' Gen says, leaning down for more popcorn. 'About five times. Mum and I watch it every Christmas.'

'Where was I?' Hugo asks, scrunching his eyes up.

'Playing Xbox,' Gen and I say in unison.

Everyone laughs.

'Mum and I watch it every Christmas, don't we,

Mum?' Xander beams, as if proud of the fact.

Nicky nods. 'I love it. One of my favourite Christmas films.'

'Evening all.' Ronnie comes in, hands in his jeans pockets.

'Did he get off OK then?' Martha says, her eyes misty.

'Flight was still showing as on time when he left to go through Security, so yeah.'

'Did you have a nice lunch?' Martha asks.

'We did, thanks. All the better because Brett paid,' he jokes.

'Oh, you! Ronnie, you're a terror.' Martha bats him on the arm.

Ronnie smiles. 'Anyone want a drink, or–' he gestures to the coffee table which is covered in snack dishes '–a snack? If there are any left, that is.'

I smother a smile.

Ronnie sits with us for a bit. Just as well we have a large living room and we watch *It's a Wonderful Life* until he declares it's time for Aria to get ready, so I redo her hair and clean her up a bit and send her out to do it all over again.

'Have fun,' I say to Gen, as she shrugs on her leather jacket and follows Aria and Ronnie to the car.

'Glass of wine, Martha?'

She goes to protest, but I say, 'Someone has to keep Nicky company, and it can't be me.'

She gives a small smile and I take that as a yes.

When I return with the drinks, she's deep in conversation with Nicky about her engagement.

'That's wonderful and yes, I'd be honoured to come, thanks for asking me.'

I exchange a glance with Nicky. Nothing will make Brett's departure make Martha feel whole, but I hope being amongst friends and being included will go some way to alleviating her pain and loneliness.

Friday 10 December

To-do list

Buy more packing tape

Ask at Tesco if they have any boxes I could have – am running out fast

Buy engagement present for Nicky and Valentin – or at least get some ideas and save them to Pinterest. What do you buy the superrich?

Buy stamps for UK cards and post those going abroad – last posting date before Christmas is around this time I'm sure

Arrange boiler check for our house – should've done it earlier. Don't want the pipes freezing.

Check if Martha wants me to send anything to Brett – must definitely be last post for Australia, although maybe she gave him his card and present before he left

Order Christmas party clothes for the kids – consult Aria and Hugo on theirs

I stand and survey the boxes around me. That's it, after this we are never moving again, at least not until the children have left home. How can we have accumulated so much stuff in a few short months? Imagine if we had to move all our furniture and other belongings from our house, how much time that would take, and effort. I dread the thought. As I seal another box with packing tape, I promise myself to stop buying so much stuff. There. That'll have to do for now. I have a nativity play to go to. At least this time Aria doesn't have the starring role. She's a sheep. So this time I can sit back and relax and enjoy the show. Mum's coming too as Ronnie's working, and Aria was fizzing with excitement at that news. I'm just a boring old mum. I don't get as many points on the cool-o-meter as a nana does.

I go downstairs to the dining room where Mum is working on some Wedded Bliss invoices.

'How you getting on? We need to leave in about fifteen minutes.'

'More or less caught up. These have to go in the post later.' She indicates a couple of parcels. 'Samples. Do you want a cup of tea before we go?'

I nod and Mum does the honours whilst I tidy a few things away. I remember before I had kids my house used to look like a show home. I can't recall the last time everything was in its place. A stray sock, or a football card, or a unicorn necklace always seem to make their way onto the table, shelf, floor. I sigh as I try to find homes for the items I pick up.

'I'm really looking forward to this,' says Mum as she brings back the drinks.

'Me too,' I say as I accept a cup from her. 'I'm particularly looking forward to there being no pressure involved.'

Mum laughs. 'Yes, being the star of the panto kind of went to her head a little.'

'A little? She was unbearable. She was offering to sign autographs last week in the playground. And she was exhausted after each show too.'

'She did well, though,' Mum says.

'Oh, I know she did, and I was amazed Behind the Mask chose her for that role, given she's only been going a few months.'

Mum grins. 'She obviously made an impression.'

'Yeah, she does that.' I roll my eyes and we laugh.

'So, who's going to your Christmas lunch tomorrow?' She's meeting some friends at the Four Springs Hotel in Hamwell for their annual Christmas bash.

'Just a few of the girls from book club and I invited Martha too. A couple of the others are bringing friends, and I thought it would be nice for her to have something else to do.'

I sigh. 'I haven't seen her the past couple of days. I can't believe in eight more days, we'll be back in our own house, and neighbours again.'

Mum nods. 'This rebuild has seemed to stretch on forever. It'll be good to have you all back home again. I'm curious to see if anything will have changed.'

'Me too, although I'm assured it hasn't. Actually, I'll miss this place.' Mum goes to interrupt, but I say, 'Not that I don't want to go home, I do, but this house has borrowed a little piece of my heart.'

'I know what you mean. It is a lovely house, but at least Benedict, his son and Tiziana will have somewhere permanent to live so he can provide them with a stable home.'

'I met him yesterday in town. He's been talking to the lawyers again. He really isn't having a fun time with it all.'

'No, I can only imagine, poor thing. Well, at least he and Tiziana will also be in by Christmas. I think he said she'll move to the school in January too.'

'Really? Oh that would be great for her. It's such a

good school, and Aria could take her under her wing. I didn't realise that. I'll talk to him about that when I see him next.'

'So, on another note, what do you want me to get the kids for Christmas? I'm late doing my shopping this year.'

'I'm not surprised. You're almost single-handedly running Wedded Bliss, so you've no time!'

Mum waves away my comment. 'I am not. Anyway, kids, presents.' She holds my gaze, willing me to answer. I have no idea. They have so much. It's always a fine balance ensuring they have enough to open, whilst not bankrupting us, especially now Hugo and Gen are older and their presents cost a lot more per item. No longer can we buy them plastic toys at twenty quid each which are half the size they are. Hugo's Xbox games start around forty quid, and Gen's clothes are eye-wateringly expensive and gadgets start at three figures.

'Vouchers?' I suggest lamely.

Mum's lips form a thin line. Not vouchers then.

'How about an experience? Tickets for something they'd really like.'

Her eyes brighten at that. 'That's a possibility. Except Aria. She's too young for that.'

She waits as if expecting an answer to miraculously drop into my lap.

'I'll come back to you on Aria.' I glance at my watch. 'Oh, is that the time? We'd better go.'

It's raining so we take the car. A queue of parents snakes around the outside of the school. Are they honestly not letting us in yet despite the weather? C'mon.

Eventually, when those without umbrellas or hoods are totally bedraggled, the office staff let us in and indicate we should head for the gym hall where the nativity will be held.

The children file in five minutes later, class by class, all of primary one to three. There must be a hundred and fifty or so in total. Aria searches the audience for us and when she spots us she waves vigorously, her mouth stretching into a smile.

She looks so cute and small up there besides her peers. A teacher has directed her to the top bench, which sits in front of the stage. It never ceases to amaze me how much noise young children can make, and as if excited by the chatter, the twins start to perform a little dance inside me. 'This will be you one day,' I tell them telepathically.

The show starts and I have to congratulate the casting director, who I know is the primary three teacher. The dynamic between Mary and Joseph is hysterical. I don't think the nativity is meant to be a comedy per se, but you'd never know it with these two. They should be a double act on primetime TV.

Baby Jesus nearly gets dropped on his head about four times, before the birth, as the 'baby' keeps slipping out of the little girl's costume. I'm guessing the teacher thought having a doll inside a flap of the costume was a good idea, but I think she may revise that for next year. One of the shepherds gets his crook stuck on a piece of the set and almost brings it crashing down on himself. Fortunately, the headteacher gets a hand to it just in time. One of the three wise men, a P1 by the looks of it, bursts into tears and runs off the stage, the pressure obviously having got to him.

The kids mainly seem to be enjoying themselves, though, which is the main thing, and the songs are fun. Overall, I'd say the production is a success.

Wait, is Aria sleeping? Oh my God, she is. I stifle a giggle and nudge Mum. 'Look at Aria. She's asleep.'

Mum checks it out and covers her mouth with a hand, whispering, 'That's those late nights from doing the panto catching up with her.'

'Look, she's leaning to the side. She's going to end up in that other wee girl's lap in a minute.' I try not to snort with laughter. It's too funny, plus, how can she sleep with all this noise around her?

Some of the other parents have noticed and murmurs and sniggers start to circulate, as the children bellow out yet another Christmas carol with their own – or their teachers' – twist to it.

Suddenly, Aria slumps to the side considerably more, and I frown. The girl next to her is almost hanging off the edge of the bench, which is three flights up. It's part of a set of stacked benches that can be stored away for convenience, but that means there's nothing supporting them on either side. Aria is second in from the end. She lists once more to the side and I try to warn the teacher, but she doesn't see me. I stand up. 'Aria! I shout to wake her, but to no avail. As if in slow motion, I watch the girl beside her topple off the bench and hit the ground with a smack and Aria follows suit.

Then there's screaming – the girl; and running – the teacher; and shrieking – Aria; and waddling – me. The piano plays a final, ominous note and the children's singing grinds to a halt as parents rush forward to see if they can help.

When I reach them, I see there's no blood, and the screaming is a good sign, I think, as I recall it's more serious from a head injury point of view if they're quiet. They could still have broken something as they fell though: an arm, a wrist.

I reach for Aria, who scrambles into my arms, her eyes wet with tears. 'Are you OK?'

She snuffles. 'Uh-huh. What happened? Why is Beatrix screaming? Why are we on the floor? Why is no one singing?'

I don't tell her that she fell asleep and knocked Beatrix off the bench unintentionally. I simply say, 'You and Beatrix fell off the bench. Are you definitely not hurt?'

She shakes her head.

'OK, let me see how Beatrix is.'

I turn to see the headteacher and another teacher tending to Beatrix. One of the parents in the audience is a doctor and has come forward to check her over and assess the damage. But as she reaches her, Beatrix bursts out laughing.

'I think we have a fit of the giggles here.' The doctor smiles at me. 'Pretty sure she just got a fright. And–' she points to the floor '–the gym mats probably helped.'

Once Beatrix has sufficiently recovered, and with a helping hand up, the teachers deem it's time for the show to go on.

As we watch the rest of the performance, I can't help but think that my girl always has to steal the show, even in her sleep.

Chapter Eighteen

Saturday 18 December

To-do list
Check all drawers, cupboards
Take elec and gas readings and submit
Diarise to speak to council about our council tax now we're moving back
Diarise to undo redirection of mail
Oh, stuff it, the rest can wait! We're going home!

It's moving day! I can't believe it. It's finally here. Bear and Patch already seem to know something's going on. They've been pacing back and forth in the living room since the minute they finished their breakfast. How come dogs always know these things? It's uncanny.

I sip my cup of actual coffee and go through my list, then add a sub-list of things not to forget like empty bins, lock windows, drop key in to Benedict, give bathrooms a final clean, run the hoover over. I know Benedict said he'll have a cleaning company come in to do a deep clean, but I don't want them thinking we're slovenly. I won't quite leave the house so clean you could eat your dinner off the floor, but it will be close.

Now that it's here, I'm so excited to see the house and to move back in. Will it feel different? Will it smell different? Will we feel different? I haven't had a flashback to the crash for ages, and I hope the fact it's Christmas means I'll be focusing only on the positives. As if in agreement, the babies move around. They're becoming more active now, not only when I go to bed. Maybe they're struggling with less room, although I'm told with two sacs, that doesn't happen.

My peace is soon shattered by Aria racing down the stairs. 'Mummy, Mummy, we're moving home today!' She clambers up onto my knee, throws her arms around my neck and snuggles in, as I inhale the scent of her baby shampoo. I kiss the top of her head and we cuddle for a moment as I say, 'Yes, we are, darling.' Pointless to ask her if she's looking forward to it, as she's buzzing.

Aria's shouting has clearly woken the kraken, as Ronnie stumbles downstairs, bleary-eyed. He stayed up late last night watching a zombie flick. I passed and went to bed to read. No zombie flicks for me, thank you very much. I'd never be able to sleep.

'Morning.' He yawns. For decorum, he's dressed in his striped navy PJ bottoms; he doesn't wear them in bed, and I note he's still a handsome man, maybe more so, at forty-one.

'Morning. Ready for the big move?'

His mouth downturns. 'As ready as I'll ever be for lugging all these boxes.' He turns to Aria then sits down beside her. 'Morning, angel. Fancy coming for a walk with me? I thought we could take Patch for a short walk in the park and then go along to Icing on the Cake to get some pastries. What do you think? Just me and you. Those guys–'

he raises a finger in the air, pointing upstairs '–they'll be sleeping for ages yet.'

She clambers off my lap and onto his. 'OK, Daddy, but first I'd like some warm milk, please.' She cuddles into him for a sec, gives him a kiss, then leans over to pick up the remote control.

I chuckle. 'That's you told.'

As he levers himself off the sofa, I say, 'Hey, if you're taking orders for the bar, I'll have a tea, thanks.'

His eyebrows raise and I smile sweetly. Wonder where Aria learned it from.

Fifteen minutes later, they leave for the village and as the door closes, the thud of footsteps on the stairs alerts me to Hugo being awake. A surge of love for him overwhelms me as he comes in, hair wild as if he's the son of a caveman rather than an engineer.

'Hi, Mum,' he says, before sitting down beside me and hugging me.

'Hi, darling. Sleep well?'

He nods. 'I had a really good dream. I was Captain America, Aria was Wonder Woman and Gen was Black Widow.'

I grin. He has such an active imagination. I wish I remembered my good dreams. Where are my dreams of Zac Efron, Kit Harington and Chris Hemsworth?

He grabs some breakfast and sits beside me, switching channels from the *My Little Pony* programme Aria was watching and flicking through until he settles on *Green Lantern.* That works for me. Ryan Reynolds is in it.

Bear lies at my feet and Patch sits on Hugo's knee once he finishes his cereal.

Eventually, Gen appears, at the same time as Aria and

Ronnie return with the pastries. That girl has a sixth sense.

'Mmm, those smell amazing,' she says, before she's even had a chance to wish us good morning.

'Well, I had to do something to mark our final morning in our temporary home,' Ronnie says. 'We need to celebrate every chance we get.'

Too true. Life throws us enough curveballs, let's at least celebrate each moment we can.

'Right, everyone in the car. Dad's following in his.' Ronnie will also make a few trips back and forth for everything else, but for now, he's in charge of transporting the dogs. Once kids, dogs, husband and myself are safely in the cars, we're off. Somehow it feels as momentous as walking down the aisle, this drive through the village, knowing that when we reach the end, a reward we've been waiting for these past few months will be waiting for us.

All the fairy lights and Christmas decorations we pass on Main Street as we head for the other end seem to be spurring us on, determined we should have a grand and cheerful entrance for our return home.

Ronnie enters the house first, just in case the workmen have left any stray nails or anything around, any electrical cables unwittingly not covered up. I smile at his protectiveness. Then it's all stations go. Everyone piles into the house, dogs with their tails wagging, kids shrieking with joy as they revisit their special places in the house, after which they retreat to their bedrooms and the playroom. With a pang, I realise, apart from his Xbox, Hugo doesn't really use the playroom to play in any more. Even in Benedict's house, that's all he did, especially since the majority of his things were still here. I wonder if he'll rediscover and enjoy playing with those toys. If not, they're going to the charity shop. It's Christmas in a week. That thought almost sends me over the edge. A move and then Christmas, whilst almost eight months pregnant? What was I thinking?

I walk around each of the rooms, rubbing the curtains between thumb and forefinger, checking for dust and dirt everywhere, but the insurance company had the house professionally cleaned yesterday in preparation for our return. The faint smell of beeswax lingers in the air. I rest my hands on the chairbacks in the dining room and simply absorb the essence of the room, drinking it in. Ronnie comes up behind me. He knows I've deliberately left this room until last. The living room. It's hard to obliterate the memory of a lorry embedded in your ceiling and pinning your friend to the wall, but here goes. I gulp as we open the door and then I'm in, we're in, Ronnie's arm around my shoulder. We look around. Ronnie, fortunately for him, wasn't here to witness the crash or the aftermath, only returning from the oilrig he was working on when he received the call. However, he'll know of the turbulence coursing through me right now. He puts his arms around me and kisses the top of my head.

'Well? How are you feeling?'

I exhale a breath I'd been holding in without realising. 'Mixed emotions. Glad to be back, but impossible not to think of what happened here.'

His hands grip mine tighter. 'This house holds all our good memories too. Let's concentrate on making more of those, particularly with our new extended family–' he rests his hands on my bump '–and hopefully we can keep any negative images at bay.'

I squeeze his hands in thanks.

The rest of the day passes in a blur of visits, texts wishing us well, phone calls doing the same, and the kids rediscovering the joy of their own home.

Nicky pops in around six, with Xander in tow. She hugs me and says, 'Let's get this over with.'

I don't know who's more nervous, her or me, as we push open the living room door. I hear her sharp intake of breath.

She stumbles to the side a little and I right her with a hand on her arm, providing support, both emotionally and physically. If it was hard for me to re-enter this room, I can't even begin to imagine how much strength it took for Nicky to do so.

'You OK?' I say.

She nods, almost imperceptibly. 'I will be. It just hit me for a second. How lucky I am to be alive.'

I know what she means. I sometimes think the same thing.

Ronnie brings us some tea through whilst Xander plays Junior Trivial Pursuit with Hugo and Gen. We haven't set the Xbox up yet, and it's good to see them showing an interest in something other than video games for a change.

'Thanks, Ronnie,' Nicky says as he hands her the tea. 'You should stay for this update, well, part of it, too.'

'Oh?' he says.

'Yes, Valentin has arranged for the engagement party to be at the Milburn Hotel in Glasgow. It's that new one, you know, the quirky boutique one on Great Western Road.'

'No,' says Ronnie. He wouldn't as he doesn't move in those circles, but I do.

'Yep, it's on one of the terraces set back from the road.'

'That's the one.' Nicky beams. 'We went a few nights ago to see it, and I really liked it. Anyway, should be perfect for the party. It's all self-contained so no need to worry about little bodies inadvertently escaping.'

'That's a relief,' I say, meaning it. Aria can be tricky that way. If she's not enjoying herself, she's likely to make her thoughts known, or try to leave to do something better. 'But how did he manage to get it at such short notice?'

Nicky raises her eyebrows. 'You really need to ask? He's a Pendragon. Everyone owes him favours. It's like currency to their kind.'

I concede the point and talk soon turns to the details of the party. Nicky apologises for not asking me to make the invitations, but says since it's so soon and I have such a lot on anyway, they decided to use the designer Valentin uses for the business and have a rush print job done too.

I wave away her apology as unnecessary. She's right. I wouldn't have wanted anything else dropped in my lap at this late stage. We have a considerable amount of unpacking to do and I promised Aria we'd do the tree 'real soon'.

'So, what's been happening with your compensation?' I ask her.

She shakes her head. 'I feel as if we're taking two steps forward and eighty steps back. Even with the might of Valentin's lawyers – yes, eventually I caved to that – it's not a straightforward process, although at least I have an excellent lawyer whom I wouldn't normally be able to afford. And if anyone can get me justice for my injuries from the crash, it's Parker Knowles.'

Everyone's heard of Parker Knowles. He's a high-profile lawyer in Glasgow, although I don't know anyone personally who has used him before, until now. Well, except for Valentin. He'd be outside of most of my inner circle's price range.

As I'm putting Aria to bed later, tucking her in with her favourite toy, she snuggles into my arm and says, 'Can we go back and visit the other house sometimes, Mummy? I like it there.'

'Well, not unless we go and visit Benedict sometime. He and Tiziana will be moving in on Monday.'

She sits bolt upright. 'Will Tiziana be sleeping in my bed?'

'Possibly. It's her home now.'

Her eyebrows pull down. 'But I love that bed. It's much better than this one.' She presses a finger into the mattress. 'This one's harder, and not as good to bounce on. I don't want Tiziana to sleep in my bed.' She pouts.

Oh no, here we go. Time to head off the drama at the pass. 'Well, she may not be sleeping in your bed. She may be sleeping in one of the other rooms, where Hugo and Gen slept.'

She regards me for a long moment then says, 'Mummy, is Tiziana going to our school?'

'Yes, I believe she is.'

She smirks. 'Good. We can have a sleepover soon then at her house. Night, Mummy.' And as if she has righted the world with that single decision, she kisses my cheek and flips over onto her side.

Children.

Hugo isn't in bed. I sent him there fifteen minutes ago. I've come up to tuck him in and kiss him goodnight, but he has disappeared. He can't be on the Xbox, as we still haven't hooked it up, preferring 'not to find it' for a day as we unpack to see how he copes. Call us evil, but hey, these are the only breaks we get. Plus, it will do him good as he has separation anxiety usually where his devices are concerned.

I look everywhere for him and finally find him in Patch's basket in the kitchen, cradling Patch.

'Hugo, come out of there in your pyjamas. I don't want you going into a lovely clean bed and getting it all covered in dog hair. Plus you'll itch like mad.'

'Mum, Patch doesn't like it here. He can't settle and he's been crying.'

When I look closely I see Hugo's cheeks are wet. I haven't seen him this upset since he found out Martha had been taken into hospital.

I sit down on the floor beside him, which isn't easy given I'm nearly eight months pregnant. Whales look slim compared with me at the minute. Hugo buries his face into my shoulder and Patch clambers across me. My two little boys. As if in tune with what's going on, the babies kick.

'Mummy, was that a foot?' Hugo says.

'It was certainly a body part.'

'Wow, it's like you have an alien inside you,' he says, scooting back from me, then a few seconds later, tentatively approaching again. He reaches a hand out. 'Can the babies feel me?' he asks.

'I think so. If you prod them gently, they may well prod back.'

His eyes narrow. Not sure he believes me.

'Go on,' I say.

He does, and sure enough, ten seconds later, I feel my

bump move, as if the babies are readjusting their position to get more comfortable.

'Oh my God, that's amazing,' says Hugo. 'Scary and kinda freaky, but amazing.'

'It is. All of those things,' I agree. I hug him to me. 'You did this too, you know.'

He draws back from me a second. 'I kicked you, like that?'

'Of course. All babies do.'

He stares at my stomach in wonder, stroking Patch's ears with one hand and tapping his fingers against my belly to see if the babies react again. I enjoy the unexpected moment with Hugo, and although I'm mindful it's late and he'll need to change his PJs before bed as he's covered in dog hair now, I revel in the moment as the three of us sit on the floor, content.

I peek in on Gen, but she's on a video call with Freya. I raise a hand in greeting and retreat. She seems happy enough. Nothing much has changed for her, not at first glance anyway. That's a relief.

Later, Patch is still unsettled. Ronnie managed, thankfully, to settle Hugo, with a new adventure story from his favourite author, which he managed to find on audio book. He's sleeping soundly now. Wish I was.

Coming home hasn't brought the horrors it could have, but neither has it offered quite the sanctuary I'd expected. I know it's early days, but I hope Aria soon remembers she loves her own bed in her own room and Patch readjusts to the smells and his favourite spot on the rug under the wall-mounted TV. Then, hopefully, it will prove more of a haven than it has today.

Chapter Nineteen

Monday 20 December

To-do list
White T-shirt for Hugo for choir
Carol concert at 10.30
Extra money for Gen for Christmas craft sale at school
Put tree up – get decorations out of loft
Midwife – 12 p.m.

'Mummy, you promised we could put the tree up yesterday, and we didn't,' Aria says, hands on hips.

God, she's becoming quite the wee nag. Honestly. Superwoman I am not, and certainly not with the size I am, and how tired I am. Yesterday morning, after having to deal with one dog who had been sick everywhere and another who had pooed everywhere – fortunately all contained to the tiled kitchen floor – I praised myself for not attacking my husband with a sledgehammer for not having put away the sack of dog food properly. The now half empty sack of dog food. Poorly dogs. Christmas. Demanding children. Nearly eight months pregnant. Appointments today. Not a recipe for tranquillity.

'Aria, I know I did, but sometimes things don't go to

plan. We will definitely do it this afternoon when everyone's home from school. But right now, we need to get ready, because I have to be at the carol concert for Hugo this morning and then I'm going to see the midwife about the babies.'

Aria knits her brow. 'What's a midwife?'

Ah, I should have simply said nurse. 'A midwife is someone who delivers a baby.'

Her eyebrows nearly disappear into her curls she's furrowing them so much. 'They deliver babies? Like the postman?'

'Postman doesn't deliver babies,' Hugo says helpfully through a mouthful of Cornflakes.

I roll my eyes at him, then turn back to Aria. 'She doesn't take them anywhere. She makes sure the babies come out of Mummy's tummy safely.'

'Hmm.' She looks at me suspiciously. 'Are you sure babies come out of your tummy, because Hugo was watching a video on YouTube and the baby was coming out of–'

'Yes, I'm sure,' I say my voice rising a few octaves. 'Now, coat on, gloves on, let's go.'

As I drive to school, the weather being particularly hideous this morning, I'm glad I dodged that bullet. She's far too young for me to be having that conversation, and I really must ask Hugo what on earth he was watching.

It seems no time at all since I dropped them at school, and now here I am again, queuing under an umbrella with other parents waiting to be allowed entry to the school for the carol concert. The choir, of which Hugo is an integral part, have been practising for weeks and everyone is buzzing about the concert. I'm really looking forward to it, as Hugo has been so excited about his role in it. Plus, for me, the carol concert shows Christmas is just around the corner.

Hugo waves manically when I enter and I smile in acknowledgement. He's near the front and as the tones of 'O Little Town of Bethlehem' rend the air, I'm thankful for my family and of the year we've had. Christmas carol concerts are a rite of passage. It's not so long since Gen was in the choir. Ronnie kept saying his angel sang like a true angel. This time, unfortunately, since he only started his new job relatively recently, Ronnie can't be here, but the memory makes me smile, and I know he'd be super proud of Hugo right now.

He holds himself with such poise as if he was born to sing. 'Hark the Herald Angels Sing' is followed by 'Joy to the World' and then 'God Rest Ye Merry Gentlemen'. And the children all sing so beautifully and look so serious and earnest, it makes my heart, well, sing.

Then my heart stops. Hugo steps forward. Isn't he feeling well? But no. The organist plays the opening bars of 'Silent Night' and Hugo begins to sing, his voice haunting and melodic. I'm transfixed. No one makes a sound. I sit and gape at my son, unable to believe my lovely boy has kept this solo secret from me. Tears roll down my cheeks and then I'm sobbing. Bloody pregnancy. Bloody hormones. And when Hugo sings that final note, the audience erupts. I look to either side of me where several other women have pulled out tissues and are dabbing their eyes. His singing touched them too, and somehow that sends me over the edge, and then I'm a blubbing, snivelling mess. What's new?

Hugo takes a bow then leaves the stage, but as he does, he looks right at me and winks. Little minx. Wait till I get him home. Poleaxing me in public like that. At least this time no one falls off the stage.

'Your blood pressure's a bit higher than I'd like,' says the midwife. 'Can you come back and see me when we reopen on the fifth of January? And if you have any problems at all before then, call me, or NHS 24 if it's out of hours.'

My eyes widen. 'Should I be worried? And why is my blood pressure higher only now? I thought gestational hypertension happened from twenty weeks?'

'It does, but it doesn't always happen at twenty weeks. The reasons are unknown, but we'll keep an eye on you. If it creeps up past a level I'm happy with, we'll start you on some medication.'

'But won't that harm the babies?' I ask, my heart racing, no doubt causing my blood pressure to rise. Just as well she'd already removed the cuff, or she'd be putting me on the medication already.

'We use the safest medicine possible when you're pregnant, so don't worry about that. For now, just take it a bit easier and try to avoid stress.'

I am worried about it, though. Hard not to be. I've had no issues at all, had top marks from the midwife in my four-weekly appointments with her. Maybe we've been a bit busier than usual. OK, we have been busier, with the move and all the kids' Christmas events. Time to put the feet up.

'Mummy, can I put the star on the top?'

'Well, no, Aria, because you're too little. We'll leave it for Daddy to put on. Normally I'd do it, but I'm not supposed to stand on chairs, because of the babies.'

'Why not?'

'In case I fall off, but also because it's hard for me to stand on a chair now, because I have this big tummy in the way.' I stroke my stomach absentmindedly.

'Can I choose which ornaments go where then?' asks Aria.

She's getting so bossy and controlling. She's going to end up like Monica from *Friends*.

'You can put some of them on. Tell you what, why don't you do the lower branches, Hugo can do the middle branches and Gen can do the top?'

She looks at me thoughtfully, then clearly deeming what I've said makes sense, says, 'OK' and rummages around the boxes of Christmas decorations. 'But I'm having these ones.' She holds aloft one of a series of miniature Swedish houses, decorated for Christmas, which Erik bought us a few years ago. They're bright and colourful and even have their own tiny lights that illuminate the insides of the houses. They're some of my favourites.

'That's fine. Right, let's dress this tree.'

'What do you think about here, Mum?' Hugo asks for the La Befana decoration I bought in Italy years ago. La Befana is a witch who brings good children treats on the morning of Epiphany, sixth of January. When Mario, Valentin's son was here a few months ago, the kids were agog as he told them how La Befana brings him treats each January, with Gen jokingly suggesting we move to Italy, and Aria in particular thinking that was a great idea.

'Perfect,' I say.

Gen needs no help. In fact, her efforts look better than mine would have. I just pass the decorations and baubles. Soon, the three children have outdone themselves and our seven-foot Nordmann fir completes the Christmas feel in our living room, where Aria had convinced Ronnie the other day to hang some decorations.

'There we go, all ready for Christmas. Now, who wants some hot chocolate with marshmallows as a reward?'

'Me, me, me,' come the replies.

'Gen, you look beautiful.' She does. She's wearing a dusky pink prom-style dress with layers of tulle, but without the eye-watering price tag, and her hair has been styled into a French roll. She looks very glamorous. If it wasn't a school disco she was attending, I wouldn't let her out of the house for fear she'd draw the wrong kind of attention.

She blushes. 'Thanks, Mum.'

I drop her off near the school gate where Freya is already waiting with her mum in their car.

'Enjoy yourself, sweetheart.'

She beams. 'I will.' She strides over to meet Freya then heads for the school gate. As she reaches it, she turns and gives me a little wave. A lump forms in my throat as I watch her. She moves with the grace of a gazelle and has the legs to match.

I'm not ready for Gen being interested in boys. I mean, she had her crush on Rain earlier this year, but somehow I feel it won't be long before she starts dating and the thought terrifies me. I make a solemn promise to myself right now that despite two new family members soon to join our ranks, I'll always keep an eye on Gen, make sure that just because she's capable and older, her needs don't get forgotten about. The maternal instinct inside me surges. I may have five cubs soon, but I will protect them all.

As I drive back to Ferniehall, my phone rings. Sam. I answer on hands-free. 'Hey! How you doing?'

Sam's out of hospital, but baby Octavia is still in the neonatal unit, where she'll stay until the doctors are happy with her, but they're both doing well. Octavia has managed to put quite a bit of weight on, and she's now nearing her original expected due date – only three weeks or so out.

'I'm good, thanks. How was the carol concert?'

'Aw, he was fabulous. He did a solo, but hadn't told me, and I was a snotty mess.'

'Wee soul. I wish I'd been there. I bet you he was amazing.'

'Oh, he was. Some other mums were crying too when he sang "Silent Night", not just me. Anyway, how's Octavia?'

'She's marvellous. In fact, she's so marvellous, she's getting home tomorrow. Whoop whoop!'

'Aw, Sam, that's fantastic news. I'm so pleased for the five of you. What weight is she now?'

'She's four pounds exactly, but she's thriving and they're really pleased with her.'

'I can't tell you how happy I am for you. Home for Christmas.'

'Yep. We're all home for Christmas, you lot and us.'

'We are.' I sigh. 'God, when you think of the year we've had…'

'I know,' Sam says. 'It certainly hasn't been boring. Imagine, you'll be able to tell Octavia when she's older that you delivered her, and I'll tell her she was born in a car.'

'Definitely a good story,' I agree. 'Do me a favour though. Don't mention delivering babies around Aria.'

'Oh?'

'That's a story for another day, but seriously, I beg you, don't. My heart can't take it.'

Sam laughs. 'Now I really am intrigued. Anyway, I'd best go. We have a lot to do. We've been here so long, we actually have quite a bit to pack. Hopefully, I'll see you before Christmas.'

'I'd love that.'

'Oh, did Nicky tell you?'

'Tell me what?' I ask, wondering if she mentioned something about the engagement party and I've forgotten. I've bought the most gorgeous midnight blue maternity dress for the party. It exactly matches the colour of a VW Golf I had a few years ago.

'The physio signed her off.'

'Nooo! Oh, that's brilliant. Thank God. Well, it certainly seems to be the season of joy: Octavia getting home, Nicky recuperating, Gen looking like a fairy princess, Hugo singing like an angel, Aria knocking people off the stage…'

'What's this?' Sam asks.

I fill her in and she howls with laughter. 'I can't believe you didn't WhatsApp me. That is comedy gold. That girl is a star for sure. Right, I'm really going this time. You all organised for Christmas?'

'No, and you were supposed to be going, for real, remember?'

'Right, right. Sorry. Just excited. OK, hugs to the kids. Bye.'

I'm laughing as I hang up.

Ronnie agrees to pick the girls up, says I should go to bed and get some rest, particularly once I tell him what the midwife said today. I don't argue. I'm exhausted. It's been quite full-on today. I had intended to wrap some presents once the kids went to bed and before Gen returned from the Christmas disco, but I'm already yawning and looking forward to starfishing in bed.

The opening and closing of the front door and murmured voices drags me to half-sleep sometime later, but I immediately go back under.

A clatter and a clang and Ronnie's raised voice finally wake me and pull me from my slumber. Ronnie's voice raises again and then all goes quieter, but faint murmurs still reach me. Realising I won't rest until I know everything is OK, I roll myself over the side of the bed – that's what I have to do now – get up a bit of momentum before I can actually manage it, grab my dressing gown and head downstairs.

The scene that greets me is not what I was expecting. Ronnie is standing in the hall with a boy and Gen. What the…?

Both teenagers look embarrassed as does Ronnie. Then I recognise the boy. He's the one who found Patch. I'm still not sure who he is. I did mean to ask around.

'Is everything all right?' I ask.

'No, it is not,' says Gen, her face crimson. 'I lost my bag at the disco, and Chris–' she indicates the boy '–found it, and brought it here, but Dad thought he was a burglar and just bawled him out.' She turns to Chris. 'Thanks,

Chris.' She turns back to Ronnie. 'Thanks, Dad,' she says, more sarcasm oozing out of those two words than I would have thought possible. She flounces past me upstairs, presumably to her room.

'Sorry,' says Chris, when she's gone. 'I didn't want to cause an argument. Maybe I should have waited until school tomorrow, but then Dad told me where you lived.'

'Your dad did?' I ask, wondering how we know his father.

'Yeah. My dad's Benedict Lamington.'

The penny drops and I groan inwardly. Ronnie's been shouting out Benedict's son. Ronnie seems to instantly 'get it' too, and says, 'Sorry for shouting at you. I thought you were trying to break in.'

'It's OK.' He smiles. 'But I may have broken your plant pot. That's what I tripped over.'

'Don't worry about that,' I say. 'And thanks for bringing Gen's bag back. That was really kind. Say hello to your dad for us.' Then I frown again. I don't even know what time it is, but it must be pretty late. 'You didn't walk, did you?'

'Well, I had a friend's dad drop me off here rather than at mine.'

I turn to Ronnie. 'Ronnie, can you drop Chris home?'

'Sure.' Ronnie reaches for his shoes.

'Oh, you don't need to do that,' Chris says, palms upwards in a 'don't bother' motion.

'Yes, he does,' I say firmly. 'Don't you, Ronnie?'

He looks suitably chastened, but he catches on quick. I need some time alone with Gen before he faces her wrath, because if I'm right, Daddy just put his foot in it with the new object of Gen's affections.

Chapter Twenty

Friday 24 December
Christmas Eve

To-do list
Wrap Ronnie's pressies and remainder of kids'
Check we have carrots and that there are some cookies left for
Santa – kids may have already eaten them all
Put 'Santa Stops Here' sign out
Look out new Christmas PJs for all
Ensure have enough milk and bread to last us until the 27th
Send any last-minute cards to people we've received them from,
but missed out when we sent ours

I pull back the curtains to a winter wonderland. Ah, the weatherman has it wrong again. They said no white Christmas and that it wouldn't snow until at least Boxing Day. Oh, the kids will love this. Ronnie finished up yesterday for Christmas so we could spend Christmas Eve together, one last time, just us and the three kids. Looks like those sledges will be out in force later today.

I sip my hot chocolate – I've had quite the penchant for it recently – and stare out of the window at the falling snow. This is my idea of bliss. Hot chocolate in hand, cosy armchair, snuggly throw and falling snow. I love being out in the snow too, but that idyllic view of it never lasts and within ten minutes I'm moaning about being frozen stiff, alternately wrapping my arms around myself, then blowing on my hands, trying to heat myself up.

This morning, I do just that as I take the dogs for a quick loo stop. I'm careful where I place my feet in case there's black ice under the innocent snow, but since it's still falling, I'm probably safe enough. No sign of a gritter though. Of course not. If they listened to the weather forecasters earlier, they'd have been convinced too that we wouldn't be seeing snow until Sunday. But here it is, and I hold my face up to the snow and try to catch snowflakes. Funny how that never loses its appeal, no matter your age.

At this time in the morning, barely anyone is around, particularly not near our house. I heard a car earlier, but they're few and far between at this time of day. Plus, I guess if the snow continues to fall, fewer people will be happy to drive. In fact, if it keeps falling, they may not be able to drive, far at least.

I listen to the stillness, feel the freshness of the air on my face, the snowflakes landing there, before I finally wipe them away with a glove. It's perfect and I wish I could bottle this moment. Soon, the idyll will be erased, literally and metaphorically, as footprints pattern the snow and cars turn the snow to slush. But for now, I enjoy it, closing my eyes for a moment and raising my face to the sky, letting the snowflakes land one by one on my face.

Ten minutes after I get back in, an elephant thuds across the ceiling. Well, Hugo, but same thing. He scrambles down the stairs, two at a time – I can tell from which boards squeak – and bursts in. 'Mum, Mum, it's snowing!' The glee on his face makes me laugh. He runs back out and shoves on his boots.

'Hey, where do you think you're going?' I ask, levering myself off the couch.

'To make footprints in the snow, of course, before anyone else does. That's the best bit,' he says.

'It is, but go put some proper clothes on first. You'll be freezing within seconds in your pyjamas, as well as wet through.'

He looks down and seems to have an a-ha moment. 'Sure.' He sprints back upstairs and returns two minutes later wearing joggers, a woolly jumper, a scarf and a hunter's hat with flaps and mitts – all too small for him and needing donated to charity. He's also trailing a sleepy Aria, who's carrying Cornie, her must-have bedtime item. It's not just a clever name, he's a unicorn.

'C'mon, Aria, it's snowing,' he shouts in her face.

'Hugo,' I say gently. 'Give her a minute to wake up.' I enfold Aria in my arms. 'Morning, darling. Sleep well?'

'Is it a snow day, Mummy?' she asks, ignoring my question, then yawns right in my face.

Technically, a snow day is a day off school due to snow, but I don't think Aria's interested in the technicalities right now, nor in a position to process them, so I simply say, 'Yes. Why don't I get you some warm milk and you can drink that whilst I fetch some winter clothes for you and you can go play with Hugo in the garden.'

'Yay!' she shouts, then bounces up and down on the sofa like a lamb in a spring meadow.

I shake my head as I walk to the kitchen for her milk,

just as Hugo rushes past me, making a beeline for the back door so he can go out into the snow.

'Careful! Come here a minute.'

He stops. I check he's dressed to my satisfaction, then give him the go-ahead. He charges out the door like a bull embarking on its first fight as a gust of frigid air encompasses the kitchen.

'Brr, shut the door!'

'I'll get it, Mummy,' says Aria, as she passes me, Cornie still clutched in her hand.

'Here, poppet,' I say, once we return to the living room. Through the dining room window I can see Hugo building a snowman.

'Mummy, I want to build a snowman,' Aria says, noticing Hugo rolling a ball of snow round the garden.

'Right. Give me two minutes so I can get you some warm clothes and you can go out and help.'

Once she's suitably attired, I decide I should probably get dressed too. I'll grab a shower later, and, well, if you can't beat them, you may as well join them.

Ronnie opens one eye as I'm fumbling around trying to find some maternity leggings and thick socks. 'Time is it?' he asks.

'Snow time.'

'Huh?' He blinks a few times as if trying to focus.

'Get up and look out the window.'

'No, I'm sleepy,' he says, cocooning himself inside the duvet until I can barely see the top of his head.

'Oh well, you're missing out. The kids are building a snowman.'

'What?' He sits up, blinking furiously, then rubs a forefinger under each eye. 'Is it snowing?'

'Pretty hard to build a snowman without snow.'

Ronnie loves the snow. He loves playing in the snow with the kids. He's essentially just a big kid himself.

He leaps out of bed, bollock naked – he'll regret that in a minute – and crosses to the window, where he peeps out of the window. Even through the double-glazed window, Hugo and Aria's shouts of joy are easily heard.

'Make me a coffee?' he asks, giving me his best puppy eyes.

I roll my eyes at him. 'OK, as long as you promise to ensure no one breaks any bones when you take them sledging later.'

He holds up three fingers. 'Scouts' honour.'

'Ready in five minutes.'

By the time I've finished making Ronnie's coffee, Gen has wandered into the kitchen in her dressing gown, stifling a yawn. 'What's all the noise?'

'Look out the window,' I say.

'Oh wow! Snow! Oh, I don't believe it. Hugo will love this, and Aria. There's enough for sledging in. Where's Dad?' Her thoughts spill out so quickly, it takes me a moment to catch up.

'Hugo and Aria are already outside building a snowman. Dad's getting dressed.' I hold up his black coffee to prove he's up.

'Why didn't they wake me?' she moans before she rushes back upstairs, presumably to get dressed.

Shortly afterwards, the five of us are in the garden building a snowman, a snow dog and even a snow cat. Hugo wants to make a snow hamster but nobody is for helping him. Gen proclaims it too lame, Aria too small, and Ronnie keeps out of it, initially.

'But we can make it a huge hamster,' says Hugo.

'What is this, Revenge of the Killer Hamsters?' says Ronnie.

'Daa-d, that was terrible,' says Gen. 'That was so terrible it couldn't even be classed a dad joke.' She shakes her head and moves away from him.

The boys and girls compete against each other building their snow creations. Although Ronnie is a 'man' down, he has Patch and Bear on his team, as they're both boys, and they provided the inspiration for the snow dog and cat, the latter because Bear likes to chase cats.

Finally, we stand back and admire our handiwork.

'The snowman doesn't have any arms,' Aria says.

Gen retrieves a couple of large twigs from the trees at the end of the garden. 'There.' She pops them in place and stands with hands on hips and gives a contented sigh. 'Right, I'm freezing. Mu-u-um, any chance of hot chocolate?'

Now it's her turn to show me her best puppy eyes. God, I give in. It's easier.

'Yes, yes. Just tie a broom to my backside too. I'm supposed to be resting.'

'Oh?' Gen asks, concern in that one word.

'Nothing serious. Midwife just said to remember I'm having two babies pretty soon and not to go skydiving or anything,' I fudge.

'Sounds reasonable,' she says. 'C'mon, you two, I'll help you out of your wet things whilst Mum gets our hot chocolate.'

Ronnie has taken the kids sledging. Whenever we have snow, we always take them to the top of the hill near the school. It's the biggest, and well, only real hill in the village. Usually, I'd be right in the midst of it all, but I'm tired, and am mindful of the midwife's words about overexerting myself. Plus, I still have some of the kids' presents to wrap and with them out of the house with Ronnie, and just me, Bear and Patch, it's the perfect opportunity.

I had started putting the presents under the tree, but Bear and Patch sniffed out their own and disaster was imminent, so I put them back in the cupboard in the hall.

I'm biting Sellotape, as I've left the scissors in the kitchen and can't be bothered to go back and get them, when my mobile rings. Sam.

'Hi, lovely. How you doing? How's Octavia? And what do Ava and Emily think of her?'

'I'm great, if a little tired, she's fabulous, and the girls love her. They both want to mother her, even if Emily does look at her sometimes as if to say "you're taking up too much of Mummy's attention. I want to talk to her."'

'I can imagine. And how's Erik with his four girls now?'

'Would you believe, in his element? He dotes on all three.'

'Four,' I correct her. 'He adores you.'

'Well, that's a given,' she says with a laugh. 'You ready for tomorrow?'

'Not yet. I'm wrapping presents whilst Ronnie has taken the kids to the Big Hill.' That's how it's known locally. Original, isn't it? 'What you up to?'

'I was trying to prepare for Erik's parents coming, but their flight has been delayed because of the weather. If they don't make it over, they'll be furious, as they're dying to see the girls, and Sweden's snow is worse than this pretty much all year round, yet it doesn't halt their transport system.'

'Very true. I know. We're total wusses when it comes to coping with bad weather. Anyway, I'm so glad I managed to see you guys on Wednesday. Octavia is so cute, so tiny, but so full of attitude.'

'Oh, she is,' Sam agrees. 'Does it make you eager to meet your two?'

'Yes, and no. Although chatting things through with Ronnie just about every second night has made me realise we will manage. Now I know he has my back on this, I feel so much more reassured. But I'm still glad I have almost another two months to get organised.'

'I know. It will be a big change, especially with Aria being five, and there being two of them. At least Emily is only three, so I hadn't quite forgotten what it was all like.'

'I don't think I forgot anyway,' I say, laughing.

'Right, I best go. This wee madam needs fed. Hope the kids have a lovely Christmas Eve, and don't let them get up at 3 a.m. Boundaries, remember?'

'But it's Christmas,' I say. 'And it wasn't three, it was five.'

'I'm a teacher, remember? Make six thirty the earliest. Before that, they have to go back to bed.'

I sigh. 'I'll try.'

I call Nicky to see how things are progressing for their engagement party next week and just to check in, then I ring Dad to check Mum is taking time off and not working on my business on Christmas Eve. They're concerned they won't manage to reach ours tomorrow if the snow doesn't stop. I tell them we'll send a tractor for them, in that case, and Dad laughs.

I work on my to-do list for tomorrow. I'm not going to stress about it. I've already done that over the past few days, and at least I do have all the shopping in. Thank goodness. Being stuck with no Christmas dinner doesn't bear thinking about.

I'm continuing with my present wrapping when I panic as I spot a figure approaching the house. No, they can't be back already. I'm not finished. Hurriedly, I hide the presents in the cupboard, then breathe a sigh of relief when I realise it's Chris, Benedict's son.

I waddle along to the front door and open it. 'Chris, what a lovely surprise. Do you want to come in? Gen's not here, I'm afraid.'

'That's OK. I'm just delivering some cards for Dad. I think he was going to drop round in the car, but that's not possible at the minute, and I fancied some fresh air.'

Likely story. He fancied seeing Gen, more like.

'Well, that's lovely. Are you sure you don't want to come in for a mince pie and some mulled apple juice?'

He's debating it, when voices reach us. He turns and spots Gen, who blushes furiously and waves shyly.

He turns back to me. 'Yeah, that would be lovely, actually.'

'Come in before the hordes descend then, or there won't be any left.'

He grins.

Ronnie and I spend a little time in the kitchen with the kids and Chris, then we relocate to the living room, leaving them eating mince pies and Christmas biscuits that I made with my three yesterday – Christmas trees, reindeer and candy canes festoon the basically Empire biscuits, but they're good, with a hint of cinnamon.

'I cleared Martha's path for her earlier,' Ronnie says. 'She wasn't going out, but I said it would help her get to ours tomorrow at least, and then I'd have less to shovel on Christmas Day, if there's any more.'

I frown. 'Have you seen the forecast?'

'Not looked yet.' He picks up his phone. 'Actually, it's meant to get pretty wild.'

'What d'you mean?' I ask, frowning.

'Well, from the looks of this, it's meant to snow all night.'

I scrunch my eyes further. 'But if that's the case, the roads may close.'

Ronnie tries to reassure me. 'Hopefully, the council will have learned their lesson after being unprepared last night, and they'll have the gritters out tonight.'

'Yeah, but whereas last night they'd just have needed gritters, tonight they'll need snow ploughs to clear the road so they can be gritted.'

'Fair point,' Ronnie says, setting his apple cider on the edge of the table.

Lucky him. I'm on the mulled apple juice, although it's still rather tasty.

The door opens. 'That's me away, Mr and Mrs Halliday. Thanks for the drink and biscuits.'

'You're welcome. How are you and Tiziana settling in?'

His face clouds over momentarily. 'As best as can be expected.'

I give him a sad smile. 'And what are you guys doing

for Christmas?'

'Well, we're meant to be going up to my aunt's in Perth, but if the snow continues, we might not make it out.'

'That's not so good, and it's also a valid point. Our family's coming from Loch Lomond They might have the same issue. Anyway, wish your dad and Tiziana Merry Christmas and perhaps we can see you all between Christmas and New Year for a get-together.'

He smiles, a genuine one that lights up his whole face this time.

'I'd like that, and I'm sure Dad would too,' he adds.

Ronnie shows him out, and when I take our cups into the kitchen to refill them a few moments later, Gen is staring into space, a wide smile on her face. Two guesses what, or rather who, she's thinking about.

Once dinner's over, I'm quick to round the kids up. 'Santa can't come until children are in bed,' I say.

'But I wanted to watch *The Grinch*,' says Aria, pouting.

'You've already watched a Christmas movie today and you can watch one every day if you like until school goes back, but right now, bathtime, young lady.'

She goes to protest, but I say, 'San–' and she stops. She clearly doesn't want to be put on the naughty list.

As per tradition, the five of us sit as I read *'Twas the Night Before Christmas*, then it's off to bed for Aria, then Hugo and even though Gen stays up a little later with us, she goes to bed relatively early too.

Soon Ronnie and I are alone, at last.

'And relax,' I say. 'Phew! That was a long day.'

'It'll be even longer tomorrow,' Ronnie reminds me.

'Thanks for that,' I say, throwing a cushion at him.

'Is everything ready?' he asks.

'Yes. Once we know they're definitely asleep, you can do Ninja Dad as you trail all the presents out from the various hiding places and I'll put them under the tree.'

'Great, but first, a glass of mulled wine, with my beloved,' Ronnie says.

'Good plan.'

I close my eyes for a few minutes as he prepares our drinks, and then I feel Bear's head at my lap and Patch's muzzle on my feet.

'Hey, don't you fall asleep already. We have presents to sort,' says Ronnie as he hands me my mulled apple juice.

'Sorry.' I yawn.

Ronnie looks at me closely. 'Are you that tired? If you are, I can manage.'

I shake my head. 'No, this is one of the best bits of the year. I want to do this.'

'Fine. Well, in that case, cheers, and let's get this party started.'

I clink glasses with him. 'Cheers.'

Chapter Twenty-one

Saturday 25 December
Christmas Day

To-do list – none. What happens, happens.

'Santa's been!'

What? No, no, no. Aria can't be up already. I look at the clock. Five o'clock. Damn. Is she downstairs?

I shuffle myself off the bed and slip my feet into my slippers, retrieving my dressing gown from its hook as I reach the door.

Aria is standing at the bottom of the stairs, Bear and Patch beside her, tails going at the speed of light. 'Santa's been,' she repeats.

I desist from reminding her she's not meant to come downstairs by herself on Christmas morning and instead should wait for everyone else. Usually that gives me and Ronnie a chance to tell her Santa hasn't been yet, but it seems this year we've failed spectacularly. Not only is she downstairs, but she's holding Rudolph's half-eaten carrot. I count to five then exhale noisily.

Pasting on a smile, despite barely being able to open my eyes as they appear to be sealed shut from tiredness, I hug Aria to me when I reach the bottom of the stairs and say, 'Merry Christmas, darling. Go wake everyone up.'

'Sure, Mummy.' She starts to run upstairs then turns and runs back down, throwing her arms around my middle. 'I love you, Mummy. Merry Christmas.' And off she dashes again. That girl. She knows how to shanghai me. My heart actually aches with love. Then I remind myself she's a minx, so I can breathe again.

Soon everyone is downstairs. I've put the two dogs into the kitchen with their Christmas presents as it will be chaos enough with the wrapping paper and new toys of three children in the living room, without the added stress of ensuring the dogs don't stand on anything or eat anything they shouldn't.

'Mummy, Mummy, I got my Little Live Pets pig!' she shrieks.

'Oh, wow! You are a lucky girl.'

She kisses me on the cheek and places her pig to the side and wades back into the sea of presents. Years ago, we tried to have the children open presents in a structured way, so things weren't as chaotic, but it always descended into bedlam, so for one day per year, we now break the rules. Christmas is Christmas, and Christmas is all about the kids.

Gen surfaces, delighted with her new FitBit, which has more functions on it than my car.

Hugo holds aloft some Star Wars Lego: Boba Fett's throne room and some scene from *The Mandalorian*. To be honest, he could be speaking a different language, that's how much it means to me. I've never been much of a Star Wars aficionado, but Hugo is. He looks so happy, he's almost in tears.

'A Barbie Dreamhouse! Thank you, Santa!' Aria screams and hugs it. At this rate, that girl will have no vocal chords left by the end of the day.

Ronnie and I exchange our gifts to each other, as the kids reach dizzying heights of elation.

'Hey, nice watch, love,' Ronnie says as he slips the Nordgreen watch on. He'd been leaving hints everywhere. Even on notes in the shower. It wasn't too expensive, a couple of hundred quid, so not pennies, but not a Breitling either, thankfully!

And I love my spa voucher for the Carrick Spa at Loch Lomond. My sisters and I have been threatening to go for ages, and now Ronnie has facilitated that.

'Thanks.' I lean over and kiss him on the lips. 'You do realise when I go on the spa weekend, you'll be left holding the babies. All of them.'

'Yeah, I didn't think that through, did I?' He grins and I snuggle into his shoulder as we watch our three beautiful children, smiles beaming, joy written across their faces.

'Right, I better take the dogs out,' Ronnie says a few minutes later. 'You manage breakfast?'

'Manage it? What am I, made of tissue paper? And anyway, do this lot look like they are remotely interested in food?' I gesture to the three children, who don't seem to know what to play with first.

'I'm going to enjoy the peace and sit back and work out a date I can go on my spa weekend.'

Ronnie's face falls. 'It won't be until the twins are a bit bigger, surely.'

I smile sweetly and say, 'That, dear husband, would be telling.'

Five minutes later, Ronnie's back, rubbing his arms and

shaking snow off his boots.

'That was a quick walk.'

'Lou, we have a problem.'

I furrow my brow. 'What?'

'Maybe we should open the curtains.' He strides over to the window and pulls them open.

'Oh wow!'

'What is it, Mum?' Gen asks, sidling up beside me. 'It's beautiful,' she says after a long moment of staring in wonder.

It's beautiful because she's never seen that much snow before and it's still falling, but it means there will be drifts everywhere, there will be people unable to get out of their houses or streets, let alone reach their destinations. And today of all days, that isn't good.

I call Wendy, Jo and Mum. Nicky's spending Christmas with Valentin and Xander, and her mum was staying overnight at Valentin's last night; Sam and the baby are safely at home with Erik and the girls. Ronnie's parents were going to his brother's in the Borders.

Thank God Martha's only next door.

Wendy answers in two rings. 'Merry Christmas, sis.'

'Merry Christmas, Wen. Your lot happy with their stash?'

'Seem to be.' After a pause, she says, 'It's not going to happen, is it?'

'Nope. If the snow over your way is anything like it is here, there's no point even trying. You might get stuck in a drift. Do you have any food in?'

'Yeah, we'll be all right on that front. Oh, I so did want to see you too. Especially as this will be our last Christmas together.' She sounds like she's about to burst into tears.

'Hey, don't worry, we can have another celebration once Christmas is over, and anyway, we have Nicky and Valentin's engagement next week. We'll be together for that.'

'True. But it's not the same.'

She's right. It's not. We talk for a bit then I tell her I'm going to call Jo.

Jo's equally upset, although at least she has Travis to cook for her. Handy having a chef as a husband. 'The kids will be so disappointed,' she says.

'Embrace the snow. That's why you moved to the countryside, wasn't it, to commune with nature more? Well, how much more natural can you get than snow?'

'Jackson's been asking to come to yours for the past two hours, and Aurora's already back on Roblox, wondering when Hugo will be online to play.'

Never ceases to amaze me how much money is spent at Christmas and then half an hour later, kids are back playing with old toys, even though sometimes they still have presents unopened.

'As soon as the weather clears, we can all get together,' I promise.

'Love you, sis. Merry Christmas. Hugs to the kids and Ronnie,' Jo says.

'And to you all. Have a lovely day.'

It's whilst I'm in the shower that it occurs to me. What are Benedict, Chris and Tiziana going to do? They supposed to be going to Perth. I don't imagine they'll be able to do that now.

I talk to Ronnie then make the call. 'Benedict, Merry

Christmas. Yes, I know, the weather's quite something. Listen, I'm guessing you can't go to Perth now, Chris told me you were going to his aunt's, so I wanted to invite the three of you here.'

'I know I don't need to,' I say at his protestations, 'but I want to, and that's what friends are for. So, will you come?'

Five minutes later, with an agreement that they'll arrive for Christmas dinner at four o'clock, I come off the phone and head down to feed the masses something that will keep them going until dinnertime.

Around two, Ronnie declares Martha's path is clear and she can now be rescued. I phoned her earlier to tell her Ronnie would clear the path and then she could come in early, rather than sit in the house like a lemon. I chose my words more carefully than that though.

'Merry Christmas, Martha.' I kiss her on the cheek and she hands over the bottle of wine and box of chocolates, plus three gift bags for the kids that Ronnie has passed to her. He rightly assumed it was safer for him to carry everything down her path and then up ours.

'Sit yourself down and I'll get you a drink. What would you like?'

'Prosecco if you have it,' she says with a sly grin.

I like her style. At eighty-eight, she's not an advocate of a glass of sherry. Thinks it puts her in a certain age bracket.

'Coming up. And I'll join you with my non-alcoholic bubbles.'

She dips her head in silent approval.

The kids come up to Martha and wish her Happy Christmas, then return to their toys, or engage her in talking about them. She hands them their parcels, and they thank her beautifully. I'm really quite proud of them, especially Aria, who is prone to grabbing things and disappearing under a table to open them. She's positively feral, usually.

Martha is wonderful with the kids, and the dogs. She always has been. It seems only a moment but it's the best part of two hours before Benedict shows up with Tiziana and Chris.

Like my children, they appear to be dressed in their Sunday best. Aria, for once was perfectly happy to wear party clothes and not dress-up clothes, so we escaped Bo Peep from *Toy Story* at the Christmas dinner table.

Benedict hands me a hamper and kisses me on both cheeks, then shakes Ronnie's hand. 'Thanks for having us. This is so kind of you.'

'Not at all. In you come. What would you like to drink? Have you met Martha?'

The conversation flows back and forth and Chris and Tiziana linger in the background until I say, 'Gen, can you and Aria go with Chris and Tiziana to get some drinks?'

Gen jumps up, a smile splitting her face. 'Of course.' She's dressed in black woolly tights, a red velvet mini-skirt and a red and white Christmas jumper. She's definitely embracing the spirit of the season, but then we all do. We all love Christmas in our family. Thank God, as I don't know what I'd do if any of my children, or Ronnie for that matter, shunned Christmas.

An hour later, everyone's sitting around the table eating goose with all the trimmings. I don't mind goose, it's Ronnie's favourite, but I love roast potatoes. I could eat them every day. And Hugo is a parsnip fiend, surprisingly, whilst Aria seems to like the baby carrots and Gen seems to have forgotten her vegetarian and vegan tendencies, and is happily munching on roast goose.

I glance around the now cleared dining table three hours later, as we're about to set up one of Hugo's new board games and I hug myself as I reflect on what a lovely time we've had. We may not have had the Christmas we expected, or been with the people we were expecting to see, but I take a mental snapshot of this scene, old friends – Martha; and new – Benedict, Tiziana and Chris – and all my family, and I am thankful for all I have, and for the people I have in my life.

'Mummy, what's that?' Aria screams.

'Bloomin' dogs,' shouts Ronnie. 'They're in it together.' He races after Bear who has entered the living room with the goose carcass on his head, whilst Patch trots along faithfully behind him.

Oh well, it keeps things interesting.

Chapter Twenty-two

Monday 27 December

To-do list
Ensure Ronnie has a fantastic birthday

The snow has finally melted and although it's not quite the tranquil birthday Ronnie had wanted or in the end got, it has still been a great day. Forty-two. I like to tease him at this stage of the year that he's now three years older than me, even if it is only for three months. We'd planned initially to spend a lazy day with the kids, a bit of family time, and we did have family time, but it was the whole family.

Since we weren't able to spend Christmas Day with our families and since yesterday was still blizzard-like conditions for part of the day, today was the first day our extended families were able to come and celebrate with us. And it was quite something. The kids had a great time, much mulled cider was drunk – not, I hasten to add by the kids – and Brandon and Ronnie bonded over a new Xbox game that Santa brought Hugo. Hard to tell who are the kids sometimes.

But Ronnie seemed happy, even though it wasn't the day we had planned, and that's all that matters. Things are really improving between us. It almost feels like I have a different husband from a year ago. And so much has happened this past year.

Mum and Dad played charades with Annabelle and Phillip and my nieces and nephews enjoyed playing with all the new Christmas gifts, as well as relieving Aria and Hugo of most of the contents of their selection boxes.

Sticky, chocolatey handprints adorn the wall in the downstairs hall, Patch has chewed through one of my new Christmas slippers already and Lyla accidentally broke one of Aria's new dolls when she fell over Hugo's gaming chair and landed on it. But all of this is part of being a piece of a large family. You have to take the good with the bad.

And talking of the good. Wendy finally told everyone around six o'clock that Ronnie and I had a table booked for dinner at a chic new French bistro in Hamwell, La Villeneuve. She's minding the kids, but since the others were happily quaffing wine and exchanging anecdotes, we told them to stay if they wished. From the looks they gave us as we left, they had no intention of doing otherwise anyway.

Ronnie and I are sitting opposite each other at a candlelit table, holding thick, leather-bound menus. Everything looks good, although I'm not much of one for frog's legs, so I'll avoid those.

'Can you recommend something?' I finally ask the waiter. 'It's too hard to choose.'

'Well,' begins the waiter, 'I see you're pregnant, so obviously the soft cheeses are out, and some of the less well-cooked dishes, however, I can highly recommend the onion soup, and the beef tenderloin is exceptional.'

'That sounds lovely. I'll have that.' I nod approvingly.

'And for you, sir, perhaps the paté en croute, one of our diners favourites, and the saddle of hare, if you are feeling a little adventurous.'

'I don't think I've had hare before, so sure, I'll give it a go.'

The waiter beams at us, recaps our orders and after recommending Ronnie a wine to go with the hare, withdraws.

Ronnie pours Evian for both of us. 'Cheers!' He clinks his glass against mine.

'Cheers.' I take a sip. 'Wow, this is weird. I keep expecting a small person to come up and ask us for something: a drink, the answer to a random question, whether I believe in God. This is bliss.'

Ronnie grins. 'Enjoy it. It won't last.'

'But it's nice just the two of us, isn't it?' I raise my glass to my lips and take a sip as Ronnie says, 'It sure is.'

'Did you ever imagine we'd be struggling to get time to ourselves, and be parents to five children?' I ask.

Ronnie laughs so hard he almost snorts.

'It's not that funny.' My eyes go wide. He's drawing attention to us, and not the good kind. People are staring.

'Oh, Lou.' He wipes his eyes. 'When I first met you, I thought it'd be me, you and maybe one or two kids. I had this grand idea of how we'd live in harmony going for walks in the countryside at weekends, having family dinners around a huge pine table each night, going swimming in the sea from April until September…'

'Ronnie, you do know we're in the twenty-first century, don't you?' I ask, my eyebrows raised. 'Walks in the countryside? It's hard enough to get them to walk to school!'

Ronnie bites his lip to contain his laughter.

'And yes, we do manage the family dinners, some nights, but more often than not everyone's eating at different times. By the time I've called on Hugo for the fourth time, Gen has come down, grabbed herself a plate and disappeared back upstairs with it. And, until recently, you were only here half the month, so missed dinner rather a lot.'

'I know. But I don't think it's too late for us to rectify that. Do you? Especially with the twins arriving too.'

I mull this over. He has a point. And why shouldn't we reach for our dreams? Why settle? If this year has taught us anything, it's that anything is possible and we can solve any problem if we put our minds to it, and talk to each other.

'You know what, Ronnie? You're right. But since we're on the subject of things we can achieve, I have a proposal to make.'

'Lou.' He looks at me seriously. 'We're already married.'

'Oh, shut up, you!' I bat him on the arm with my napkin.

Ronnie laughs and puts his hands up in a surrender motion. 'Just kidding.'

'What? We're not married?' I ask, deadpan.

Ronnie rolls his eyes. 'I think it was better when I cracked the jokes. Anyway, what's this proposal?'

'Well–' I stall '–I propose we don't allow ourselves to forget that we need time to be on our own. Life's moving too fast and it's about to get a lot busier if not faster, although it'll probably do that too, knowing our luck.' I reach my hands across the table and take Ronnie's long fingers in mine. 'So, what do you say, birthday boy, are you with me?'

'Sounds like a plan.' He sips his wine. 'Very nice. I wonder what year it is.'

Now it's my turn to roll my eyes. 'Right, steady on, don't start pretending you know about stuff you don't.'

Ronnie feigns outrage. '*Moi*?'

Then he seems to recall he's in a French bistro and this sends him into a fit of the giggles. '*Moi*? I said "*Moi*!"'

I shake my head like the long-suffering wife I am, but I'm smiling.

'Any more of your nonsense and I'll be booking you a sommelier course for your next birthday, not a trip to the Monaco Grand Prix.'

He grins. 'You know Brandon already asked me who I was taking with me.'

'Ha! That doesn't surprise me. I hope you told him you were taking me. Even if you aren't.'

Ronnie's brow furrows. 'Do you want to come?'

'Eh, Ronnie, even if I did, logistics… Small children. Ours. Twins.'

'Yeah, sometimes I think this will only really hit me once they're born.' Ronnie rests his glass back on the table.

'Yep, that's how I feel too. Occasionally shell-shocked. God knows what it will actually feel like when they do arrive.'

'Sore, I imagine,' Ronnie says, nodding.

'Ronnie! It may well be, for you, if I crush your fingers when I have contractions.' I smile sweetly at his appalled face.

And as I gaze into my husband's handsome, slightly lined face, I can't help the surge of happiness that shoots through me at us being here, tonight, on his birthday, alone, taking time to reconnect.

'Happy birthday, Ronnie.' I lean forward until he does the same, then our lips meet and one chaste kiss is all it takes for me to remember exactly what I have, and precisely how much I love my husband.

Friday 31 December
Hogmanay

To-do list

Ensure there's a lump of coal near the front door for whoever first-foots us – even if it's Ronnie. Don't want to have bad luck for a whole year.

Don't forget Nicky and Valentin's engagement present and card

Aim to leave thirty minutes before need to – that way we won't have to worry about traffic

Sew Hugo's new trousers – he burst the seam at the butt on Christmas Day

Take spare clothes for Aria – that's if I can get her out of the witch's costume she put on this morning and into her party dress. It's not looking good at the minute.

My heart swells with happiness. Finally, Nicky has met someone who deserves her. No more Sebastian and all the expletives I'd become accustomed to using whenever I thought of him, or heard his name mentioned. Now it's Valentin – kind, funny, friendly, caring, successful, reliable, not to mention very sexy, Valentin. The whole package. And tonight we're going to celebrate their love for each other. So romantic. And, Nicky's told me, she'll also reveal the date of the wedding, which is helpful, since we're bridesmaids. I'm just glad it's after I give birth, as I am currently the size of a small country, and I still have almost a month and a half to go.

Finally, we're all ready for tonight's party, and everything in our house is as prepared as it can be for tomorrow's New Year's Day dinner. Everyone who missed us at Christmas is coming for New Year. Most of them tend to come for both anyway, and most of those we'll see tonight at the party too. But tomorrow will be more relaxed than tonight's swish affair, although I'm very much looking forward to it, desperate as I am to show off my midnight blue maternity dress. I love it. I may even have it taken in so it becomes an ordinary dress once I'm no longer pregnant with twins.

My brood scrub up well and as we enter the Milburn Hotel, my heart swells with pride. They look beautiful, all of them. Wendy and Jo are already there, with their kids and husbands. I'm surprised Travis took the night off from Solitude, but then he and Nicky have always got on really well as friends. He'd want to be here for this happiest of occasions.

I spot Nicky off to one side of the main function room, deep in conversation. She catches my eye and smiles. I give a little wave, then head for the bar. Her glass looks empty. I'll get her a refill and I can 'interrupt' that way.

The younger children are already dancing to the strains of Duran Duran's 'Rio'. Busting some moves, as Hugo likes to say. The pre-schoolers are dancing round and round watching the light move across the dance floor, swishing their party dresses this way and that.

My eyes take in the room. I don't know so many

people, apart from my immediate circle. Sam's there, with Erik and the girls. His parents finally made it over from Sweden and they're babysitting.

'Hi, Erik. How you doing?' I ask once I've kissed him and Sam on both cheeks.

'I'm good, thanks, Louisa. I never did thank you properly for delivering my baby girl. I was too much in shock afterwards.'

'It was my pleasure, Erik. Well, once I stopped panicking about the responsibility of it.' We all laugh.

'Oh my God–' Sam's hand flies to her mouth. '–I never did pay you for the deep clean of the car.'

'OK, well, that part wasn't such a pleasure, but I won't hold it against you.'

Sam reaches into her bag for her purse.

'Sam, don't be silly, I don't want your money.'

'But I don't want you being out of pocket–'

'Shh,' I say, putting a finger to my lips. 'I don't want to hear another word.'

She goes to protest, but Valentin chooses that moment to tink his champagne glass with a teaspoon.

'Good evening, everyone, and thanks to you all for coming, from far and wide. I think a special mention has to go to Sunil who has come all the way from Doha in Qatar. Thank you. And the prize for the person who had to make the shortest journey goes to Eddie, who lives about a hundred and fifty metres away.'

That raises quite a few laughs as Valentin smiles. 'Now, before we start the evening proper, my fiancée–' cheers go up all round at this, possibly his first public pronouncement of their relationship '–Nicky would like to make an announcement.'

Nicky takes the mic from him. She's beautiful, resplendent in a flowing magenta halterneck evening gown with criss-crossed straps at the back. She wouldn't look out of place on the red carpet.

'Hi, everyone. As my fiancé Valentin has already said–' a few giggles and murmurs go around at her parroting Valentin's comment '–thanks everyone for coming. It means so much to us. It's rare to have so many friends gathered in one place, so we absolutely want to make the most of you having made the effort to come here tonight. And with that in mind, I'd like to announce the date of the wedding. Drum roll, please.' She smiles as the band obliges.

She takes an envelope and opens it. 'You are cordially invited to the wedding of Valentin Pendragon and Nicky Cussans on Saturday the fourth of June at the Pendragon Estate. Invitations will be sent out in April, but please, save the date. We would love to have you there with us.' She looks up from the card she's been reading from. She meets my eyes and when I give her the thumbs-up, she grins.

Everyone cheers. Valentin takes the mic back and says, 'Right, folks, let the party begin. Dinner will be served presently.'

I smile. Presently. Only Valentin, coming from such a distinguished family, could get away with saying 'dinner will be served presently' and it not coming off as if he's a butler in a posh country house.

Everyone heads off to find their tables, but I make a point of waylaying the woman of the hour before we sit down to eat.

'So, soon-to-be, Mrs Pendragon, how are we feeling?' I ask.

Nicky couldn't stop smiling if she tried. Her smile is so

wide and her teeth so white, she's in danger of some producer asking her if she'd like to star in a toothpaste commercial.

'Honestly, Lou? On top of the world. Like Kate Winslet in *Titanic*, you know, the bit where she has her arms outstretched on the bow of the ship. Well, I think it was the bow. My nautical knowledge isn't exactly my forte.'

I smile, then I hug her tight. 'I love you, Nic, and I'm so happy for you, for you both.'

'Oi, babies, you're squishing me,' she says, pulling back a little. 'Crikey, Lou, I know it's not the done thing, but you really are pretty huge. What on earth…?'

I turn pale, I know I do. I look at Nicky. 'Nic, my waters just broke.'

'What!'

'You heard,' I say helplessly as amniotic fluid pools around my feet.

'Give me your hand,' she says. 'I don't want you bloomin' slipping in it.'

She waves to our table, but they don't notice us, so deep in conversation are they.

A waiter passes and she stops him. 'Can you fetch Mr Pendragon, please? We have a situation.'

The waiter looks at Nicky in alarm, then my no doubt stricken face, then spots the pool on the floor, then he goes as pale as I'm sure I am. 'Certainly, Madam.'

I fumble with my phone to attract Ronnie's attention, but just then Sam gets up and heads in our direction. She frowns at my furious waving and hurries over.

'What's…? What the actual…?'

'Yes, quite,' I say dryly. I'm glad some part of me is still dry. My knickers are…OK, too much information. Suffice to say, my lovely midnight blue dress probably won't be rescued by a visit to the dry cleaner.

'Is that–?' Sam starts.

'Amniotic fluid? Yes,' I confirm. 'Do you think you could ask Ronnie to come over? I think I'll need to go to the hospital. I can't bloody believe it. Tonight of all nights.' I gaze at the menu, which is helpfully on a stand behind us. My mouth waters at the menu. I was looking forward to my tournedos of beef most, but the chocolate and honeycomb ice cream terrine was a close second. And the mushroom duxelles starter sounded lovely too. I don't want to miss all that. 'Can't I at least stay until the main course?' I ask hopefully.

Nicky gives me a stern look. She knows I'm not kidding.

'We could clean me up. It's not as if the babies are likely to arrive right now, or anything.'

'Seriously? You're going to go all naïve on me with regards to how long it takes babies to arrive? They don't always arrive on schedule. Sometimes they miss the memo,' Sam says.

'All right, all right, just because your daughter was born in the car,' I say part jokingly, part grumpily.

'I'll get Ronnie. He'll need to drive you,' says Nicky.

'He can't,' Sam points out. 'He's had a beer.'

'Oh no, really?' I gasp. Someone up there doesn't like me. I raise my eyes heavenward in supplication. Please give me a break.

'What about Erik?' suggests Nicky.

'No, he's had a few. He knew I was driving. I'll need to take you. Ha, payback for me having my baby in your car. But listen, none of that nonsense tonight. I can't handle having to deliver two babies.'

'I'm coming too,' Nicky says.

'You bloody well are not,' Sam and I chorus.

'It's your engagement party, or hadn't you noticed?'

'And what does that matter? You're bringing life into the world,' she says dramatically.

'Nicky, I have another seven weeks to go before–'

'Is that more amniotic fluid coming out?' Nicky asks.

'Right, right, I get it, we have to go. Nic, can you tell Erik and Ronnie for me? And please have a good time. We'll keep you updated.'

Mouth downturned, Nicky finally accepts we're going without her. 'Fine. But let me know what's happening.'

'We will,' Sam and I chorus.

Valentin arrives just then. 'What's going on? Ooops! What's…?'

'Amniotic fluid,' Nicky, Sam and I say together.

His eyes widen. He raises a finger and a waiter comes over. 'Can you see to it that the floor gets cleaned so no one slips, please?' He turns back to me. 'Louisa, how can we help? Are you OK?'

'I'm fine. Babies are just being difficult, clearly. And tonight! It had to be tonight. Please, go back and enjoy your meals. Sam's taking me to the hospital, as no doubt they'll want to monitor me.'

'Are you sure?' Valentin's earnest face leans towards me.

'Yes, I'm sure. Sorry I've spoiled your evening.'

'Oh, Louisa, you haven't. It's exciting. Let us know how things go at the hospital.' He pats my arm, his eyes shining. I smile. I can see him and Nicky having a kid together in the future. He clearly wants more, and he doesn't see Mario very often, even if he will see Xander all the time.

'Right, lady, let's get a move on,' Sam says as Valentin walks off, summoned by one of his guests.

'Lou.' Ronnie's eyes are full of concern as he reaches me. 'You're not going without me. Wendy and Jo are taking the kids.'

'Oh, c'mon, Ronnie, you know how boring it'll be. They'll hook me up to monitors and leave me there for days. Well, it always feels like days. And poor Sam's missing the party, but she may be able to come back later, once she's dropped me off, so there's no point you wasting your time. Go and enjoy your dinner. I'll be fine.'

Ronnie frowns. 'I don't know…'

'Well, I do,' I say decisively. 'So on you go. Sam, are we ready?'

'Yep.' She picks up her clutch.

'If you're sure.' Ronnie bends down to kiss me on the cheek.

'I am, and mind and divert my sisters too, or we'll never get out of here.'

He laughs at that. 'True. OK, on you go. But call me as soon as you know anything.'

'I'll make sure she does, Ronnie.' Sam puts her hand on my back.

Valentin comes back just as we're leaving. 'Here, you may find these useful.' He thrusts a bundle of towels at us.

'I hope they're not an engagement present,' I say.

Valentin laughs. 'No, they're the hotel's. Now, get to hospital before I take you myself.'

'OK, fine, my goodness, you guys are all so uptight tonight.' I turn and waddle after Sam.

Fortunately, depending on which way you look at it, we are

already in Glasgow, so it only takes us ten minutes to reach the hospital. When we arrive, Sam explains the situation and fetches a wheelchair. It's not long before I'm being whisked up to a triage ward waiting room, where they give me scrubs to put on and some clean underwear, of the lovely paper variety, and some maternity pads. It's a palaver holding them in place with no leggings to do the job.

'Bloody glad the hospital was so close, weren't you?' she says.

'And then some,' I blow out a breath. I'm feeling a burning sensation in my gut. Hmm, do twins feel different? I've never had my amniotic sac break this early. And I'm a little apprehensive about not being one hundred per cent sure what to expect.

Sam and I sit and talk for a bit, whilst we're confined to the waiting room. We are the only ones here, so it's no big deal being here, but my stomach keeps tightening. It's an odd sensation.

'You OK?' Sam asks.

'Hmm, I'm not sure. Would you mind finding a nurse?'

'Sure.' She wanders off.

Ow. Now I'm really getting discomfort in my stomach. I exhale and inhale. I mean, crikey, this is almost as painful as contractions, but it can't be contractions. Surely. No two friends are this unlucky to have their babies this early. I have this sinking feeling, call it a sixth sense.

'Ronnie,' I say when he answers the phone. 'I think you better come to the hospital. It's not confirmed yet, as I haven't seen a doctor, but I honestly think I'm in labour.'

By the time Ronnie arrives fifteen minutes later, his face flushed from exertion – he's clearly been running – I'm no longer in triage, but in a bed.

'You OK?' he asks, kissing my head then taking hold of my hand.

I nod. 'Just about. I'm waiting for the doctor to come and check me over, or the midwife, or whoever, someone, anyone. But I feel as if I'm having contractions.'

'Do you want me to go chase them up?'

'I don't think you can chase doctors up,' I say ruefully. 'It's not a report.'

'Well, you should be able to.' He sits down heavily in the chair next to me. 'I saw Sam on the way in. I told her to go back to the party.'

'Yeah, they wouldn't let her in here. It was OK in the waiting room, but not once I got a bed. Ow!'

Ronnie pats my arm. 'Right, I'm going to find someone.'

It's 11.53 p.m. on Hogmanay, Elodie Halliday has just entered the world. Ronnie holds her up. She's perfect. I'm exhausted, but I still have her twin to deliver, so I grit my teeth and get on with it.

Ronnie holds my hand throughout, and then at 12.08 a.m. on the first of January, Elijah Halliday joins his sister. What a start to a brand new year. Happy New Year to us.

After the midwives and the team of neonatal specialists have done their checks and ensured the babies are OK, a midwife places them on my bare chest. Skin-to-skin contact. Ronnie strokes their backs and kisses me on the lips. 'Well done, darling. They're perfect. You were amazing. Hello, Elodie.' He curls her tiny fingers in his. 'This is your twin, Elijah, but you're actually his big sister, by fifteen minutes, so you'll have to look out for him. Got it?' He strokes her head.

'Did they mention what weight they were?' I ask Ronnie.

'Elodie is four pounds exactly and Elijah is three pounds twelve ounces,' Ronnie rhymes off.

'That's decent for thirty-three weeks, and for being twins,' I say, relief apparent in my voice. 'I can't believe they were born on different days.'

Ronnie shakes his head in disbelief. 'I know, but you know what this means, don't you?'

'Double trouble?'

'No, two-day birthday celebrations every year. Twice the partying.'

I smile, then yawn. Giving birth to one baby is exhausting. I can't even begin to explain how shattered I am after delivering two, and two who've caused quite a stir right from the outset.

'Congratulations, Mum and Dad,' says one of the midwives. 'And you also have the first baby born in the hospital this year.'

I smile at Ronnie. I'm only now taking in the fact we have a boy and a girl. We didn't know if it would be two girls, two boys or one of each. I'm so glad Sam chose Octavia for her daughter's name, as I think Elodie and Elijah fit together like jam and cream on a scone. Perfectly.

What a whirlwind few hours.

'Happy New Year, Ronnie,' I say.

'Happy New Year, Lou.' He bends down to kiss me. 'It's going to be a good one.'

Epilogue

Two weeks later

'Here we go,' says Ronnie as he carries one car seat over the threshold and I follow him with the other.

'We're home,' I call.

'Yay!' Aria runs up to us.

The twins had to stay in hospital for two weeks because they were pre-term, but now we're all back together.

Hugo and Gen arrive seconds after Aria, everyone crowding around the twins.

I glance up. Wendy and Jo are in the living room. Mum and Dad are too.

Wendy comes over to hug me. 'We left the kids with Brandon and Travis. We thought it might be too overwhelming for everyone to be here at once.'

'Thanks.' I'm grateful for her foresight. It would have been. As it is, it's going to be wild with these three having a new brother and sister. It may take a while for the novelty to wear off.

'Tea?' asks Jo, coming forward to hug me.

'That would be lovely, sis.'

Mum comes over and puts her arms around me. She whispers in my ear. 'Well done, my clever girl. They're beautiful. And they complete your little family perfectly.'

'It's not such a little family now.' I hand her Elodie to hold at her request.

Mum laughs. 'True, but we wouldn't have it any other way.'

And I wouldn't. She's right. They've been here two weeks and I can't imagine life without them. They're so cute when we place them next to each other, reaching their tiny hands out, as if they're already aware of their unbreakable bond. I don't have a twin, but I have the next best thing. I look up at my two sisters, different from each other in virtually every way, and I smile. If my kids, twins included, can have even half of that relationship, I'll be happy, and they'll be very lucky indeed.

Dad comes over and hugs me. No words. He just hugs me. We don't need words. Then he says, 'Thank you.'

I hug him tight, then I look at the various members of family around me. My world is complete. They are all I need. I couldn't ask for a better family. I pass Dad Elijah and he cradles him like a natural.

Ronnie wanders back over to me and puts his arm around me. I gaze up into his face, whose lines I know so well. I love this man. Sure, we've had our problems, particularly this year, well, last year, but we're still together and that's what counts. Things will never be perfect with Ronnie and me, but that's OK. We're doing so much better, and whilst it's OK to strive for perfection, ultimately it can be setting us up to fail, so now I've decided to be happy with my lot – and what a lot it is – a lot of love, life and family. And I couldn't ask for a better family than the one I have.

The doorbell rings and Ronnie says, 'I'll get it.'

He ushers his parents in a moment later.

'Hello, everyone,' Phillip says.

'Where are my newest grandchildren?' asks Annabelle. She fusses over the children for a moment, irrespective of the fact my parents are currently holding them, and have only just been handed them. I bristle. I can't help it. Annabelle has such a sense of entitlement, it rubs me up the wrong way. Every time.

'Anyway,' she says, 'we have news.'

'Oh?' Ronnie's eyes flick to mine for a second.

'Yes.' Annabelle claps her hands together and announces, 'We've bought a house in the village. Next door to Benedict's, in fact.'

My jaw drops. Ronnie's does too. Just when I thought everything was perfect. Oh my goodness, I want to hit her. The prospect of her coming round unannounced on a daily basis embeds itself in my brain. This can't be happening.

'And breathe,' Ronnie whispers in my ear. 'We'll get through this, we always do.' He grips my hand and swings it gently back and forth.

He's right. We have each other, our little family, and we'll manage, taking it just one day at a time.

THE END

Author's Note

Well, what can I say, it feels like the end of an era, although it's only been a year in the life of Louisa and her family, and around two years in mine. But for those past two years I have lived, breathed and dreamed the Halliday family. It means so much to me that so many of you have taken Louisa and her friends and family into your hearts and laughed and cried with them. I have to admit to feeling deflated for around a week after finishing the series. I felt as if my best friends were emigrating – maybe I just need more friends!!

Did you enjoy *Just One Day – Autumn*?

I'd really appreciate if you could leave a review on Amazon or Goodreads. It doesn't need to be much, just a couple of lines. I love reading customer reviews. Seeing what readers think of my books spurs me on to write more. Sometimes I've even written more about characters or created a series because of reader comments. Plus, reviews are SO important to authors. They help raise the profile of the author and make it more likely that the book will be visible to more readers. Every author wants their book to be read by more people, and I am no exception!

Did you get your free short stories yet?

TWO UNPUBLISHED EXCLUSIVE SHORT STORIES.

Interacting with my readers is one of the most fun parts of being a writer. I'll be sending out a monthly newsletter with new release information, competitions, special offers and basically a bit about what I've been up to, writing and otherwise.

You can get the previously unseen short stories, ***Mixed Messages*** and ***Time Is of the Essence***, FREE when you sign up to my mailing list at www.susanbuchananauthor.com

Have you read them all?

Sign of the Times

Sagittarius – Travel writer Holly heads to Tuscany to research her next book, but when she meets Dario, she knows she's in trouble. Can she resist temptation? And what do her mixed feelings mean for her future with her fiancé?

Gemini – Player Lucy likes to keep things interesting and has no qualms about being unfaithful to her long-term boyfriend. A cardiology conference to Switzerland changes Lucy, perhaps forever. Has she met her match, and is this feeling love?

Holly is the one who links the twelve signs. Are you ready to meet them all?

A tale of love, family, friendship and the lengths we go to in pursuit of our dreams.

The Dating Game

Work, work, work. That's all recruitment consultant Gill does. Her friends fix her up with numerous blind dates, none suitable, until one day Gill decides enough is enough.

Seeing an ad on a bus billboard for Happy Ever After dating agency 'for the busy professional', on impulse, she signs up. Soon she has problems juggling her social life as well as her work diary.

Before long, she's experiencing laughs, lust and … could it be love? But just when things are looking up for Gill, an unexpected reunion forces her to make an impossible choice.

Will she get her happy ever after, or is she destined to be married to her job forever?

The Christmas Spirit

Natalie Hope takes over the reins of the Sugar and Spice bakery and café with the intention of injecting some Christmas spirit. Something her regulars badly need.

Newly dumped Rebecca is stuck in a job with no prospects, has lost her home and is struggling to see a way forward.

Pensioner Stanley is dreading his first Christmas alone without his beloved wife, who passed away earlier this year. How will he ever feel whole again?

Graduate Jacob is still out of work despite making hundreds of applications. Will he be forced to go against his instincts and ask his unsympathetic parents for help?

Spiky workaholic Meredith hates the jollity of family gatherings and would rather stay home with a box set and a posh ready meal. Will she finally realise what's important in life?

Natalie sprinkles a little magic to try to spread some festive cheer and restore Christmas spirit, but will she succeed?

Return of the Christmas Spirit

Christmas is just around the corner when the enigmatic Star begins working at Butterburn library, but not everyone is embracing the spirit of the season.

Arianna is anxious about her mock exams. With her father living abroad and her mother working three jobs to keep them afloat, she doesn't have much support at home.

The bank is threatening to repossess Evan's house, and he has no idea how he will get through Christmas with two children who are used to getting everything they want.

After 23 years of marriage, Patricia's husband announces he's moving out of the family home, and moving in with his secretary. Patricia puts a brave face on things, but inside, she's devastated and lost.

Stressed-out Daniel is doing the work of three people in his sales job, plus looking after his kids and his sick wife. Pulled in too many different directions, he hasn't even had a chance to think about Christmas.

Can Star, the library's Good Samaritan, help set them on the path to happiness this Christmas?

Just One Day – Winter

Thirty-eight-year-old Louisa has a loving husband, three wonderful kids, a faithful dog, a supportive family and a gorgeous house near Glasgow. What more could she want?

TIME.

Louisa would like, just once, to get to the end of her never-ending to-do list. With her husband Ronnie working offshore, she is demented trying to cope with everything on her own: the after-school clubs, the homework, the appointments … the constant disasters. And if he dismisses her workload one more time, she may well throttle him.

Juggling running her own wedding stationery business with family life is taking its toll, and the only reason Louisa is still sane is because of her best friends and her sisters.

Fed up with only talking to Ronnie about household bills and incompetent tradesmen, when a handsome stranger pays her some attention on her birthday weekend away, she is flattered, but will she give in to temptation? And will she ever get to the end of her to-do list?

Just One Day – Spring

Mum-of-three Louisa thought she only had her never-ending to-do list to worry about, but the arrival of a ghost from the recent past puts her in an untenable position. Can she navigate the difficult situation she's in without their friendship becoming common knowledge or will it cause long-term damage to her marriage?

When a family member begins to suspect there's more to her relationship with the new sous-chef than meets the eye, Louisa needs to think on her feet or she'll dig herself into a deeper hole. But the cost of keeping her secret, not only from her husband, comes at a high price, one which tugs at her conscience.

With everyday niggles already causing a further rift between Louisa and husband Ronnie, will she manage to keep her family on track whilst her life spirals out of control? And when tragedy strikes, will Ronnie step up when she needs him most?

Just One Day – Summer

List-juggling, business-owner mum-of-three Louisa is reeling after a tragedy, as well as learning how to cope after a life-changing revelation. With oil worker husband Ronnie possibly being able to move onshore, she hopes he can help her manage the burden.

But the secrets she keeps are causing her headaches and she's unsure if her ability to make good decisions has deserted her. All she seems to do is upset those around her.

With Louisa's to-do list gathering pace at an incredible speed, will she manage to provide a stable home for them all, embrace her new normal as well as rebuild their life from what's left?

And if she gets what she has always wanted, will it match up to her expectations?

Printed in Great Britain
by Amazon